DIET SODA CLUB

Chaz Hayden

CANDLEWICK PRESS

Copyright © 2024 by
Chaz Hayden Weiner

First edition 2024

Library of Congress Catalog Card
Number 2024930333
ISBN 978-1-5362-2312-5

APS 29 28 27 26 25 24
10 9 8 7 6 5 4 3 2 1

Printed in
Humen, Dongguan, China

This book was typeset
in Arno Pro and Intro.

Candlewick Press
99 Dover Street
Somerville, Massachusetts 02144

www.candlewick.com

FOR MELINDA.
YOU WOULD HAVE LOVED THIS.

ONE

MOST KIDS probably wake up to the sound of an alarm clock or the smell of breakfast cooking. Maybe, if they're really lucky, they get woken up by their parents with kisses and hugs and all the things parents are supposed to say to make their children believe it's going to be a great day.

My sister, Beatrice, mostly knows waking up to the beeps of hospital machines and doctors poking at her during their morning rounds. And since I spend almost every minute next to her, that's mostly all I've known, too.

"I'm just going to take your temperature," a nurse whispered to Beatrice.

It was barely light enough in the room for me to see that Beatrice was already awake and sitting up. After ten years of the same routine, your body starts to anticipate the disturbance, but that doesn't make it easier.

Beatrice waved good morning to me. Then she opened her mouth for the thermometer and uncovered her arm from her blanket so the nurse could wrap a blood pressure cuff around it. Everything was a sad reflex.

"How long have you been awake?" I asked her.

"Maybe an hour. I'm so excited, I couldn't sleep."

Beatrice was getting discharged today, which was a pretty big deal since she hadn't been home in almost two weeks. The nurse smiled at Bea's enthusiasm, but I've dealt with hospitals long enough to realize her smile wasn't one that expressed any agreement with what Beatrice said. Instead, it was just full of pity. My heart sank.

"Bea, you could've woken me up," I said. "We could've talked instead of you just sitting alone in the dark."

"It's okay. You looked like you needed rest."

I laughed. Sometimes Beatrice sounded more like my parent than my ten-year-old sister.

Hospitals are an easy place to lose track of time. The rooms only have one small clock, and you try your hardest not to look at it because then you'll know exactly how much of your life you've spent in this place, which is a scarier reality than the reason you're even in the hospital. For Beatrice, it was pneumonia again.

My sister has a disability called spinal muscular atrophy—she was born with it. There's a whole bunch of medical jargon that goes along with SMA, but the idea is Beatrice has weak muscles. She's never walked and probably won't ever walk. And SMA affects her respiratory system, which is common, from what her doctors tell us. Hence all the pneumonia.

Anyway, the nurse finally left, and before there was even a moment to get my bearings, the doctor came in and flipped on all the lights. The fluorescent bulbs made sure I was definitely awake. But that's how mornings are in the hospital. There's no time to hit the snooze button or slowly come to your senses while watching cartoons. One moment it's silent and all the patients are sleeping, and the next it's a full-fledged, nonstop business.

"How are we feeling today, Ms. Beatrice?" Dr. David asked. He was flipping through her chart and didn't even acknowledge my presence, which I actually liked. All of his focus was always on my sister.

"I feel great," she told him. "I'm ready to go home."

"Yeah, I bet. Let me take a listen to your lungs."

Bea followed every order to take a deep breath in, cough, and breathe normal. After a few repetitions, Dr. David took the stethoscope out of his ears and wrapped it around his neck. I believed Bea when she said she felt better. I mean, she's been sick enough that she really understands her body. At least that's what other doctors have said, including Dr. David, but after he finished listening to her lungs, he had almost the same expression as the nurse.

Dr. David looked at me. "And how are you, Reed?"

"Fine." I kept my answer short. I knew he was stalling.

Dr. David noticed my foot anxiously tapping the floor. He sighed. "Fair enough."

"So, what? Am I getting discharged today?" Beatrice impatiently asked.

"Your labs show that the infection hasn't fully gone away. And when I was listening to you, I heard a lot of congestion rumbling."

"But I feel fine," Bea tried to argue. But then she coughed and it sounded wet, and we all knew it didn't help her case.

"I'm going to schedule a respiratory therapist to come do more chest PT," Dr. David said. "I also want another X-ray of your lungs."

Beatrice pulled the blanket over her head, and Dr. David recognized that was his cue to leave. I was disappointed just like my sister, but there was nothing I could do. We'd been through the routine so many times that I understood that truth.

"Yo-Yo"—that was Bea's nickname for me—"can you give me

your laptop, please?" Her tiny voice barely made it out from under the blanket.

"Sure." I reached into my backpack to grab the computer, but all my crap inside was a mess and everything came spilling out, knocking over an empty can of Diet Dr Pepper that was next to my feet.

In hindsight, I should've picked up everything immediately, but I felt bad for Bea and I was focused on giving her the one thing I knew would distract her. So, I left all my notebooks and homework on the floor, grabbed Beatrice's favorite unicorn pillow, and got her set up. Her fingers immediately went to work.

"What are you doing on there?" I asked.

"Checking the respiratory therapy schedule. Yesterday I was waiting all day."

"Bea, you can't hack the hospital." Now *I* was sounding more like the parent.

"I don't think you mean *can't* because you know I could if I wanted to. But I don't need to. The other day I saw Dr. David type in his password on the nurse's laptop."

"That's still hacking and it's illegal. Not to mention you're only ten and shouldn't know anything about that."

Bea ignored me. Honestly, I don't know what else I expected her to do. I mean, she spends most of her life in a hospital, and there's only so much basic cable and Disney movies a kid can handle. So, last year I let her start playing around on my computer, and then one day we watched a show about the dark web and hackers. After that she was obsessed with becoming "the best white hat," whatever that means.

"Ugh, see, I told you." Beatrice pointed at the screen. "They scheduled me for the afternoon, which really means evening."

"Well, now you know and don't have to wait."

"No way. I'm going to change it. The sooner the mucus is gone, the sooner I can go home."

I was going to argue with Bea that there were other factors that determined when she'd be discharged, but I caught sight of the clock on the wall and confirmed the time with my phone: I was going to be late.

"Crap, I gotta go," I said as I shoved my notebooks and stuff back into my backpack. "Are you okay to be alone until Mom gets here?"

Beatrice nodded, refusing to break concentration on the laptop.

I didn't like the idea of her doing shady stuff on the internet without some kind of supervision. So, to distract her until our mom arrived, I ripped out a page from one of my notebooks and threw it onto her bed.

"Here," I said. "Read my history paper. You can fact-check me before I turn it in tomorrow."

Beatrice finally glanced away from the screen to the essay—the only ten-year-old whose concentration could be stolen by homework. She frowned. "World War Two didn't end in 1948."

She always fell for the mistakes. "Now you have something to keep you busy that won't have the police busting into your hospital room." I kissed her forehead. "I love you." Then I raced toward the door.

"Love you, too, Yo-Yo."

Sadly, I knew my way through the hospital hallways, which came in handy when I was rushing to get out. Like, I knew by the north-side elevators there's a vending machine stocked with Diet Dr Pepper. So I headed that way and grabbed a fresh can for my morning caffeine.

Once I was in the elevator, I checked my reflection in the

mirrored walls and gave my hair a quick comb with my fingers. It honestly didn't help much.

But I kept staring at myself the rest of the ride down. I'd been making this same trip since I was a kid. I didn't understand everything back then, but I knew my sister was sick all the time, and I knew my parents were scared all the time.

Not much had changed since. Beatrice still got sick all the time, and we were still scared all the time. The only difference was I had one less parent. And now I had a beard. At least I'd convinced myself it was a beard.

As soon as I exited the elevator, I recognized a voice I unfortunately couldn't ignore.

"I can park wherever I want," she said. "I practically live here."

I turned to see my mom arguing with hospital security. First the news Bea wasn't getting discharged and now that. I should've known it was going to be one of those days.

I walked over to them. "Hey, Chuck, what's going on?"

"I'm trying to get your mom to move her car," Chuck told me. "She's parked in an ambulance spot."

Through the glass front doors, I saw our car parked crookedly across the red painted lines. It was taking up almost two spots.

"And I'm trying to tell you there's no handicap spots," my mom said. "I've got a wheelchair in there and a daughter who's getting discharged today."

"Mrs. Beckett, I don't know what to tell you. You can have the valet park it for you or—"

"I'll handle this," I interrupted. "Thanks, Chuck." I pulled my mom away from the security desk. "Give me the keys."

"I'm not paying for valet. They charge a fortune, *but it should be*

6

validated for parents of a patient!" She made sure that last part was loud enough for everyone in the lobby to hear.

"I'm not going to valet. I'll find you a spot. I think I see an actual parking space right in front."

I didn't have my license yet and had hardly even practiced driving, but I figured I could handle a parking lot. And it's not like I had much of a choice, anyway.

Mom started digging through her purse for the keys. I'm not sure how they could be lost so fast. "Well, I'm not waiting for you to come back. I wanna go see my baby."

"Fine. I'll leave the keys with Chuck."

Finally, she handed over the keys. "What time did Dr. David say she'll be discharged? Because I have—"

"She's not getting discharged today. The infection is still in her lungs."

Mom buried her face in her hands, rubbing her eyes and then fixing a messy ponytail. "Sorry, I'm just . . . exhausted."

I knew she was telling the truth. It wasn't just the dark circles under her eyes or the fact that she just got off a double shift. I recognized something deep inside her because I felt the same way.

"I have to go," I said. "I'm late for school."

Mom nodded and I left. My own day hadn't even begun yet.

TWO

MY MOM used to do all the mom things like bake sales, PTA, and help with my homework. A lot of people will think our life started going downhill when Beatrice was born, but that's the furthest thing from the truth. My parents were really proactive when she got diagnosed and never fought about her care. At least I never heard them if they did.

No, Mom didn't fall apart until Dad died. After the accident, I watched her slowly start to drift away, until she was only a floating body; around but not really present—though even that wasn't really true anymore. Most of the time she was either working or sleeping, which meant I became the person who took care of my sister and did all the things that needed to be done to keep her alive.

Things had gotten even worse over the past couple of weeks. Something about this latest trip to the hospital seemed to have hit my mom harder than usual, and she'd been acting more erratic and detached since then.

Honestly, it was almost worse knowing that our mom had it in her to be a good mom—a *great* mom, even. I couldn't help feeling like she was choosing to let us down, which I knew wasn't fair but was how I felt a lot of the time.

Anyway, after riding a public bus to the apartment and then pedaling my bike the few blocks to school, I was, in fact, late. All the side doors to the building were already locked, which meant I had to check in with the main office and get judged by the secretary.

"Don't you have an alarm?" she asked.

"Not a conventional one."

"What does that mean?"

"Never mind," I said as I signed the attendance sheet.

"I'll need to see your student ID."

I flopped my backpack on the floor and started rummaging through it. I searched every pocket and crevice until I figured my ID was probably lying on the floor next to Bea's hospital bed.

"I don't have it," I said.

She sighed, now utterly disappointed in me. "I can't let you in without a valid ID."

"So, what? I'm just supposed to miss an entire day of school? You know who I am. I've checked in here before."

"I guess you can get another ID. They're printed in the art room, but hurry. She usually leaves before the end of homeroom."

I took off down the hallway.

"And come back so I can properly check you in!" the secretary called after me.

My footsteps pounded on the linoleum as I raced to the art room, which was on the opposite side of the building. When I got there and saw who would be printing my ID, I seriously considered ditching and just taking a full day of absence. Unfortunately, she saw me before I could make my escape.

"What do *you* want?" Helena Shaw asked.

"New ID. I forgot mine and apparently that's a big deal."

"It's for everyone's safety. I suggest putting it on a lanyard with other important items like a house key."

"Noted."

Helena walked over to a computer at the far end of the room and clicked around a few times. A minute later a large printer started making noise and shook the table it was standing on.

The new ID wasn't some chintzy, temporary paper one. It was a legit piece of plastic identical to the one I'd left at the hospital.

Helena caught me staring at it. "What's wrong?"

"Nothing. I just thought these came from some professional printer."

"Nope. They're all done here by me."

I chuckled. "Like you don't waste enough of your time for this school being student council president and prom queen."

"We haven't had prom yet."

"You know what I mean."

Helena clicked her tongue like how girls do when you get them all annoyed. "Is there anything else you need, or can I move on with my day?"

As reluctant as I was to spend another minute in Helena's company, I did have a question for her. "Actually, yes. Why did you get rid of all the vending machines?"

"Do you know that almost twenty percent of teens are considered obese?"

"Do *you* know that some teens don't have the ability to make lunch every day? Grabbing something from the machines is the only chance they get to eat."

Helena rolled her eyes. "They can use that money to buy lunch. The school just cut lunch costs."

"Trust me, a candy bar and a bag of chips is a lot healthier than anything the cafeteria is cooking up."

Helena looked like she wanted to continue arguing, but lucky for me the bell rang. I headed back to the office to prove I was actually a student.

THREE

HELENA SHAW was one of those students who put a lot of effort into school—doing all the extra-credit problems, spending weeks on her reports and dioramas, working on the yearbook, and running for student government and whatever else. But people like her never realize how lucky they are that they have nothing else to worry about but what goes on within the four walls of a classroom.

I didn't have that privilege. When the final bell rang, I had to think about how I would get back to the hospital.

Did I have enough bus money?

Would there be a lot of traffic?

Would I make it there in time to have dinner with Beatrice—and what would I have to deal with once I got there? Had Mom pissed off any of the nurses or Dr. David with her attitude? Had the authorities finally arrested Beatrice for hacking?

Even with all that, I was still a good student and in some top percentile or whatever. Part of the reason I was able to still get good grades was because of Beatrice, actually. She was a pretty decent study buddy.

Beatrice barely let me enter her room before rolling over to me in her wheelchair. She skidded across the freshly cleaned floors and almost crashed into me. "Watch it, daredevil," I said. She never eased up, which is what I loved most about her.

"Sorry." She backed up.

"It's okay. I missed you today." I gave her a kiss on the head and plopped my backpack in her lap. "Bring this over to your table. I have some English reading and calculus. We'll start in a few minutes. I just want to talk to Mom first."

While Bea meticulously lined up my homework, I sank into the chair next to our mom, who was pretty distracted by her phone. I wasn't even sure if she noticed I arrived.

"How'd she do today?" I asked.

She didn't look up.

"Mom?"

Finally, her thumbs paused their typing. "What?"

"How is Beatrice?"

"Fine. The respiratory therapist came in and got her to cough up a bunch of crap, and then they took her to get X-rays."

"Any updates from Dr. David?"

Mom shook her head.

For a few minutes, I just watched Beatrice read through my class notebooks. I wasn't sure she understood any of it but, honestly, who the hell knew. One time she hacked into a TV station and changed the schedule so she could watch a movie before her bedtime.

"Who are you texting?" I asked Mom.

"Nobody."

"It's obviously not nobody. You've barely stopped typing since I got here."

She sighed. "His name's Seth. We met at the bar a few weeks ago."

"You work with him?"

"No. He's a customer."

Now I sighed.

"He's different."

After Dad died, our mom tried to date more times than I cared to count. The majority of the guys were jobless boozehounds or creepy businessmen, like this one guy who brought me and Beatrice random toys that seemed used, like they were taken from his actual children. It goes without saying that I never liked any of them, and thankfully none lasted more than a week. But now I was expected to believe this new guy was somehow different.

"Whatever," I said. I needed to change the subject. "I think we should send Beatrice to school."

Mom shook her head. "Your sister is way too fragile to go to school."

"I mean after she gets better. Just look at her." We both pivoted our heads toward Beatrice, still poring over my homework. "She wants to learn. Beatrice is ten years old and has never been in a classroom."

"Because my baby is sick. That is why I chose to homeschool her." Mom got up from the chair and ran over to give Bea a hug. Beatrice smiled, even though it looked like Mom was practically squeezing the life out of her.

"You mean *I* homeschool her," I corrected our mom. "Dad would want her in school."

Mom quickly released her hug. "Don't tell me what you think your dad would want. He's not here, and I'm alone making the decisions. Your sister isn't well, Reed."

"Stop saying she's not well." My voice started to get loud. "I mean, she gets sick, but other than that she just has her SMA. There are plenty of kids at my school who are in wheelchairs and they're doing great."

14

I noticed Bea was getting upset with the yelling and Mom was a second away from totally exploding. I was about to drop the fight, but I didn't need to since Dr. David walked in.

"Oh, good. The whole family is here," he said.

Bea instantly forgot the fight and rolled over to Dr. David. "Are you here to say I can go home now? I did really good with the chest PT, even though the respiratory therapist was mean."

Dr. David laughed. "I'm afraid you still can't go home. But I do have your X-rays." He held up the photos to the light so we could see them. "I had them take images of Beatrice's chest and spine. You can see here that her scoliosis has gotten worse."

Mom gasped like it was a death sentence.

"Don't be too alarmed. It's common among patients with spinal muscular atrophy, and it's fixable. The problem is the curve of her spine is pushing on her rib cage." Dr. David pointed at the other X-ray. "The left side of her ribs are caving in on her lungs. That's why she keeps getting pneumonia."

I looked over to Bea, who was taking in all the information. She didn't look scared, just observant.

"So, how do we fix that?" I asked.

"Well, first I want to get your sister in to see a spine specialist. But she'll need surgery to correct the scoliosis and open her rib cage so she can breathe better."

"Surgery!" Mom cried.

I had the same panicked reaction as my mom, only I knew I had to remain composed for Beatrice. Though my grip tightened around the chair I was standing next to, turning my knuckles white.

"Okay," I said. "And when can she get the surgery?"

Dr. David sat down next to Bea and took off his glasses like doctors do when they are about to deliver more bad news. "We can't schedule the surgery until her pneumonia is gone. Then I'll want her to recover and get stronger before putting her under anesthesia."

"But I'm already strong." Beatrice held up her arm and tried to flex her muscles.

"I know you are." Dr. David chuckled. "That's why I know you'll do great when it comes time for the surgery."

Dr. David stood up and left, and it was barely a second later before our mom headed for the door, too.

"Where are you going?" I asked.

"I need to get out of here," she said, looking at her phone. "I have somewhere to be."

"Somewhere to be? Your daughter was just told she needs major surgery! Don't you want to process with us for a minute?"

"I really can't stay, Reed. I'm already running late."

I couldn't believe what I was hearing, but then I saw Beatrice had already moved on to digging through my backpack again. It was like I was the only one who understood the seriousness of what Dr. David said. I thought I was losing my mind.

"Mama, can you bring me some chocolate cake from the restaurant?" Beatrice asked.

"Mama's not going to work," she told her.

"So, you're not going to work, but you have somewhere more important to be?" I asked. "Are you going to see that guy you're texting?"

"Reed, I am the parent. Don't talk to me like that. And his name is Seth."

"Whatever. Just go."

After Mom bailed, I just stood in the middle of the room and stared at the floor, and it felt like my chest was going to explode. I tried to breathe, but it wasn't helping. I was almost hyperventilating.

"I'm gonna go get some ice chips from the machine," I told Bea. "You want some?"

"Yes, please."

I raced out of the room and down the hall to the ice machine I knew better than I wanted to. For a moment I just stood there and stared at the machine. But then I started kicking and punching the metal box, tears pouring down my face.

I couldn't stop. It was like something took over my body, and I kicked and punched, wanting to scream at the machine and scream at the sky. Wanting to scream at my dad for not being there and beg him to come back.

But I couldn't scream. I had to be strong for Beatrice. I guess I was the only one who wanted to.

Eventually, I calmed down and filled up a cup with the classic hospital crushed ice. When I got back to the room, Bea was trying to read my chemistry textbook.

I sat next to her and just watched.

"Why do you and Mom fight so much?" she asked.

"We just care a lot about you. You know we'll do anything to get you better, right?"

Bea nodded.

"And you know we love you a lot, and we're going to keep you better once this is all over?"

Bea nodded again.

"Everything is going to be okay."

"I know." Bea looked at me and smiled, and for that split second, I actually believed everything was going to be okay.

For the rest of the night, we ate crushed ice and pretended we were professional glass swallowers. Eventually, I put Beatrice in bed and lay next to her until a nurse came in to slip on the mask for her breathing machine.

None of it was normal, but it was our normal.

FOUR

I'VE NEVER been close to normal long enough to really know what it looks or feels like. But I had a better sense of what it *wasn't*. It wasn't sleeping next to my little sister in a freezing-cold hospital room.

It also wasn't wearing the same clothes for three days straight because you hate hospital showers and hate going to your apartment because it's so empty and depressing. But that morning Beatrice told me I was starting to smell and kids in class sat farther away from me than usual, so after school I stopped by the apartment to take a shower.

When I got there, I saw Mom's car in the parking lot, even though she was supposed to be with Beatrice. My temper flared. How hard is it to spend time with your kid?

Inside, I saw my mom making out with some guy I'd never seen before.

"What the hell?" I yelled.

Mom jumped off the couch and struggled to button her shirt. "Reed! I didn't know you were stopping by today."

"Stopping by? I live here!"

"I just didn't know you were coming home. I'd thought you'd be with Beatrice."

"*You're* supposed to be with Beatrice! I've been at school all day."

Mom looked somewhat guilty, though how she could've forgotten a routine we do literally every day was beyond me. There was a pause long enough for me to remember there was another person in the room with us. The famous Seth, I assumed.

He hadn't even moved from the couch and just sat there with his shirt open, acting like a family crisis wasn't happening two feet away from him.

Who doesn't at least stand up when someone walks in on you making out with their mom?

Mom caught me eyeing him. "That's Seth. Seth, this is my son, Reed."

Seth nodded at me. "What's up, man?"

I really hated that guy.

Mom sat back down next to Seth. "So, how was school today?"

"Don't do that," I told her.

"Do what?"

"Act like you care or want to hear about my day."

"Well, I do. I'm your mother."

I laughed. "I'm going to take a shower and then I'm out of here."

"You don't have to leave so fast. Do you want to grab a bite to eat with us?"

I looked at Seth, who still hadn't buttoned up his damn shirt. "No, I don't want to grab a bite to eat with you and Seth. Beatrice is still alone at the hospital."

My mom didn't argue or even offer to drop off food. I heard them leave as soon as I got in my room, which I actually didn't mind. It was probably best for everyone if they weren't there when I came back out.

The bus ride to the hospital was when I finally started to cool down. For most of it, though, I was so pissed, I tried not to punch a hole in my seat.

Were they even dating, or did they just meet at the apartment and grope each other on the couch when Mom was supposed to be with Beatrice?

"How long have you been alone?" was the first thing I said when I got to Bea's room.

She was sitting on her bed, occupied by the computer. "I don't know. A few hours, I guess."

"Beatrice, you gotta tell me when Mom doesn't show or when she leaves, so somebody is always with you."

"You understand I'm in a hospital, right? What could happen to me?"

"That's not the point."

"Then what is the point, because you're always saying I can't be left alone, and then it's either you or Mom here or the nurses and doctors. I don't get any privacy."

"You're ten years old. You don't need privacy."

"Well, I at least should get *some* time to myself. It's really not fair."

I sat in the recliner next to her bed and took a moment to breathe. She was fine, obviously. I know Bea is feeling well when she still has her sass.

"Dad used to sit with you in the hospital all day and all night," I told her. "Did I ever tell you that?"

She shook her head.

"Well, he did. And he used to say that it doesn't matter if you're in the hospital and surrounded by doctors and nurses. You don't deserve to be alone."

"So, Dad told you to never leave?"

"He didn't have to tell me. When he died, I just took over. I knew he'd want somebody to."

Beatrice lowered her eyes. She practically sank into herself. "I don't want you to be stuck with me all the time."

"I'm not stuck with you. If anything, you're stuck with me— even when I smell."

That made her laugh. "You don't smell today."

"That's because I finally took a shower." I climbed into Bea's bed and put my armpit in her face.

"Gross, Yo-Yo. You're so immature."

I rested my head on her unicorn pillow. "But you still love me, right?"

"Not when you block me from using the computer. Move your big head."

"What are you doing on there, anyway?" I asked.

"I was talking to Zigzag."

"Zigzag? Your dark web friend?"

"Don't say dark web. But, yes, they're helping me reconfigure the firewall I built because it had a pretty big back door."

I didn't understand a single word she said. "I really don't like that you talk to people on the dark web, especially someone named Zigzag. You have no idea who they are."

"So?"

"So, you're a little kid and they could be some internet perv. Who knows what kind of people hang out on the dark web?"

"I told you to stop saying dark web. And, second, you don't have to worry. Zigzag can only see my username."

"Which is what?"

"WheelieCool. Get it? Because of the wheels on my wheelchair."

"I got it." I sighed. "But you seriously think Zigzag hasn't hacked into the computer and knows exactly who you are?"

Beatrice shrugged. "Maybe. Although my VPN is registered in Canada under the name Larry. Also, this is your laptop, so Zigzag probably thinks I'm some teen boy named Reed Beckett. Either way I'm safe."

She wasn't making me feel any better. I closed the laptop and moved it to the end of the bed where she couldn't reach it.

"Hey," she whined.

"Chill. You can go back on it later. It's homework time." I rolled out of the bed and went digging through my backpack. "Here, I brought this for you." I placed a crumpled piece of paper on her pillow.

"What is it?"

"It's algebra homework from my freshman year. I found it when I was going through my locker today."

"Someone scribbled out all the answers."

"Yeah, I did. It's so you can solve the problems again. You think you can do it?"

Beatrice's eyes narrowed, and she poked out her tongue like when she's concentrating really hard. "Definitely," she declared. Bea never backed down from a challenge. She got that trait from our dad.

One way or another, I had to get her in school. For now, my version of homeschooling would have to suffice—and I have to say that I was doing a decent job, because when Beatrice handed back the algebra homework, I realized she did way better than I originally had. I would never tell her that though. I still had to maintain the smarter older brother persona, at least for myself.

FIVE

BEATRICE MAY HAVE had Zigzag—though I'm not sure that some shady dark web character really counts as a *friend*—but my everyday routine didn't really provide me with an opportunity to have friends. I'd had a best friend in elementary school, but when we stopped being friends, I didn't bother trying to make new ones because everyone was doing things that I couldn't do, like going to baseball practice or birthday parties on the weekends. It was easier for me to slide into the background and pretend I was still experiencing the same childhood as them, even though my life looked a whole lot different from theirs.

Don't get me wrong, I'm not blaming Bea or my dad dying for my lack of a social life. Honestly, I think I always saw myself as more of a lone wolf. Plus, my ten-year-old sister was a lot cooler and more interesting to talk to than anyone at my high school.

"You think Miss Havisham is manipulative?" Beatrice asked me. She was reading my most recent English paper.

"She definitely is. She uses Pip in her sick game with Estella."

"Well, did you ever consider that maybe she's just a heart-broken old woman? Maybe she just desperately wants to be a part of a love story."

"That doesn't make her any better."

Bea rolled her eyes and kept reading.

"There's no right answer to the essay question," I told her. "I picked the side that was the easiest to argue."

"That's just being lazy."

I snatched the paper out of her hands. "Whatever. I didn't ask for your opinion."

It had been one of those days where it felt like every doctor and nurse in the hospital had been inside Bea's room, so both of us were on edge. Plus I was still in a bad mood from having walked in on Mom and Seth the day before, and realizing that Mom was leaving Bea alone to hang out with her new boyfriend. And whether Beatrice would admit it or not, I know she got more anxious when our mom wasn't around for all the testing.

"Yo-Yo, can you go to the cafeteria and get me some ice cream?" Beatrice asked.

"You have a tray of food next to your bed."

Beatrice glared at the hospital lunch: a crusty turkey sandwich, apple juice, and an underripe banana.

"I'm not eating that gross stuff," she said.

"Well, I don't think you're even allowed to have ice cream right now. The dairy usually makes you have more mucus."

Suddenly she was screaming. "This is the worst day ever! I just want to go home!"

Beatrice looked like she was about to totally lose it. There was always a day during one of her hospital visits where nothing goes right, and today seemed to be that day. Those days usually meant she was on the brink of either getting better or falling and landing deeper than where she was originally.

My phone buzzed. "Mom's on her way up," I told her. "She says she brought food."

"I don't care." Beatrice wouldn't look at me. One moment she was judging my literary theories and the next throwing a tantrum like an average kid her age. My sister was exhausting.

"What do you mean you don't care?" I tried to be playful. I gasped. "Maybe Mom has fries from the bar."

The smallest smile broke out on her face, even though she fought against it.

"You want me to get you in your wheelchair?" I asked.

"No."

"Yes. You eat better when you're sitting up." That was a sentence I'm sure nobody my age had ever said before.

I yanked all the blankets off Beatrice. Her hair was a mess, and it was so long she could almost sit on it.

"When was the last time a nurse gave you a bath?" I asked. "You smell like an enchilada."

"Don't be mean, Yo-Yo."

"Hey, you called me out when I stunk. I'm just making things even."

That finally got Bea to laugh and relax enough so I could get her dressed easier. I lifted both her arms to take off the oversize shirt she sleeps in.

"What do you want to put on?" I asked.

I held up a pink top with a rainbow and another shirt covered in mini pineapples. All of Bea's clothes were girly with way too much glitter and fit her personality perfectly. I pretty much religiously wore black. I wondered what that said about me.

Beatrice pointed at the pineapple shirt, and I chose a pair of sweatpants that I knew wouldn't be impossible to get on her. I gently rolled her side to side on the bed, making adjustments until everything fit okay.

Then Bea wrapped her arms around my neck. I picked her up and carried her over to her wheelchair. For a ten-year-old, Beatrice luckily didn't weigh much, but I knew eventually she would get too heavy for me, and I wasn't sure what we would do then. I knew there were lifts or other things to help, but I didn't know how we could possibly afford them. Maybe I just needed to start lifting weights.

"Doesn't it feel better to be in your chair?" I asked.

Beatrice nodded. She was too stubborn to agree out loud. I remember our dad was like that.

One of the nurses came in to do their hourly check, and I asked if they could give my sister a bath later. Once again, I felt older than I should've. There's definitely a fine line between childhood and being an adult. People think that you're only an adult when you turn eighteen, as if an arbitrary number can somehow determine a person's ability to act mature and function independently. It's really not that cut-and-dry, though.

I'd been doing "grown-up things" for probably longer than most new parents, but they'd be seen as more adult than me just because of their age. I would even argue my sister was more of an adult than most adults. We were just the products of our circumstances.

And our circumstances were a dead dad and a mom who thought it was fine to bring her sketchy boyfriend to the hospital.

27

Because trailing behind our mom, who was carrying two bags of food from the bar, was Seth.

"What's he doing here?" I asked.

"Seth bought us the food. Isn't that nice?"

I turned to Seth. "Do you even have a job, or do you just live at the bar?"

"Reed, be nice," Mom told me. "Seth has a great job that lets him be flexible during the day."

She sounded chipper, and that disturbed me more than the sight of Seth standing in Bea's hospital room. I hadn't seen my mom chipper since my dad died, even with other boyfriends. In the past ten years, my mom has had two moods: careless and sleeping. Now some guy came along, and suddenly she could act like a functioning human again.

I probably should've been happy for her, for us. But all I felt was anger and resentment. Why could she act like that for him but not for us?

The question festered in my mind while I ate in silence. Pretty much everyone was silent including Beatrice, who didn't take her eyes off Seth. He sat at the small table in the room and ate a burger, and once he was done, he whispered something in my mom's ear. She shook her head and told him she wasn't in a rush. A few minutes later, he tried again. Eventually, after the fifth time Seth whispered something to her, my mom got up and grabbed her purse.

"I'll be back later, baby," she said to Beatrice, following Seth out.

She didn't even kiss Beatrice goodbye.

SIX

USUALLY I DIDN'T listen to the school's morning announcements. I especially never paid attention when Helena was sounding off another one of her student council president rules.

"Starting today, all students who leave campus for lunch must sign in and out with the main office." Helena's voice echoed through every room and hallway.

The kids in my homeroom all simultaneously groaned like they had practiced it or something, and they pretty much had. It seemed like every morning Helena was announcing a new rule. First it was getting rid of "unhealthy" vending machines, and then came the rule about no open-toed shoes, as if that fashion choice personally offended her. Last week she handed out lanyards in the cafeteria, and all students had to start wearing their IDs around their neck. I tried not to take that one personally, though it was hard not to suspect that she'd made the rule specifically to avoid having to print me another ID.

There was a pause over the loudspeaker, like Helena knew everyone was complaining and she needed them to finish so she could continue. "This new policy has been enacted to ensure all students are accounted for in an emergency situation or school lockdown."

I'd never heard of a high school student council president who actually had the power to make changes. Most of them just passed out flyers about global warming or when to show up for pep rallies. If there was ever going to be a person who took the responsibility of being president of a bunch of teenagers a little too seriously, it was going to be Helena Shaw.

Except for the vending machines, the new rules didn't really affect me. I mean, I literally never wore sandals, and I had no car to drive to get lunch. And, to be honest, the rules kind of made sense. God, I couldn't believe I was actually on the same side as Helena about something.

Anyway, homeroom ended and the bell cut off Helena, who clearly wasn't finished talking. There was definitely going to be another announcement tomorrow. My bet was it would be a rule to not leave homeroom until we were officially dismissed by President Helena Shaw.

On my way to lunch, my phone rang. And it kept ringing and ringing in my pocket like a legit call.

My stomach flipped and I felt like I was about to throw up. Only one place ever calls me.

"Hello?" I answered.

"Hi, this is Nurse Catherine from East Memorial Hospital. We're trying to reach your mom. Do you know where she is?"

"She's supposed to be with Beatrice. Why? What happened to my sister?"

"Oh, nothing. Beatrice is completely fine. We actually want

to discharge her today, and we've been trying to get ahold of your mom, but she's not answering our calls."

"I'm on my way," I told the nurse. My mind began racing, trying to figure out where my mom was and why she wasn't at the hospital again.

"Great, but we actually need an adult present to discharge your sister."

"Okay. I'll try to find my mom. Just tell Beatrice I'll be there in twenty."

As annoyed as I was with my mom, I couldn't really hold it against her for not being prepared for this. Usually we'd get a heads-up about Beatrice getting discharged, and we'd be as prepared as my family possibly could be.

This time was a surprise, since it had been less than a week since Dr. David said Bea's lungs were still infected. If Beatrice was really getting discharged today, it would be one of our shortest hospital visits: under three weeks.

I raced down the hall with only one priority: tracking down my mom and getting to the hospital. I didn't sign out with the main office like Helena said we had to. There was a long line, and I just wanted to get my sister home—though there wasn't much I could do without our mom.

The hospital didn't understand that I *was* the adult.

SEVEN

RUNNING DOWN the street to the bus and then sitting on the bus, I probably called my mom fifty times. I'd call and it would ring a few times and then go to voice mail, so I would text her and then try calling again. And they weren't just basic texts like "Where are you?" I literally spelled out that Beatrice was getting discharged and the hospital needed her there. At one point I even called the bar where she worked, forgetting it was too early for it to be open.

People on the bus must've thought I was a maniac or something because I kept nervously tapping my legs and asking the bus driver how long until we'd exit the highway. Part of me honestly thought they'd throw my sister in the parking lot until someone came to get her. I know that sounds absurd and from experience I knew that getting discharged takes hours, but those were my thoughts when the bus driver stopped every block for a pickup even if the bench at the bus stop was empty.

"Yo-Yo, what are you doing here?" Bea asked as soon as I burst into her room.

"You're getting discharged. I came to help bring you home."

"But you're supposed to be in school."

"It's fine. It's lunchtime."

"You'll go back later?"

"Yes."

"Do you promise?" Beatrice asked.

I rolled my eyes. "Yes, I promise, Mother."

Beatrice giggled and maybe it relaxed her a little, but I could see her face was still really anxious. And it wasn't because I ditched school; that was just the thing she focused on to ignore everything else, like the fact she was actually going home. Getting discharged is nerve-racking because you're going to a place that might be more comfortable, but it also doesn't have a staff of doctors and nurses in case of an emergency. And you keep wondering when the next emergency will be.

"Is Dr. David coming in?" I asked a nurse.

"Yes, he's just finishing the discharge orders, and then he'll be in to explain everything. But we need your mom here before you can leave."

"I know." I checked my phone. Still nothing.

When our mom finally showed up, she was wearing a tennis outfit, the kind with a white miniskirt and matching top. I'd never seen her look at a tennis racket, let alone play. And she had on a visor and brand-new sneakers—I didn't even recognize whoever she was trying to be.

Before I could say anything, Mom looked at me, frantic. "What's going on?"

"Beatrice is getting discharged today. You didn't read any of my texts?"

"My phone was off. When I turned it back on and saw all your messages, I came straight over. Jesus, Reed, I thought something had happened!"

33

"You shouldn't have been gone in the first place."

She waved me off. "Beatrice told me I could go."

I looked at Bea, who avoided my gaze. But I didn't need her to actually say anything to know our mom was lying.

"So you chose to play tennis instead of taking care of your daughter," I said. "I didn't even know you *liked* tennis."

Mom sighed. "Beatrice, honey, do you care that Mommy left?"

"Well, um—"

"It's not about whether or not Beatrice cared," I interrupted. "It's about doing what you have to do for our family."

"Excuse me, but I do a lot for this family. I work very long hours to make sure we have a roof over our heads and food on our table. I think I deserve a little break from time to time."

"Dad never wanted Beatrice to be alone," I said quietly but sternly. "You know that." I wanted to say more, but just then I noticed something else was different. "Where are the earrings that Dad got you?"

Mom touched her ears. Where gold hearts once were, a pair of diamond hoops now dangled. "Oh, Seth gave these to me today for our one-month anniversary."

"That's not a thing. And where'd you get the money for that outfit, anyway? Or did Seth buy that for your month-iversary, too?"

"I don't appreciate your tone, young man," Mom said, trying to sound like an actual mom. But she didn't answer my question, and I didn't press the issue, since I was pretty sure I didn't really want to know, anyway.

I debated getting away from her for a bit by hitting up a vending machine on another floor to grab a Diet Dr Pepper and a bag of Doritos—I hadn't eaten lunch and was feeling pretty hungry—but I didn't want to miss Dr. David talking to my mom. She never fully absorbed what the doctors said; that had been my dad's job and then became my job. I had to be there, as much as I wanted to disappear.

Thankfully, Dr. David showed up quickly. "Great, everyone's here now," he said as he entered. "Today's your lucky day, Beatrice." He said that every time she got to leave the hospital. "The infection that was in your lungs is almost gone, and you seem strong enough to recoup at home."

"That's great," I said. "And when do you think she can have the surgery?"

"We'll see what the specialist says. I'm hoping at the end of next month, but that really depends on how quickly she regains full strength."

"What exactly does the surgery entail?" Mom asked nervously. "Does she really need it? It sounds so risky, and it's not like it's going to cure her."

"No, we can't cure Beatrice's SMA," Dr. David said patiently.

He walked over to my sister, pointing at her sunken side and twisting spine. Those were things I'd seen for years and known were strange, but a doctor explaining the details raises the stakes to another uncomfortable level.

"The surgery will try to correct Beatrice's spine and rib cage," Dr. David told us. "The hope is that her expanded rib cage will allow her lung to heal and lessen the number of times she gets pneumonia."

"What if she doesn't have the surgery?" Mom asked.

"Then Beatrice will continue to get serious cases of pneumonia, which will eventually cause permanent damage to her lungs as well as other parts of her body. She will also develop serious spine issues."

"Will I die without the surgery?" Beatrice asked.

"Beatrice!" Mom exclaimed. "Don't even *think that!*"

I saw in Bea's eyes that she wasn't scared. She just genuinely wanted to know, like any good hacker trying to hedge the risk.

"I'm going to be honest with you all," Dr. David said. "There are risks to both decisions. The surgery is long and risky, but not doing it is an even bigger shot in the dark."

"We're doing it," I decided. Mom stayed silent, which was as close to an agreement as we were going to get from her.

Dr. David nodded. "In the meantime, I want to set you up with private-duty nursing to make sure Beatrice doesn't have any setbacks."

"Private-duty nursing?" Mom asked. "What does that mean?"

"It's just nurses who will visit Beatrice at home. They'll administer her breathing medication and do chest PT like she got here. Honestly, it'll be a nice break for you and Reed."

Obviously, I thought it sounded like a great idea, and I wouldn't have to worry about who's with Beatrice and rushing home from school. But my mom was shaking her head through all of it.

"No. No, I don't think that's something we can do," she told Dr. David.

"Well, if you're worried about paying for it, I already checked and your state insurance will cover a few nursing hours each day."

Mom kept shaking her head.

"I'll just get you the information in case you change your mind," Dr. David said. He left and I hoped he wasn't thinking we were terrible people.

"Why don't you want the nurses?" I asked our mom.

"I just don't want anyone in our house and in our business."

"But it's for Beatrice. Someone to help take care of your

daughter." I turned to Beatrice. "Tell Mom you want the nurses. They'll help you stay healthy. Plus, we need someone we can trust to be there." I glared at our mom.

"Well, I guess if it'll help . . ." Beatrice said. Her voice was quiet.

"Strangers in your house just want to snoop around," Mom interjected. "We've been doing fine on our own."

"How would you know?" I mumbled.

"What was that?"

"Nothing."

The upside of the fight about the nurses was that Beatrice forgot all about my returning to school, which was good because it was another two hours until we were finally leaving. Beatrice rolled down the hallway toward the elevator and said goodbye to every nurse she passed. I wondered if she realized she had now stayed in every room in the pediatric ICU. I did, and I recalled each visit and its reason like I could see our ghosts lingering in the rooms. I was actually jealous of the people in the memories. They were naive and had hope that somehow that room would be the last room.

One room still had a dad in it, and I hated that one the most.

EIGHT

MOM DROPPED Bea's bag of clothes on the couch and walked out before I could ask where she needed to head back to, or who.

"Where's Mom going?" Beatrice asked.

"Not sure."

"But I wanna watch a movie with her."

"I don't know what to tell you, Beatrice." My voice got loud, angry. I fought to control it. My sister didn't deserve to be my punching bag. "Are you hungry? You want me to make something?"

"Yes, please!" I went to reach for the back of her wheelchair to push her into the kitchen. "Stop, I can do it."

I let her go and although the kitchen was barely fifteen feet away in our tiny apartment, Bea had a hard time getting herself there. She definitely lost a lot of strength while stuck in the hospital, which sucked and made me angrier than I already was. Just a few days ago, she was practically flying around her hospital room and almost crashed into me. Now she could barely move.

There were too many ups and downs, and nobody ever seemed to know whether it was her muscles getting weaker from SMA or if she was always battling getting over being sick.

What if she didn't get back to full strength before her surgery?

What, exactly, was she supposed to look like when we went back to the hospital?

Those were the sorts of questions we should've asked Dr. David.

"Can you make pancakes?" Beatrice asked.

"Um, let me check what we have."

We had nothing. Literally not a single edible item in the whole apartment. All that was in the fridge was a Styrofoam container of leftover fries, but those were growing mold on them. Mom convinced me she had been going to the apartment to nap and take showers. Obviously, it wasn't *our* apartment she'd been going to.

I tossed the container of moldy fries in the overflowing trash. "I can go get you something."

"How? You don't have a car."

"I can ride my bike to Cheap Check." That was the convenience store down the street and our only option until Mom came home.

Beatrice didn't even take a second to consider that. "No, thanks." She yawned but I could tell it was fake. "I'm tired. I think I just want to take a nap."

"Well, first I want to give you a bath."

"No, Yo-Yo," she whined. "I'm too tired for a bath."

"We always wash the hospital grossness off you when you get home. Besides, I don't know why you're complaining. You just have to sit there. I'm doing all the work."

Beatrice groaned again and locked her tires as if I couldn't easily unlock them myself. I'll admit I didn't really want to give her a bath and would've rather taken a nap, too, but I knew the nurse only gave her a subpar sponge bath after I had to ask a hundred times. And my mom definitely wasn't doing it whenever she got back later, even if she was in the right headspace.

While the bathwater was heating up and I got organized with towels and clean clothes to put on Beatrice, I realized those were all things a nurse would do. My sister would definitely prefer having a nurse give her a bath over me. She was still young enough where I think it was all right for me to give her a bath, but eventually she'd get older and then it would be strange for me, her brother, to do that.

Maybe not, though. I guess you hear about siblings taking care of each other when one of them is sick, but most of the time that's temporary because they'd either get better or they'd die. Beatrice wasn't getting better. If she had the surgery, maybe she'd stop getting pneumonia so often, but she'll always have SMA, which means someone will always need to care for her.

Was that somebody me?

I didn't mind; it was just another thing I wanted to know.

Anyway, right then neither of us had a choice. I was the person there and Beatrice smelled, so I gave her a bath.

"Are you gonna go back to school?" Beatrice asked while I shampooed her hair.

"You mean today or, like, ever?"

"I mean after I'm done with the bath. You can go back while I'm napping."

"The school day ended almost an hour ago."

Beatrice pouted. "I don't like that you miss things because of me."

"We've talked about this. I don't care about missing things."

"Well, then, what do you care about?" Bea asked. I couldn't tell if she was crying or if the bathwater was running down her rosy cheeks. "People your age are supposed to care about things, right? But you don't do anything. You're just always with me."

Then she lost it, in the bathtub and surrounded by bubbles. And I didn't know what to do.

I couldn't hug her, not when she was naked. Plus, I wasn't even sure if Beatrice was actually upset about my lack of hobbies or if there was something else going on.

"I'm scared, Yo-Yo," she whispered, watching a rubber duck float past. "I'm really scared."

"I know. I'm scared, too, and so is Mom. I think that's why she hasn't been around much. But you're going to be okay."

"How do you know?"

"Because somebody has to hack into my school and change my attendance record."

A small laugh escaped her. "That's not funny."

After a few more minutes, at which point Bea determined her fingers were pruney enough, I took her out of the bathtub. I draped one towel over her wheelchair so it wouldn't get wet and had another warm one waiting to wrap her up in. Our dad always warmed our bath towels.

Beatrice slept for about four hours. She pretty much passed out as soon as I plopped her in her bed, and I thought about joining because I was exhausted, too, but I kept noticing how filthy everything was. It's kind of a strange thing for a teenager to care about, but I really couldn't ignore it. I mean, layers of dust had their own layers of dust, and it seemed like the garbage hadn't been emptied in weeks.

Did we always live like that? Or had things gotten worse since Mom had become distracted by Seth?

Either way, Beatrice for sure wouldn't stay healthy in a place this dirty. That was just common sense.

41

So, I spent the entire afternoon cleaning our apartment, trying to quietly vacuum so I wouldn't wake up my sister, and I had to empty the canister like twelve times.

By the time I finished, the sun had almost completely gone down. I peeked into my bedroom, which was directly across from Beatrice's. My bedsheets hadn't been touched in weeks. Even when I was home, I didn't usually sleep in my own bed; I had nobody to turn off the lights for me.

So, I did what I always do: collapsed on the floor next to my sister's bed.

We were silent, the only sound being both of our stomachs growling. Our mom didn't return until the next morning.

NINE

THE ONLY GOOD thing about the apartment was I could sleep in a little and not have to worry about catching public transportation. We lived right down the street from my school, so I just rode my bike.

The downside of being home was literally everything else. It was even more depressing than being at the hospital. There wasn't any food, which I was kind of used to, but at the hospital I could swipe something off Bea's cafeteria tray that got delivered to her room. And the vending machines came in handy a lot.

But that was all gone. Still, I guess it was a decent compromise for Beatrice not being sick.

"You have any extra cash for lunch?" I asked my mom.

She was occupied, chugging cups of black coffee, and pointed at her purse.

I rummaged through it but found only a few bucks. I'm not sure why I expected more.

"You have to stay home with Beatrice," I told her. Reminding my mom to be a mom had to be done even more when we were home, sadly. That was another thing that sucked.

"I know. I'm off from work today."

She'd said that other times, and then I'd find out she abandoned Bea to go be with Seth. I was starting to think my mom didn't even work anymore. Before Seth came into the picture, she practically never had a day off.

Beatrice called from her room, probably wanting to get up for the day. I took that as my cue to exit, leaving Mom to finally do mom things for once. No doubt my sister would give her instructions if she forgot.

When I got back from school, I thought I'd walked into the wrong apartment. The smell of actual food cooking greeted me and transported me back to my childhood. I could almost hear the music playing in the background and see the silhouette of my mom in the kitchen preparing dinner with my dad. I was just waiting for him to walk out and ask me about my day. He didn't.

"Hi, Yo-Yo," Beatrice said, focused on the TV. "Mom's making meat loaf."

Meat loaf? I didn't even know Mom knew how to make meat loaf.

I walked over and kissed the top of her head, but my eyes were quickly shifting around the apartment. Somehow it seemed brighter.

"How are you feeling?" I asked her.

"Good! Do you like my clothes? Mom and I went to the grocery store, and then we stopped at the mall and I got this new outfit."

Nothing was making any sense. My mom barely ever went grocery shopping—we survived on food from the bar, takeout, and whatever we could get from Cheap Check, plus hospital food, of course—let alone going to the mall. It was eerie.

And then it got more surreal, which I hadn't thought was even

44

possible. My mom came out of the kitchen wearing an apron and hugged me.

"Reed, honey, how was your day? Are you hungry? We're having an early dinner."

"Okay" was all I could say.

My mom smiled at me, like really smiled. The same smile from when I was a kid and she'd tuck me into bed. I thought I'd never see that smile again, and when she walked back to the kitchen, I kept playing it in my head and comparing it to the one I used to know. Maybe they weren't exactly the same, or maybe I just told myself this one had to be different somehow.

Either way, it was a smile. My first in almost ten years.

"Do you need any help?" I asked.

"Nope. I've got everything under control."

I'm not joking when I tell you I legit pinched myself a few times. There could only be two explanations for my life suddenly flipping over and finally landing on the right side. Either my bike is a black hole to different dimensions, or our mom got hit in the head with a tennis ball and realized we needed her to be a mom again.

To me, one of those is obviously more plausible than the other. It's not the one you're thinking.

While my mom finished making dinner, I joined Beatrice, who was watching some boring technology show on the Science Channel. Honestly, I didn't know what to do with myself. My mind was telling me to lean back and sink into the couch, but my body wouldn't let me.

"Has Mom been acting like this all day?" I asked Beatrice.

"Not the whole day. She was kind of grumpy after you went to school and when she was getting me dressed. But she was in a better mood when she came back home."

"What do you mean 'when she came back home'? She was supposed to be with you all day. You said you guys went shopping together."

"That was after."

"After what?" I asked.

Beatrice sighed. "This morning Mom got me in my chair, and while I was watching TV, she left. She wasn't gone for very long. Like less than an hour. And when she got back, she took me shopping."

It didn't take a genius to figure out that Mom had seen Seth while she was supposed to be watching Beatrice. Suddenly the apartment didn't seem so bright anymore.

"Dinner is served," our mom called out.

Beatrice let me push her over to the table, which meant she was lying when she said she was fine. Or maybe she was just tired from her day out. It might have been the most active my sister had been in one day that didn't involve doctors.

"Meat loaf, mashed potatoes, and green beans." Mom pointed out the spread on the table. She was proud of herself and, in spite of myself, I kind of was, too.

"Thanks," I said. "It looks great."

"Yeah, I'm starving," Beatrice added.

She was ready to dive face-first into a plate of food, and so was I. The last time I had a home-cooked meal might've been the casseroles our neighbors brought over after my dad died.

"Before you dig in, I have some exciting news," Mom said.

Beatrice and I looked at our mom, concerned and confused, because nothing exciting ever happens to us. I didn't even remember what excitement felt like.

But I guess our mom did because she grinned so wide, we could almost see all her teeth. She glanced back and forth between us, trying to get us to smile, I think, but I definitely wasn't joining in until I heard the news. Beatrice didn't budge, either.

"Seth and I are going on a vacation!" Mom announced.

"How is that exciting?" I asked.

"It means we're taking our relationship to the next level. He told me when we get back, he might ask us to move in with him."

I had so many different things I wanted to say, but for some reason I settled on: "He 'might'?"

"Well, we'll have to figure out the logistics and everything. But we're gonna be a family! Isn't that great?"

"We already *are* a family," I reminded her.

She waved that aside. "You know what I mean—you're going to have a mom *and* a dad again."

"Do I have to call him Dad?" Beatrice asked.

"No," I told her.

Mom glared at me. "Only if you want to, sweetie."

The room was spinning and so were the meat loaf and potatoes, and I realized I hadn't come home to a dream or a better alternate universe. This was a nightmare. This was hell. I mean, the guy had barely said one word to me and my sister, and suddenly he wanted to be a part of our family?

I wanted to puke.

Mom checked the time on her phone. "Crap, he's probably waiting for me outside."

She tossed her apron on the kitchen counter and smoothed out the dress she was wearing.

How had I missed that?

Then she raced over to the couch and grabbed two rolling suitcases.

How had I missed those?

"We're just supposed to stay home?" I asked.

"It's only for the weekend. We'll be back Sunday night."

"And this day of shopping and making us dinner was for what? So you could pretend you're a mom before you bail on us again?"

Looking at a mirror by the front door, Mom fidgeted with putting in the pair of earrings Dad had bought her—as if that made up for what she was doing. She disgusted me.

"Reed, I need this," Mom said. "Everything's just been a little too much lately."

"You've got to be kidding me right now!"

I looked over to Bea for backup. Her eyes were fixed on the uneaten food.

"Can you watch your sister until Sunday?" our mom asked.

"Do I have a choice?"

She ignored that and walked over to kiss Beatrice on the head. "Bye, sweetie. Keep your brother out of trouble, okay?" She glanced at me, but I looked away. "I'll be back before you know it."

And just like that, she was gone.

I couldn't move for what felt like an eternity.

"The meat loaf is dry," Beatrice announced.

Somehow I was able to collect myself to get us in bed. I hoped I'd wake up to my life before, which was pretty sad because that one sucked, too.

But I didn't. My stomach was still growling, my dad was still dead, and now so was my mom, at least to me.

TEN

AFTER MOM took off for her romantic getaway with Seth, I couldn't help wondering how, exactly, they'd met. The story of my parents' meeting was legend. My dad used to tell the story over and over again to our neighbors or random people we'd see. He'd always have a different spin each time or give details I hadn't heard, so I never got sick of listening and he never got bored telling the story, either. However he said it, my mom was always blushing at the end. Sometimes she'd get teary-eyed.

The gist of the story is that my dad was set up on a blind date by some of his buddies from college. Apparently, he was pretty nervous about the whole thing and decided to show up to the restaurant early to have a drink.

At the time, my mom was also bartending. Now that I think about it, serving drinks is probably the only thing she's good at. That and running away.

Anyway, she saw my dad sitting at the end of the bar, sweating through his blazer and just looking like a total wreck. She kept bringing him drinks and coaching him on what to say to girls and how to not act like a goof. I guess it worked because my dad did go home with a girl that night, it just wasn't who he originally expected.

My dad always said he got stood up, but Mom insisted she saw a girl wandering around the restaurant but kept my dad distracted because she liked him so much. Either way, they both agreed they ended up with the right person, which was the part that always made people gush over how cute they were.

Nine months after they met, I was born and Mom dropped out of college. Dad graduated and they settled down in the suburbs like a perfect family, and for a while we basically were.

Occasionally I have a dream that I'm with my parents at the bar where they met. I'm myself but they don't know me, and in most of the dreams, I'll just watch them talking or sometimes I'll sit next to my dad and point out my mom bartending before she even notices him.

That night after my mom left, I had that dream again. But this time I sat far away from my dad and only talked to my mom until it felt like my tongue was going to fall out. And any time she would turn around to serve someone else or look at my dad, I'd demand another drink or pretend like I was going to faint.

Eventually, my dad left with another woman. Maybe it was the date he was originally supposed to meet. Maybe it was someone entirely different. It didn't matter.

"Yo-Yo" I heard through the fogginess of sleep. "Yo-Yo, wake up."

Flat on my back, I opened my eyes to the white of Bea's bedroom ceiling. We still existed, which proved dreams aren't real. "What? What time is it?"

"It's eleven o'clock. I want to get up."

As soon as I looked at the clock on the wall and confirmed it was actually almost the afternoon, I got to my feet as quickly as possible. There were things Beatrice had to do hours ago, like take her medication—not to mention it's bad for her to lie in one position for so long.

The first time I'm truly alone with my sister, I mess it up.

"Why didn't you wake me up earlier?" I asked.

"It looked like you were in a really deep sleep. Were you dreaming? What were you dreaming about? I had this dream where—"

"Beatrice, you have to be up at a certain time so we can follow the medication schedule Dr. David wrote."

"But I feel fine." She coughed. "I mean, I'll be fine."

I rolled my eyes, half blaming myself and half blaming her. Even though the routine was different after she got discharged, Bea knew what needed to be done.

"Let me just wash up quickly and then we can start," I told her. "Where's the paper we took home from the hospital?"

"On my dresser, I think. Mom was looking at it yesterday."

I grabbed the paper that was already crinkled from a coffee stain and took it into the bathroom. I studied it while peeing and brushing my teeth and had it almost memorized by the time I splashed some water on my face.

"Okay, first thing you have to do is a nebulizer breathing treatment," I announced as I walked back into her room. "Where did Mom put the medicine?"

Beatrice's eyes were closed. She was a terrible faker.

"Stop. This is serious. We have to do all of this stuff, and you're already three hours overdue."

That only made her pretend to have a really annoying snore, and Beatrice was so bad at it, she made herself laugh. It was funny, but I was too exhausted and anxious to laugh.

I pulled off the mask to her breathing machine that she always uses while sleeping and sat her up in the bed, propping her head with her unicorn pillow. She was still committed to the acting-asleep skit.

"Beatrice, seriously. What is your deal?" I asked.

She wouldn't fully open her eyes, but I saw her peek at me. I guess this was a version of a hissy fit. Sometimes I forgot she was only ten.

"Are you still thinking about last night?" I asked.

Bea nodded.

"Yeah, me too. That kind of sucked, right?"

"Does Mom not love Daddy anymore?" she asked.

I slid down to the floor with my back against her bed and faced a picture of our onetime family. Our dad was holding Beatrice, and Mom had her arms wrapped around him. I was standing in front of them, but you couldn't see my face. I was turned around, admiring everyone I loved. I know I was smiling. I remember.

"I don't know," I told her. "Maybe. It's hard to love someone who's not here."

"Do you still love him?"

"Of course. And I know he still loves us and is with us every day."

"Mom doesn't think so."

"Well, maybe Mom is just feeling really lonely."

"Are you lonely?"

"No." I jumped up. "That's impossible with you around."

Beatrice opened her eyes and stuck her tongue out. That was the signal we could finally start our day.

It took about ten minutes for me to find the medicine for Bea's nebulizer. Mom had put it in one of the kitchen cabinets, but as I was going through the new morning routine, I tried to organize everything next to my sister's bed. In addition to the medicines, she had a machine to help her cough and another that was like a tiny vacuum that sucked out all the mucus and boogers. It was kind of gross but had to be done.

"So, I just turn the machine on and put this mask over your face?" I asked.

"Yeah. And then use that other tube to suck out whatever I cough up."

I nodded, confident and terrified. I mean, it wasn't a big deal; I'd seen the respiratory therapists do it tons of times. But obviously I'd never tried doing it, and everything medically related is a lot more intimidating when you're on your own.

I covered Beatrice's nose and mouth with the mask and watched her tiny body jolt from every forced inhale and exhale. It felt like I was torturing her.

The instructions for the cough-assist machine were spelled out very clearly: five sets of five coughs. I yanked the mask off after only two coughs.

"Yo-Yo, what are you doing?" Beatrice asked.

"I'm not pushing too hard, am I?"

"It's fine. You're doing a good job."

I took a deep breath and we continued.

Halfway through, Beatrice's face was getting red from using so much energy, so we took a break. But she was getting up a lot of mucus, and after each round, her voice was a little bit stronger and louder.

"Did Mom do this yesterday?" I asked.

"No. She just did the nebulizer."

"Well, we're going to do it every day. Look how much you coughed up." I pointed at the canister, which was already half-full.

Beatrice shifted her eyes to get a look. "It's like aliens floating around."

I laughed. "We should incubate them and see if we can grow another Beatrice."

"That doesn't make any sense, Yo-Yo."

"I mean, it came out of you." I tried to make myself sound like a mad scientist. "The mucus has your DNA."

Beatrice wasn't buying it. "That's disgusting. I like the hospital where the suction is behind me so I can't see it."

I picked up the mask. "You ready for more?"

Bea nodded confidently, or as confident as someone can be who has to go through all that she does. But like me, she realized the new routine was making her feel better already. We just had to stick to it. I'd make sure we did, alone for two days or not.

"An hour and a half," Beatrice said as she rolled herself out of her bedroom and toward the living room.

"What?"

"That's how long it took from when you woke up to getting me in my chair."

"You were timing me?"

"Yes. But I don't think it's accurate. It felt more like two hours."

"Do you have somewhere to be that I don't know about? Hacking date with Zigzag?"

Beatrice ignored me, her eyes flickering around like she was doing some quick mental math. "Ten minutes for the neb and then another fifteen doing cough assist. But then we slowed down drastically because you had to stop to use the bathroom."

"Sorry, I had to poop."

"It's fine. You made up time giving me a bath and getting me dressed."

"I could do that with my eyes closed."

"True. Those are definitely your strongest events."

"Thanks, Coach, I guess. Should I be writing these times down?"

Bea nodded and I raced into the kitchen to grab a pen. I noted the duration of every step of her morning routine as estimated by my sister, who was having a little too much fun critiquing me. Some of them seemed harsh, like how she had me timed down to the second for how long it took to brush her teeth. But I played along because it was keeping her mind off our mom.

"So, all together about eighty-eight minutes," I told her.

"It's a start."

I rolled my eyes. "Bea, you know getting you ready isn't a race or decathlon or whatever you think it is."

"I know. But I was thinking about what time we'll need to wake up so we can do everything and you won't be late to school. Right now you'll be very late unless we wake up at five o'clock."

"Don't worry about that," I told her. "Mom will be back to help."

Beatrice didn't answer me. She just turned around and focused on the Science Channel. It was like she knew something I didn't, and suddenly I was the little sibling that needed protection.

"You want breakfast?" I asked, trying to fill the silence.

"Sure. What do we have?"

"Meat loaf."

"That's it?"

"Pretty sure. Unless other food magically appeared in the fridge overnight." When I'd put away the leftovers last night, I'd noticed that Mom hadn't bought any other food at the grocery store besides whatever it was she'd needed to make dinner. I don't know why I'd been surprised.

"Well, can you check?"

I think Beatrice was too occupied by the TV to remember that she'd gone shopping with Mom and therefore knew that we literally had no other food, but I went into the kitchen anyway just to appease her.

Obviously, when I opened the fridge nothing had changed. A pan of meat loaf and a bowl of potatoes stared back at me, both virtually untouched. Neither Beatrice nor I had had much of an appetite last night after Mom ditched us, and neither of us liked the idea of seeing that meal again, given everything it represented. But my stomach seemed to think it was on the verge of starvation. It felt like a canyon was being carved into it.

Whether I liked it or not, spite wasn't a part of the four main food groups. I heated up two plates and called over my sister. If I ate, then she would, too.

ELEVEN

THE REST OF the weekend went pretty smoothly. Beatrice played on the computer, and I actually got some homework done. Maybe other kids in my situation would've thrown some huge party, but not me. Beatrice probably would've loved it, but I had nobody to invite.

Anyway, my sister and I were watching TV when she randomly pressed the mute button. "What time is it?" she asked.

"Almost seven," I said, though I knew that wasn't really what she was asking. She was asking when Mom would be home. It had been exactly two days since Mom had left, but there was no sign of her yet.

And every time I cut off a sliver of meat loaf to heat up and eat, the sliver of chance that she would return also got pulverized in the microwave. Still, I couldn't quite believe that she would actually leave us.

"I'm gonna call her," I said.

The phone rang four times—I counted. It seemed like the only way to stop myself from totally freaking out.

When she answered, I didn't even waste time saying hello. I went straight to "When are you coming home?"

"Reed?" Mom responded. It sounded noisy wherever she was.

"Yes, it's your son. Are you on your way back? It's Sunday."

"Oh, funny story. Seth actually knows the manager of the hotel we're staying at in the city. They're old college friends. Small world, right?"

I didn't answer. My stomach dropped, predicting what was coming next.

"Anyway, he upgraded us to a suite, so we're extending our stay," she told me.

"What? How long?"

"I don't know. We're just sort of playing it by ear."

"I have school tomorrow. And Beatrice and I need food."

"There's meat loaf."

"We already ate all of it."

"Already?"

"Mom, it's been two days! It was the only food in the apartment."

Mom sighed. "Reed, I don't know what you want me to do. I'm not there."

At that point in the conversation, I was ready to chuck my phone across the table. Somehow I resisted.

"Yeah, I realize you're not here," I said. "But Beatrice and I are hungry."

She sighed. "There's some cash in my dresser drawer. Feel free to help yourself." I could tell she thought she was being generous. "Listen, I have to go. Seth bought tickets to a show."

Then she hung up—and then I really did throw my phone at the couch cushions.

I searched through my mom's dresser drawers, starting with the bottom ones. But, of course, the money was stashed in her underwear drawer, which I dug through just to find a lousy twenty bucks.

I was putting the things I wish I hadn't needed to touch back in place when I felt something hard slide around the bottom of the drawer. I pulled it out and had to sit on the edge of Mom's bed when I realized what I was looking at.

It was my dad's driver's license. I had no idea that she'd kept it or why. But I stared at it a while longer before sliding it into my back pocket.

"You up for walking down the street to the Cheap Check?" I asked, heading back into the living room.

"Why do we need to go there?"

I sighed. "Do you have to question everything?"

My sister just stared at me, eyebrows up like the answer to that was obvious.

"We need food, Beatrice," I said.

"Why can't we just get a pizza delivered?"

I held up the small wad of cash. "A pizza costs more than twenty dollars to get delivered."

"We can just wait for Mom to get back, and then she can go get us something."

"Didn't you just hear me on the phone? Mom's not coming back tonight."

"Why not?"

"I don't know. They're staying on their vacation longer."

"Well, when *is* she coming back?"

"I don't know, Beatrice."

My sister got quiet, almost sinking in her wheelchair. "Maybe we can go to Cheap Check later," she told me. "Zigzag's supposed to teach me about micro services in an hour."

I knew that was a lie. The night before, Beatrice had told me she was taking a break from Zigzag and her dark web friends. She'd said something about too much drama, whatever that means.

"I can push you," I said, "if you're worried it's too far."

"No. I just don't understand why we can't drive over."

"I don't have a license. And I don't know how to drive."

"Oh, yeah. You should really learn how to do that."

"Thanks for the tip."

I shut off the TV, which of course was followed by some whining from Beatrice. Apparently, now she'll never know the six types of malware.

But I didn't care. I transferred her off the couch and into her wheelchair. We both needed some fresh air.

Cheap Check was only three blocks from our apartment, but like I predicted, Beatrice got tired before we were halfway down our own street, so I pushed her the rest of the way. I didn't try to make her feel bad, though. She obviously knew she'd lost strength and didn't need me to remind her. Really, she just needed me as a sounding board for her lecture on the origins of cybersecurity—which was thankfully cut short when we got to Cheap Check.

Of course, my sister took off as soon as we were in the store, rolling up and down the aisles without any problems. That made me smile.

"Can we get these?" Beatrice held up a bag of Doritos.

"No. We're here to get something for dinner, not junk food."

"I hate to break it to you, but that's all we got here," said Poolio, manning the cash register. He was in his midtwenties and had been working there since I was Bea's age. His dad owned the store so he never left. And his first name was Jared, but no one called him that. "This isn't a restaurant."

I ignored him. "Go over by the cereals and pick out something," I told Beatrice.

"Still junk food," Poolio butted in again. "It's just sugar and corn syrup. The closest we have to real food is that fridge with pre-packaged sushi."

"Is it any good?"

"That depends on what you need it for."

"What does that mean?" I asked, walking over to Poolio. When I got closer, I realized he was reading the *Sports Illustrated* swimsuit issue and didn't even try to cover it up. He winked at me. "Inventory quality control."

I chose to ignore this.

He shrugged. "Anyway, the sushi sucks as food, but it's a great bowel detox. Yesterday I was feeling a little backed up, so I popped a few pieces and cleared everything out."

My eyes still glued on Poolio's goofy face, I yelled, "Stay away from the sushi, Bea!"

"I don't even like sushi!" she yelled back.

Heading over to Cheap Check, I thought twenty bucks would make me feel like a millionaire in the store. Like we could probably buy enough to last us a few days. But it was the complete opposite.

A pack of four frozen breakfast burritos was almost ten bucks. A half gallon of milk was around five, and then a box of cereal was over seven dollars.

Beatrice zipped past me, her lap piled with various chips and cookies. She definitely wasn't looking at any prices.

"Poolio, why's everything so expensive?" I asked.

"Convenience," he told me. "It's in the name of the store."

"Dude, the name of the store is Cheap Check. Nothing in here is cheap."

Poolio didn't answer, occupied by a customer who wanted to buy an overpriced pack of gum.

I'd been in the store dozens of times, so I shouldn't have been so surprised at the extreme markups. Occasionally, my dad would stop there with me, and we'd grab a slushie and some chips to snack on. Cheap Check supplied endless possibilities for getting hopped up on sugar, but that was when I was paying with someone else's money. I guess I still was in a way, but I wasn't as nice as my dad when I saw Bea over by the slushie machine.

"We can't afford that," I told her, walking back over to the front counter.

Poolio slowly rang up our box of Frosted Flakes, carton of two-percent milk, bag of Doritos, and a six-pack of Diet Dr Pepper. Every time he bagged an item, he'd eyeball me like some righteous judge of what people should put in their body. I should note he wasn't exactly a fitness model.

While I waited for my sister to finish whatever she was doing at the back of the store, I noticed a pile of employment applications next to the register.

"You hiring?" I asked.

"Always, my man. Can never seem to fill the position, though."

It's not like I had time for a job—and surely Mom would be back before things got *that* desperate—but my hand still grabbed an application and stuck it in my pocket. "Beatrice, come on."

"Relax. I'm right here." Her arms struggled to reach high enough to put her overflowing slushie on the counter.

"I told you we can't afford that. I only have a few bucks left."

"What flavor is it?" Poolio asked.

"I mixed them all."

"That's exactly what I do! I call it the Brainfreeze Blast." He smiled. "Take it with you. It's on the house."

Beatrice obviously didn't push herself back home, either, since both of her hands were busy holding the slushie and trying not to drop it whenever her wheels hit a bump. At the end of the block, while we waited for the walk signal, she poked out her tongue so I could examine the color change.

"Is it blue yet?" she asked.

"Your whole mouth is blue."

"Perfect." She chugged a little more. "By the way, you were ten minutes faster getting me ready today."

Beatrice said it like she knew that fact might ease my stress. And it might've if I had more than two bucks in my pocket and some kind of idea of when our mom would return.

TWELVE

THE STORY OF my parents doesn't just begin at a clichéd smoky bar and end with a death. There was obviously a whole bunch of other life events in between.

Apparently, my dad's parents are pretty conservative people and weren't totally on board with their son having a baby with a "one-night-stand type of girl." At least that's what I used to hear my parents say when they thought I couldn't hear, and even though at the time I had no idea what a one-night stand was, I understood enough to know it insulted my mom. Dad didn't stand for that. As long as I knew him, he protected the people he loved, and he loved my mom so much that I never met my grandparents. It was their loss, though. Besides never getting to meet me or Beatrice, they also missed out on seeing my dad's face every time he told the story of how he found the love of his life. If they'd seen it even one time, they'd have realized he'd made the right choice.

As for my mom's parents, she'd told us she left home at eighteen because both her parents were "selfish pieces of crap." Like parents, like daughter, I guessed.

So Beatrice and I really didn't have anyone to call. Maybe I could've looked up my dad's parents, but when I thought about it, I'd probably be better off asking a rando on the street to help us out. If my grandparents didn't care back then, then I'm sure they wouldn't care now. All that "blood is thicker than water" stuff is nonsense, as I'd unfortunately come to learn.

Anyway, I sat on the couch until almost midnight, waiting for my mom and Seth to walk through the door. I despised myself for wasting all that time and energy believing in something I knew wouldn't happen. I had tried calling her all night, but the calls had gone straight to voice mail. Before I went to sleep, I decided to try her phone one last time.

To my surprise, she answered right away.

"Oh, honey, I'm glad you called."

I perked up, naively thinking my mom had missed us and was coming home.

"The Broadway show was spectacular," she told me. "I've been dying to tell you and Beatrice all about it! Put me on speaker, would you?"

"Speaker?" I repeated numbly. "Mom, Bea's asleep. It's after midnight!"

"Oh. Well, I guess I'll just tell you, then. You can fill her in in the morning."

"Mom, no, I—"

But she cut me off before I could tell her that I'd only found twenty bucks and that we'd run out of food if she didn't come back by Wednesday. So I just stayed silent and let her ramble on about Broadway until I couldn't take it anymore.

"Mom, when are you coming home?" I asked.

"I already told you that we extended our stay."

"But what does that mean? One day, two days—a week?"

"I don't really know yet. Seth is handling everything. He said I deserve a break. I think he's right, that it'll be good for me and good for *us*. Don't worry; I'll send you some money. In the meantime, try to make the money from my dresser last. You'll need to step up and be responsible while I'm gone—"

I hung up.

I wasn't upset or angry or terrified. Truth was, I had to move on quickly for me and especially for my sister. I had to move on the same way it seemed our mom had moved on from us. And, honestly, she'd been gone way before leaving for her vacation.

Since I had no clue when (or if) our mom would end her narcissistic gallivant, I had to quickly figure out how Bea and I would survive in the meantime. So, before going to bed that night, I quietly ransacked our apartment looking for more than the twenty bucks I'd found, but I came up empty-handed, without even a single penny tucked under a couch cushion. It seemed my only option was to fill out the Cheap Check employee application. Maybe Poolio had afternoon shifts, and I could bring my sister with me to hang out or something.

I don't know what time it was that I finally fell asleep, but I know that it was far too early when the alarm in Beatrice's bedroom began blaring. I groaned.

"You have to go to school," Beatrice told me. "It's Monday."

"There's no way," I said, sitting up and groping on her night-stand for my phone. When had Bea managed to set an alarm? "You can't be alone for eight hours."

"Yes, I can. It's safe here and I know how to do my nebulizers

66

myself. You just need to leave the medicine and Frosted Flakes where I can reach them."

"What about if you have to pee? You can't get on the toilet by yourself."

"I won't drink anything." She said it like that was an obvious solution.

I rubbed my face, not believing I was actually having that conversation. "Beatrice, you can't just not drink all day. That's not healthy. I'll come home and find you passed out from dehydration."

"Well, I don't know. But you have to go to school."

She nagged me about school all through our morning routine, pausing only during her nebulizer treatment. My sister wasn't going to let up unless I caved and went to school, or at least left the house for a few hours. For all she knew, I could've sat out front all day and watched her through the window.

"Okay, I'll go," I told Beatrice, once I'd gotten her dressed and all set up for the day.

She beamed like a proud mom who'd convinced her son that kindergarten won't kill him.

"But I'm gonna check in on you every half hour."

Beatrice gasped. "You bought me a cell phone?"

I chuckled. "No, you're on my laptop all day, so I'll just email you to see if you need anything." Technically I'd be emailing myself since Bea was too young to have her own email address, but since she already treated my inbox as joint property, I knew she'd receive any messages I sent.

Beatrice frowned, clearly upset that I hadn't bought her a phone, even though we could barely afford a box of cereal the day before. Anyway, I kissed her head and left.

Honestly, I *was* actually planning on going to school, but first

I stopped in at Cheap Check. When I got there, it was like Poolio hadn't moved since I last saw him. He wore the same clothes, and the only difference was that he was reading a *Maxim*.

"Where's your partner in crime?" he asked me.

"Home."

"By herself? What if she needs you? What if something happens?"

I wasn't sure why he assumed Beatrice would be alone. Did we ooze some kind of orphan pheromone?

Poolio didn't seem astute enough to pick up on something like that. On the other hand, he knew how to use convenience store sushi as a bowel cleanser, so perhaps I underestimated him.

"She'll be fine," I told him and myself. I slid the application across the counter. "I'm looking for something part-time. I can work afternoons and weekends."

Poolio examined the paper as if I was applying for something legit, like a passport. He would look at what I wrote, then flick his gaze up to me and then back down to the application. In between he would make a strange grunt.

And in between us was an open *Maxim* magazine. The whole thing was very uncomfortable.

"You have impeccable handwriting," he said.

"Thanks. Is that a necessary qualification?"

"No, but I thought I should mention it. Do you mind if I ask you some interview questions?"

"I guess not."

Poolio took a deep breath. "If a customer came in and handed you a twenty-dollar bill to pay for three items that total eighteen dollars, how much change do you give them?"

"Um, two dollars?"

"Correct. If I announced everything in the store is fifty percent off, how much would a ten-dollar item cost?"

"Five?"

Poolio nodded and finally exhaled. "It seems you have a good grasp on American currency and economics."

"So, do I have the job?"

"Let me just check one more thing." Then he sighed a different type of sigh. The type I didn't want to hear when applying for a job. "You're not eighteen?"

"No. Is that a problem?"

"There are items here that can only be distributed by a legal adult." He eyed the magazine and pointed at the selection of cigarettes behind him.

"Well, if someone wants to buy those, then I'll just call you over to ring them up."

Poolio laughed. "Why would I hire you if I still have to be here? That doesn't make any sense."

I ran my hands over my face. If only the world trusted me to pass out cigarettes as much as my mom trusted I would take care of Beatrice and myself.

"Listen, man, I really need this job," I said, practically begging.

"Sorry. There's nothing I can do. But maybe check out the grocery store over on Crossing."

"It's too far. I can't drive."

"Oh. You should really learn how to do that."

"Thanks," I spat.

I was about to leave when a group of kids my age came in and blocked the exit. They were all oddly jittery for the morning and whispered among themselves. I recognized the kid in the front named Tucker Walsh.

He stepped up to Poolio at the counter. "A pack of Lucky Strikes."

"Identification?" Poolio asked.

Tucker's friends turned beet red as he fumbled in his pocket for his wallet. I was interested to see how this would play out.

"Got it right here." Tucker tossed the plastic card onto the counter.

Poolio examined the ID even more intently than my job application, which I didn't think was possible. He held it up to the fluorescent ceiling lights and brought it so close to his face, he almost ingested the thing.

"This is fake," Poolio announced.

Tucker fidgeted with his hands. "No—no, it's not. That's legit."

"Dude, *New Jersey* is spelled wrong on this thing. Also, there's no way you're twenty-nine."

"I'm telling you, that ID is real. Just give me the smokes."

Poolio shook his head and pulled out a pair of scissors from under the counter. "You come in and demand cigarettes with a fake ID. It's sad. And Lucky Strikes? Seriously? Who are you, my grandpa?"

With one quick snip, the card was halved. Tucker and his friends were horrified. Poolio was having the time of his life.

"Bro, I spent eighty bucks on that!" Tucker yelled.

"Well, you wasted your parents' money. Now, get the hell out of my store."

The four of them stomped out like children who were banished to their bedrooms. I don't exactly know what possessed me, but I chased after them.

Actually, I know exactly what possessed me. As soon as I heard Tucker say he spent eighty dollars on his crappy ID, I knew it was a sign, an answer to my money problems. It was like the universe had put me at the Cheap Check for this perfect moment of spiritual guidance.

"I can make you a fake ID!" I called out in the parking lot.

Tucker and his friends turned. "What are you talking about?"

"I can make you fake IDs. All of you. Better than the crap that just got cut up."

"How?" Tucker was visibly confused, but I had his attention.

"I have access to the right equipment," I lied, my mind already whirling with possible ways to gain access to the printer in the art room, the one that made our student IDs.

"That doesn't mean you can make a legit driver's license."

"I'm good with Photoshop," I told Tucker. It was true. I took a graphic design class sophomore year and did pretty decent— decent enough to design an ID, I figured. Plus I remembered I had my dad's old license to use as a template. "Trust me; it'll work." He had to believe me.

"How much?" one of the friends asked.

I blurted the first number that popped in my head: "Hundred bucks. Each."

"No way," Tucker said. "That's more than the other one. We don't even know if yours'll be half as decent."

"True. But I'll definitely spell *New Jersey* correctly."

Tucker huddled with the rest of the group to discuss.

"Have you ever made one before?" Tucker asked.

I shook my head.

"Then make yourself one and try it out here first."

"Can't. The guy in there knows my age."

"Fine, then test it on the liquor store down the street. The owner is a hard-ass. You'll get our money if you can walk out with a six-pack—of *beer*," he added unnecessarily.

71

I nodded, my palms already sweating as the gravity of what I was agreeing to hit me, and then Tucker and his friends got in their car and drove away.

My dad always said that if you jump, the universe will put out a net. I definitely jumped high and far, and I couldn't tell if there was a net waiting to catch me and Beatrice, or if I was going to land straight in jail.

THIRTEEN

OUR STUDENT IDs were the same size as driver's licenses and made from the same high-quality plastic—unlike Tucker's cheap forgery. If I could get time alone in the art room, I had no doubt I could make a better one, once I'd spent a bit of time figuring out the design. But first things first. I knew from watching Bea's cyber-security documentaries that all criminal activity starts with a plug.

Unfortunately, I realized my plug had to be Helena Shaw. She controlled the art room and the printer.

Despite her being student council president, Helena ate lunch alone. It was the perfect opportunity.

I nonchalantly sat down across from her.

"What do you want, Reed?"

"Wow, is that any way to greet one of your constituents?"

Helena put down her sandwich and forced a fake smile. "Hello, Mr. Beckett. How may I help you?"

"You're in Yearbook Club, right?"

"Yes, I'm the president."

"Of course you are. Anyway, Yearbook meets in the art room, right?"

"Yeah. Why?"

"I wanna join."

"You want to join?" Helena was more surprised than I expected. "What are you going to do?"

"I don't know. Whatever you need, I guess. I'm good at Photoshop. Anyway, does it really matter? I thought it was open to all students."

"Well, it is but—" Helena stopped when she noticed me unpacking my lunch. "Is that really what you're going to eat?"

I nodded.

"A bag of Doritos and a Diet Dr Pepper?"

"Yes. That is what I'm holding."

"Is that what you normally eat?" She inflected her interest with a not-so-subtle hint of contempt.

"No, it's not what I normally eat, actually," I said. "Usually I have Doritos, a Diet Dr Pepper, *and* a Kit Kat. But, you know, you got rid of all the vending machines."

I took a loud slurp of my soda, making sure I drove home the message that I didn't care what Helena thought about my lunch. She was visibly disgusted.

"I don't know why this is freaking you out," I said. "I've seen you drink soda."

Helena had no response and finally returned to our original topic. "Fine. You can join. We meet twice a week."

"Great."

"And we're meeting today after school, and you have to be there."

"No problem." I didn't love being away from Beatrice even longer, but I didn't really have a choice.

Helena got this crazed smirk on her face, which I'd seen before,

74

and it scared the hell out of me. Then she pulled out a thick binder from her backpack and flopped it on the table.

"What's that?" I asked.

"My vision for the yearbook. I usually review it by myself, but now that you're a member, we need to get you up to speed."

Her yearbook lecture consumed the rest of lunch period, almost forty minutes. She rambled about page weight and different types of finishes, like gloss or matte, and through it all I just nodded. Really, though, I wanted to stick my head in the huge pot the lunch lady was stirring.

Instead, I kept thinking about Beatrice. This was our ticket. Well, at least a small first step. But the next was a doozy.

How the hell was I going to convince Helena and the rest of the Yearbook Club to leave me alone in the art room for long enough to make an authentic-looking driver's license?

FOURTEEN

WHILE I'D LEFT Beatrice alone before for an entire school day, she'd either had doctors or nurses checking on her constantly or Mom was home with her. Now that we were truly on our own, I couldn't stop worrying about her.

I probably emailed her about a hundred times throughout the day, mostly to ask if she'd been drinking and if she needed me to come home so she could use the bathroom. Apparently, she was fine, though, based on the fact that she'd told me she joined a non-stop Hackathon with Zigzag and couldn't leave the computer even if she wanted to. I made the decision that I'd eat lunch at the apartment the next day to make sure she drank some water and didn't spend all day on the computer.

I let Beatrice know that I'd being staying late at school, although I didn't tell her why because if I did, she'd start asking questions. Plus, my sister knew me too well to accept the excuse that I'd voluntarily joined a school club.

The art room where the club met was empty when I got there, and for some reason I was surprised. I wasn't sure how many people it took to put together a yearbook, but I was assuming it was more than just Helena Shaw. If it was only going to be the two of us, then the school definitely wasn't getting a yearbook—though I'd seen Helena accomplish more than that by herself, so who knew.

On the upside, if it was just the two of us, that made it a lot easier for me to figure out how she printed my student ID and scope out a way to make another without being seen.

"Hello?" I called out into the empty room, then immediately felt ridiculous. Did I expect someone to climb out of a closet or something?

And then someone actually did. A door at the back of the room opened, and Helena Shaw appeared.

"Oh, good, you came," Helena said. I couldn't decide if it was sarcastic.

"I told you I would. Are you the entire club?"

"Pretty much. And Ms. Gold, our club mentor. And now you."

As if she'd been waiting for her cue, Ms. Gold walked in. I had her for graphic design last year. She was definitely the kooky art teacher and looked exactly how you'd expect an art teacher to look, with retro glasses and strange knitted ponchos. Not to mention she kind of smelled like weed. I bet she told the other teachers it's because she burns sage.

"New recruit?" she asked Helena.

"Yes, this is Reed Beckett."

"Oh, I know Reed. He was in my graphic and illustrations class last year. He was my best student."

"I was in that class, too," Helena added.

"Yes, you were, dear."

I probably shouldn't have enjoyed their back-and-forth as much as I did.

Ms. Gold winked at me and then whisked over to her desk.

I never use the word *whisk*, but it perfectly describes the way Ms. Gold moved and how her poncho flapped behind her.

"I can't stay," she announced. "Helena, are you okay to train Reed by yourself? I'm late for tantric yoga."

Helena sighed. "Sure."

Ms. Gold left, and I dry-heaved a little, thinking about her at yoga. Helena laughed.

"I never thought I'd hear a teacher say *tantric*," I said.

"Soon she'll ask you to call her Barb," Helena told me.

"Wow, can't wait for that."

Helena smiled, which made me feel pretty good for some reason. Maybe she wasn't as uptight as I thought. But her face quickly morphed back to business. "Come with me."

I followed her over to a table with a stack of papers that was easily three feet high. Obviously, I was getting stuck with the tasks Helena and Ms. Gold didn't want to do.

"These are yearbook order forms. And this is a list of every homeroom and the number of students." She handed me a piece of paper. "I need you to group the order forms with the correct amount for each homeroom so we can deliver them tomorrow."

"Seems easy enough."

"Yup. Let me know if you have any questions."

"I think I know how to count," I told her.

I started making piles across the table and labeling each with the room number. I'd gotten through about five or six when I realized Helena was still standing behind me.

"Helena, seriously, I got this," I said. "Go do whatever it is you do in that closet."

"It's not a closet. It's a darkroom."

I knew what it was, but I felt like giving Helena a hard time. "Obviously, it's a dark room because it's a closet."

"Oh my God." She flopped down on the seat next to me. "That's the name of the room, darkroom. It's where you develop photos."

I wanted to keep going, but I couldn't stop myself from laughing. "Helena, I know what a darkroom is. I'm just giving you a hard time."

"Oh." She jolted up from the chair. "Just let me know when you're done."

I wondered if maybe at one point Yearbook Club had more help, but Helena babysat everyone so they left. That could be true, though the more logical explanation was nobody joined in the first place because it's boring.

Either way, both explanations left me stranded.

Grouping order forms was the most tedious activity I'd ever done, and the whole time I was tormented by the computer and printer behind me. Somehow I had to get Helena to show me how she made the ID because it wasn't like I could just randomly ask. I mean, maybe if it was anyone other than Helena Shaw, but I knew she'd get suspicious. Beatrice and Helena would probably get along great.

But then a miracle happened. There was a knock on the door, and some random student was standing in the room. "Um, the guidance office said this is where I come if I lost my student ID."

Helena came out from the darkroom. "Just tell me your name, and I can print a new one."

The two of them huddled over by the computer that was right next to me, and I secretly watched Helena scroll through hundreds of student yearbook photos. There were folders meticulously labeled by graduating year.

The dollar signs added up in my brain, making that *cha-ching* sound like in cartoons. But I snapped out of that daydream to focus on the Photoshop template Helena opened.

It looked exactly like the ID I had, except it was missing a picture and a name. Helena pasted in the kid's photo and a few clicks later a new ID was printed.

I was mesmerized. The process was like magic. I figured it wouldn't be too hard to make a few tweaks to the template, but it had to be without Helena or Ms. Gold around. That part was going to be tricky, considering it seemed like Helena lived in that darkroom.

FIFTEEN

HELENA TEXTED ME before I even got back home to say that I had to show up to school an hour early the next day to help deliver the order forms to all the homerooms. I assumed she was joking, but her request turned more insistent until finally it was a full-on military order. I could just imagine how she acted during student government meetings.

Like, I remember in second grade Helena was in charge of what game our class would play at recess. Don't ask me why that was her job—I'm pretty sure she elected herself—but she kept a strict schedule. On Mondays and Wednesdays, we'd play kickball; Tuesdays and Thursdays was tag; and then on Fridays, our class would go to the jungle gym.

One day somebody brought in a skateboard for show-and-tell, and obviously everyone in class wanted to try it at recess. Helena had a total meltdown that we weren't following the schedule, and our entire class got in trouble for not playing with her.

Anyway, all of that meant I really had no choice but to show up early. Especially if it meant the possibility of unsupervised time in the art room.

"You couldn't get two carts from the supply closet?" I asked Helena as I pushed at least fifty pounds of paper down the hallway.

"Mr. Milton said he only had one available."

"Who's Mr. Milton?"

"The school's head custodian," she said, like it was common knowledge.

"Do you know everyone in this place?"

Helena smirked. "It's just part of being president."

"Well, Ms. President, can you at least help a little? I'm gonna get a hernia trying to push this."

"I am helping." Helena nodded toward one measly stack of forms in her left hand. The other was holding a banana she'd been nibbling on.

It was so early in the morning that barely any teachers were in the school. It might even have been just me, Helena, and Mr. Milton, who so kindly lent us a cart that pulled to the left and had an obnoxious squeaky wheel.

"Isn't the school nice when it's empty?" Helena asked.

I shrugged. "It's kind of creepy."

"You get used to it."

"You've done this before?"

"Only when I'm doing stuff like this, or I need to set up for a pep rally or a school dance. Luckily, the back door to the gym is always unlocked." Helena froze. "Forget I told you that."

"Told me what?" I joked, trying to act like she hadn't just solved my biggest problem: how to get alone time in the art room.

I dropped another box of order forms on a teacher's desk. For some reason, the cart didn't feel like it was getting any lighter, and we still had another twenty stacks in the art room.

"What'd you get on your last English paper?" Helena asked out of the blue.

"Which one?"

"The one Mrs. Kapoor passed out after class yesterday? Our assignment on Miss Havisham?"

"Oh, I don't know. I didn't look."

Helena narrowed her eyes at me. "You're lying. The grade is right at the top. You couldn't miss it even if you tried."

I sighed. Helena was never going to stop unless I told her my grade, which I seriously didn't know. I stuck the paper in my backpack and forgot all about it. My grade was whatever it was.

I yanked my backpack off my shoulder and tossed it to Helena. "Here. Since you care so much, you can dig through my crap and find it."

Oddly, Helena didn't take offense to that. She was so nosy, she actually knelt on the floor and went searching through my backpack. I just left her in the middle of the hallway, continuing our deliveries and dropping order forms in front of homeroom doors that were locked.

"You got a hundred?" Helena called out.

"I guess. Is that what it says?"

She held up the crumpled paper. "You got a hundred." Helena sounded shocked—and disgusted.

"So?"

"So, I only got a nighty-eight."

I walked back over to Helena and grabbed the paper from her hand. It actually had the number one hundred at the top. Mrs. Kapoor even drew a smiley face and wrote BEST IN CLASS.

Seeing the look on Helena's face was better than the actual grade. But rubbing the paper in Beatrice's face was going to be priceless.

"I didn't know you were smart," Helena said.

"Thanks."

"No, I don't mean it like that. I mean, I remember you being smart when we were kids, but I didn't know you were *that* smart."

"It's an AP class," I reminded her.

Helena just stared down the length of the hall. Between this and hearing Ms. Gold say I was the better graphic design student, Helena must've felt like her world had suddenly exploded. I felt bad for her, but it was also a little pathetic.

Finally she snapped out of her existential crisis and looked at me. "I brought you something." She dug through her backpack and pulled out a small baggie. It was a sandwich.

Helena handed it to me, and I just stared back at her, speechless.

"I don't want you to think I'm being intrusive or anything, but I was making my lunch this morning and had extra so I made you one, too. I hope that's okay?"

"It's cool. Thanks—a lot."

Helena blushed. "It's peanut butter with Marshmallow Fluff and bananas. I remembered you used to eat that all the time. Not the healthiest but better than chips and diet soda."

I rarely get emotional over stuff like that, but my throat tightened and my eyes started to fill over a peanut butter sandwich. Thankfully, Helena didn't make a big deal of it.

She just smiled at me. It wasn't her fake smile she flashed in the hallways or during her student council president speeches or even the big cheesy one she gets when she knows she got the highest grade. This smile was human, and I'd seen it a hundred times when we were younger.

I hadn't realized how much I'd missed it.

SIXTEEN

HELENA AND I were neighbors for the first seven years of our lives. We practically spent every waking moment of our childhood together, chasing each other outside or building blanket forts in her bedroom and laughing until we fell asleep. We were best friends. At least I thought we were.

But Helena was different back then; we both were. Apparently, though, she still remembered my favorite sandwich.

"Where'd you get the sandwich?" Beatrice asked me.

When I came home for lunch, she was exactly where I left her: glued to my laptop. I'd debated eating the sandwich on my own, but in the end, I decided we'd split it. My sister deserved to eat something other than Frosted Flakes.

"I got it at school," I told her. It wasn't a lie, but there was no need for her to know we were at the point of accepting handouts.

"Well, what is it?"

"Peanut butter with marshmallow and bananas."

Beatrice's eyes lit up.

"We'll eat it in a little bit. First you need to use the bathroom and do a nebulizer."

Any other day, my sister would've groaned for no reason other than just being a pain in the ass. But she didn't make a peep. She was desperate to sink her teeth into that sandwich. I was too.

"Your pee is too dark," I said, flushing the toilet. "You have to drink."

"I did." She batted her eyes at me.

If there's anything I've learned from all the time we spend in hospitals and around doctors, it's that urine doesn't lie.

"I'm gonna fill up two glasses of water before I leave," I said.

"I can't drink that much. I'll pee in my pants."

She had a point. "Fine. But you're finishing a glass with lunch, and then I'll help you in the bathroom again."

I rolled Bea into her room and turned on her neb. The mask almost covered her entire face, and when she talked, she sounded like Darth Vader.

"Why are you being so bossy?" she asked.

"I'm not being bossy." My voice was unnecessarily loud. I caught myself and took a deep breath. "There's just a lot we need to do before I go back to school. I don't want you to get sick again."

Bea nodded, audibly taking in deep breaths of her medication. Sometimes I forgot she didn't want to be sick just as much as I didn't want her to be sick.

"What have you been doing today?" I asked. "Busy with Zigzag?"

"Oh, yeah. Someone made a replica of the original Yahoo! firewall. Thousands of people are trying to complete the re-hack challenge. Me and Zigzag teamed up."

"I thought you wanted to be a good hacker?"

"I do, but first I need to understand how the bad guys think."

I started to laugh, but then I recalled my own attempts to think like a criminal, and suddenly it didn't seem so funny.

"Hey, check this out." In need of a distraction, I dug around in my backpack and fished out my English paper.

"Nice. But you probably could've gotten above a hundred if you wrote about Miss Havisham being a lonely romantic."

"You can't get above a hundred."

"Well, maybe your teacher would've given you extra credit."

"There's no way. Besides, I got a better grade than this girl who's, like, the smartest person in my school."

Beatrice just shrugged me off. I kind of loved that she never fueled my ego or even let me have one.

Anyway, her breathing treatment fizzled out, and after it was done, she followed me back into the kitchen. Both of us ogled the sandwich that was sitting on the counter. I carefully unwrapped it and handed Beatrice half.

We devoured the thing. I mean, we didn't talk or blink or even breathe. The sandwich was the best thing I'd tasted in years. Something about the marshmallow melting with the peanut butter made it grossly delicious.

And the baggie it came in smelled like Helena, which I obviously didn't point out to my sister and was also a little mad at myself for realizing. But it was a smell I recognized from when we were kids, a mix of her mom's perfume and all the other scents that made Helena Shaw.

Maybe that's what made the sandwich taste so good to me.

"Do you think Mom is ever coming back?" Beatrice asked, bringing me back to reality.

"You miss her a lot?" I asked.

Bea nodded.

Unfortunately, I couldn't bring our mom back any more than I could bring our dad back, which was tough to accept because one of them was still alive. And it's not like I didn't try. These past couple of days, I've called and texted Mom almost constantly, sending her a quick message or leaving her a voice mail between classes when I was at school, or ducking into the bathroom when I was at home. I did everything to protect Beatrice from knowing that I was failing to get ahold of our mom.

I told myself that she'd forgotten to turn on her phone or had misplaced her charger. That she was on her way back and wanted to surprise us, and that's why she wasn't picking up or texting me back. That she just needed to escape everything for a little bit longer before she was ready to face it all again.

But as the days dragged on with no word from her, a dark fear had started to creep in: What if she liked her fantasy life with Seth more than she liked being a mom?

What if she was never coming back?

I didn't care if Mom wrote me off; I could take care of myself. But my sister needed her mom. Maybe not to do her medicine or say the right things to Dr. David or have money to buy her gifts to make her feel better, but just to be a mom.

In between small sips of water, Beatrice glanced at the front door. I knew how she felt, like if she looked hard enough, then the door would magically open.

I opened the refrigerator and took out two of the cans of Diet Dr Pepper I'd bought from Cheap Check. The cold aluminum reminded me of Helena, and I told my brain to block her out.

Beatrice eyed the can I set in front of her. "Didn't you say I have to finish this glass of water?"

"I did, but I think you deserve something more fun right now. You know, Dad used to sneak me a soda when I was sad."

"Really?" She started to perk up, like she always did when I told her something about Dad.

"Oh, yeah. It was our little secret from Mom."

"But Mom doesn't care if we drink soda."

"She did back then. So Dad and I would hide in my bedroom and drink Diet Dr Pepper." I lowered my voice to a whisper and looked around as if people might be eavesdropping. "He called it Diet Soda Club."

"Diet Soda Club?"

I shushed her. "Keep your voice down. It's a secret."

Bea giggled, then tried to look serious.

"Do you wanna join the club?" I asked.

"Definitely. What's the initiation?"

"Who said there's an initiation?"

"Well, there has to be. Especially if it's a secret club."

I tried not to laugh and diminish her seriousness. "You're right. I was testing you. The initiation is you have to take a huge gulp of the soda and then burp your name."

Beatrice narrowed her eyes, but she was eating up every second of Diet Soda Club, even the parts I made up. After I popped the tab for her, she brought the can up to her mouth. The delivery was shaky, but she got it there.

Then Bea chugged almost the entire can before setting it back on the table. Her cheeks puffed and her eyes bulged. It was building inside her.

"BEATRICE!" she belched.

We both lost it, tears running down our faces. My sister wouldn't stop burping. She'd take a sip and burp her name or my name or any other word that would pop into her head. It was a pretty incredible talent for someone with breathing issues.

I tried to join in, but I wasn't nearly as good. We laughed anyway and drank our Diet Dr Peppers and forgot all about being alone.

SEVENTEEN

"**WE GOTTA GET UP**," I told Beatrice, rolling her over on her back.

She could barely open her eyes. "What are you doing, Yo-Yo? What time is it?"

"Four in the morning. I have to get to school early."

"Again? You did that yesterday."

"I need to work on a project," I told her. It was a small fib.

The truth was I needed to get there before anyone else so I could work on making illegal government identification. Tucker cornered me in the hallway yesterday and asked what was taking me so long. Besides, we were running out of food, and with Mom still not answering her phone—or making good on her promise to send us money—we needed a source of income, stat.

Beatrice groaned.

My hands and mind were going wild, rushing to get everything organized for our morning routine. I hadn't slept well, too worried I'd sleep through my alarm.

"Can't I just sleep for, like, five more minutes?" Beatrice begged.

I finally slowed down to realize she still hadn't fully woken up. "Fine. I'll take a shower and you can sleep more, but when I come back, you're getting up."

I took her silence as confirmation that she agreed.

In the bathroom, I walked myself through the process: find the open gym door Helena mentioned, get to the art room unseen, make the ID in less than a half hour, and get out.

As soon as I got out of the shower, I grabbed my dad's old license and put it in my backpack; I didn't want to forget to take it. I couldn't afford to.

Now everything was in place. I just had to get Beatrice ready for the day. She was thankfully a little more cooperative when I returned but definitely knew something was up.

While I knew Helena had been telling the truth about the unlocked gym door, I was still shocked to see for myself just how unsecure the school really was. Luckily, not a single teacher was in sight—though I glimpsed Mr. Milton, who lent us the cart the day before. I slipped into the art room without him noticing me.

The glowing computer screen called my name like it'd been waiting for me. We had business to take care of, and I got right to work.

First, I took out my dad's ID and placed it directly in front of me so I'd have a reference the entire time. I'd noticed it had a symbol printed on the plastic that reflected in the light. That part was going to be tough to nail. But I'd stayed up half the night researching ways to mimic iridescent ink, and I felt reasonably confident I could pull it off.

I opened the Photoshop template for our student IDs and, as I'd expected, the format was very similar to the one for the driver's license. It was like whoever had designed our student IDs *wanted* someone to forge driver's licenses. I was only too happy to comply.

I moved around a few elements, making sure I removed the name of our school and replaced it with *New Jersey*—spelled correctly, of course.

Information like the ID number I stole from my dad's license, and every time I'd glance at it, it felt like his eyes in his picture were following me, judging me. Eventually, I flipped over the piece of plastic so he couldn't look at me.

"Sorry, Dad," I mumbled. "I have to do it for Beatrice."

And it was a good thing I flipped it over, because I realized the back of the card had stuff on it, too, including a couple of barcodes, which were definitely important to have but which I had no idea how to replicate. I started to panic as the clock in the classroom ticked louder and louder with every passing second. But I had no choice. I had to figure out a way.

To buy myself some time, I imported my photo from the yearbook pictures folder. If I stared long enough, maybe I didn't exactly come across as twenty-one, but maybe I wasn't too far off. It definitely helped that on the day those were taken, Bea had a bad night so I was up with her and got no sleep. Between the bags under my eyes and the stubble, I definitely looked older.

I probably wouldn't get so lucky with Tucker and his friends' photos. But that would be tomorrow's problem, hopefully.

Now for the barcode issue. One of the barcodes was the same style as the barcodes on our student IDs, so that was easy enough to import. As for the other barcode—some weird pixilated one that looked kind of like a stretched-out QR code—I did the best I could at creating a reasonable approximation. So long as no one actually tried scanning the barcodes, I figured I'd be okay. The rest of the elements on the back were child's play compared to the barcodes.

Finally, I pressed print and waited for the first test to shoot out. When it did, my stomach plummeted. It looked like crap! The state emblem didn't shimmer, and overall the colors were way brighter than on my dad's license.

I decided to put a filter over the ID to tone it down. That worked for the text and my picture, but the emblem still looked too phony to pass any serious check.

Then I figured that maybe I could first print the card without the emblem. After that I'd put the plastic through the printer again to finish with the emblem on top.

The idea came to me from a movie I'd watched with Beatrice about counterfeit money. Those printers went through a two-step process, and while I knew it was just a movie, I was running out of ideas along with the confidence that I could actually pull this off.

By some chance miracle, though, it worked. The shimmering emblem, text, and photos all looked legit. I held the fake ID next to my dad's, and there really was no difference.

I did it. I actually did it.

I wanted to scream and jump and run around the room, but obviously I couldn't do any of that.

Instead, I stuffed both IDs in my backpack, along with the test ones, cleared out the printer's history, and slunk out of the room like the criminal that I was.

EIGHTEEN

BEFORE I LEFT school that day, I caught up with Tucker in the hallway and told him to meet me outside the liquor store around ten o'clock. I also told him not to bring any of his friends because it'd look really sketchy if a bunch of teen boys were waiting in the parking lot. But I was confident. At least I hoped I came across that way.

I waited for Beatrice to fall asleep before I left the apartment. Luckily, it didn't take long; the upside of getting up so early that morning. As I walked toward the liquor store, I felt a sense of power that I'd never experienced before. Like, just carrying that thin piece of plastic changed me, even though I had no intention of using it except to prove to Tucker it worked. But even though it was fake, it still felt like proof that I was an adult.

Tucker had smartly parked his car on the opposite end from the liquor store. "A real six-pack," he reminded me through the open window as I passed. "Don't try to pull any of that non-alcoholic beer bullshit."

I didn't answer him. I didn't even acknowledge him or look his direction. I just grabbed the cash he held out and kept walking.

Nobody else was in the store, which made sense considering it was the middle of the week. The owner, some skinny old guy with a bald head and gray beard, sized me up as soon as I entered. I pulled down the hood of my sweatshirt and waved so I wouldn't seem too suspicious.

"Six-packs?" I asked.

"Cold or off the shelf?"

"Cold," I answered quickly, confidently. That seemed like something a real adult would be sure about.

The old man pointed to the back of the store where three refrigerators stood. His eyes were on me the entire time; I could almost feel them.

Because of that I had to be deliberate, certain about what to grab. Problem was there were about twenty different kinds of beer. Some were in cans, some were in bottles. Some said light, whatever that meant.

Tucker had only given me eight bucks, which apparently wasn't a decent amount, because it narrowed my choices to only two beers. One of them I recognized as the beer my dad drank. I grabbed the other option.

"Is that all?" the old man asked when I returned to the front.

"Just a midweek pickup," I said, chuckling.

The owner didn't laugh. I'd thought useless chitchat might help, but clearly it didn't. He just rang up the beer, his scowl never budging. "I need to see ID."

"Of course."

I pulled out my masterpiece from my front pocket and then I started to think that might appear too convenient and maybe I should've put it in a wallet. But I didn't have a wallet—mostly because I had nothing to put in it, like a driver's license or money, but also because I didn't have a dad. Buying your first wallet seemed like something you do with your dad.

My mind jolted into panic overdrive, and I felt my cheeks get hot. But it was too late. The ID was out and the old man was already holding it.

Thankfully, he didn't examine it nearly as intently as Poolio had. He just gave it a brief once-over and handed it back. Maybe he wasn't such a hard-ass. Maybe Tucker and his friends were just jerks.

Or maybe my ID was just that good.

"Have a good night," he said, pushing the bag of beer over to me.

I must have blacked out for a second. All of a sudden, I was almost at Tucker's car when I realized I actually did it. The beer was in my hand and, most importantly, I wasn't getting arrested.

In that tiny moment between the sidewalk and Tucker's car, my entire outlook on life flipped on its head. I was actually going to save me and Beatrice.

"A hundred bucks each," I said, handing over the beer.

"What? It actually worked?"

I nodded.

Tucker tore open the six-pack and popped one of the cans. He took a sip. "Shit, this is real beer!" He looked at me. "You're a genius."

"A hundred bucks," I iterated. "Each. You'll have your IDs before Friday."

Then I left him, walked back to my apartment, and lay down next to Beatrice's bed like nothing happened. That night I slept like a baby.

The next day, when I opened my locker after lunch, there was a wad of cash waiting for me. Tucker must've stuck it through the slit in the door along with a sticky note that had his name, three others, and their corresponding locker locations. We never talked about how to pass the money or IDs, but that seemed like a decently incognito system.

For a moment I stood there at my locker, holding the money and just feeling the weight of the stack of bills. Suddenly, anything seemed possible.

"What you got there?" Helena popped up next to me.

I chucked the cash back in my locker and slammed the door shut. "Nothing."

"It didn't look like nothing."

"Well, it was. So just drop it, okay?"

Of course, Helena couldn't. "Was it the pop quiz from history? Did you fail?" She sounded giddy at the thought.

"Yup," I lied, and started walking toward my next class. The effects of her sandwich had worn off, maybe because I didn't need her charity anymore.

"You know, I got a hundred on that quiz," she bragged, desperately trying to walk stride for stride with me.

"Good for you."

"I can help you study if you're having a hard time."

I wasn't having a hard time. Actually, I got a one hundred and five on the quiz because I answered the extra credit. Beatrice would be proud. But if I told Helena the truth, then she'd go back to asking what was in my locker, and she for sure wouldn't give up unless I showed her, which I would never in a million years do.

"I'll keep that in mind," I told her.

She smiled. "And you're coming to Yearbook today, right?"

Now that I knew about the gym door, there wasn't a reason for me to be in the club anymore. I could've told her I'd realized I wasn't really Yearbook Club material or that I had to be home right after school—both of which were true.

"Yup," I said. I told myself it was because if I quit too quickly, that would seem suspicious.

"Perfect." Helena spun around, her ponytail almost whacking me in the face, and walked away.

I had to make Tucker and his friends their IDs, but I didn't want to wake up at the crack of dawn again to do it. That part had really sucked, and my sister would've probably killed me if we did it one more time.

Thankfully, something incredible happened during the Yearbook Club meeting. Helena told me she had "business to take care of in the darkroom" and so I'd be on my own. To keep me busy, she asked me to categorize a stack of group photos by club type.

"They're pretty obvious," she said. "The Chess Club is posed with a bunch of chess sets. The Marching Band is in uniform. The Drama kids are being dramatic. You get the idea. But put any ones you're not sure of in a separate pile, and I'll go through them later. I'm probably in most of them, anyway."

This was it. If I could somehow get rid of Ms. Gold, then this could be my moment with the printer. But I couldn't just use it, could I? Helena would definitely hear it and get suspicious. Somehow I had to get permission, hide in plain sight.

"If somebody stops by for a new student ID, should I come get you?" I asked, hoping the answer would be *no*.

Helena studied me longer than necessary and then shook her head. "I'm sure you can handle it," she said, and gave me a quick rundown on what to do. I listened, nodded, and asked questions as if I didn't already know all the answers.

The only other problem was Ms. Gold, who was distracted by crocheting another poncho. But I still couldn't risk it. I prayed for another tantric yoga class—as much as the idea made me shudder.

So, as I was categorizing the group photos that Helena had left for me, I tried to think of excuses to get Ms. Gold out of the room. If I knew what kind of car she drove, I could tell her I thought I saw its lights still on in the parking lot. Or I could've stepped into the hall and called the main office, pretending to be a family member with an emergency, although that was way more diabolical than I wanted to get.

But then the loudspeaker crackled to life.

"Can all faculty please report to the auditorium?" a voice echoed over the loudspeaker. It might as well have been the voice of God; too perfectly convenient to believe.

Ms. Gold moaned. "What do you think it's about?"

I shrugged.

"You think I should go?"

"Seems like you have to."

"It's gonna be a snooze fest. Nothing like my tantra class."

"I truly hope it's nothing like that."

She begrudgingly stood from the wicker chair at her desk. Yes, Ms. Gold had a wicker desk chair. It was covered in all sorts of beads and fabrics. She chose one of her ornaments and wrapped it around herself.

"You'll behave?" she asked. "I'm bound by a teacher's oath to ask that when I leave a student unattended."

"Yes, I promise."

"Fabulous. If there's a fire, ask Helena what to do."

"Got it." I was desperate to get her to leave before Helena came out for light.

Ms. Gold had a foot out the door before she turned and looked at me. "Just don't peek in my top left drawer. Or the cabinet by the window."

I promised her I wouldn't — I had no interest in discovering the things that even Ms. Gold felt were off-limits. Finally, she was gone and I could get to work. I didn't know how long I had, so I gave myself only fifteen minutes to bang out the four IDs.

I started with Tucker, who had the right amount of scruff on his face to pass as a believable adult. His friends weren't as lucky, which made my job a lot more difficult. One had a huge zit on his cheek that I had to airbrush out. Adults can have acne, too, but for the fake IDs to work, they couldn't draw any unnecessary attention to the photo.

Another kid wore a T-shirt with our high school's name on it. That was easy to cover up, though.

The biggest challenge was the last name on the list, Fletcher Gross. Besides his name being unfortunate, he didn't have a recent photo that I could find. I mean, I scanned the folder about twenty times until I came to the conclusion that he must've been out the day yearbook photos were taken.

So, I went back to the previous year and found him — only he had a deranged smile and a mouth full of braces. At that point I thought about giving up on that ID and returning the extra hundred bucks. Maybe I didn't need it; three hundred bucks could feed me and Beatrice for a month or more, if it came to that.

But then I remembered Fletcher had a brother who was a year older than us, and from what I could recall, they looked pretty similar — or at least resembled each other enough to pass as related. This saving epiphany only came to me because last year Fletcher's brother ran against Helena for student council president. His slogan was VOTE GROSS. I ROCK THE BOAT or something equally as ridiculous. He won by a landslide against Helena, whose greatest rebuttal was YOUR MA AND PA LIKE HELENA SHAW.

Anyway, my hand gripped the computer mouse and jolted into action, clicking and opening files until I found the older Gross's picture. I tried to imagine Fletcher and if the two looked as similar as I remembered, and I guess if I squinted my eyes, it could be the same person. At least I hoped.

In general, though, the IDs printed flawlessly. Each emblem shimmered like it was supposed to and looked even more impressive in actual daylight. I smiled, then frowned. I was both proud of and angry at myself.

Just as I finished the final printing and stuffed the IDs in my backpack, Helena appeared from the darkroom. "Were you printing something?" she asked.

"Why?"

"Because I thought I heard the printer go off twelve times."

"You were counting?" I don't know why I was so surprised.

"It's loud and vibrates into the darkroom."

I thought quickly. "Sorry about that. Some people came by for new IDs, and I messed up a few times."

Helena's head turned toward the trash can by the printer, like she was actually going to look inside to inspect my so-called mistakes, which obviously wouldn't be there. I jumped out of my chair.

"Hey!" I yelled with no plan of what to say next. But the random outburst shifted Helena's attention away from the trash can.

"What?"

"Um." My mind searched for the perfect Helena topic. "You know, I just realized you haven't told me about the yearbook cover. What's it going to be?"

"I haven't decided yet. But don't worry; there's plenty of time." Then she let out a long sigh. "Sorry."

"Why are you sorry?" I asked.

"For nagging you about the printer. You were just doing what you're supposed to."

Technically I wasn't, but what was really throwing me off was Helena being that self-aware. In all the years I've known her, she's never said sorry for anything, and there were things she definitely needed to own up to, especially when it came to me. Maybe this printer incident was a start.

"I'm just really stressed out right now," Helena continued. She walked over and sat down in the chair next to mine. All I wanted to do was escape with the IDs, but it seemed Helena had other plans. "I applied to a summer program where my dad went to college, and I haven't heard back yet."

If ever there was a sentence I couldn't relate to, it was that one. Imagine wanting to go to college before you even went to college!

"Well, you know what they say: no news is good news, right?"

Helena shrugged. "Not always. Acceptances were supposed to get emailed today."

"The day's not over yet," I reminded her. "Besides, it's just a summer program and not a real college acceptance, so I wouldn't stress too much."

She glared at me. "It's a pretty big deal, Reed. This program is basically a pipeline into the school's prelaw major. Without it, I'll have no chance when I apply next year."

It was getting harder for me to empathize with Helena. I wanted to tell her that *real* problems were things like figuring out how to feed yourself and your younger sister while your mother was off pretending she wasn't anybody's mother. But I knew better than to say any of that to Helena.

"I don't know what to tell you," I said at last. "You'll hear when you hear, and stressing about it won't change that."

She sighed and this one was different than before. This one seemed to relax her. "You're right. I just need to chill. So, what colleges are you looking at?"

"None."

"What? Why?"

"Because I'm not going to apply anywhere."

"Like, anywhere?"

I shook my head.

"Reed, you have to apply. I mean, it's college. You have to go."

"Maybe you do. It's just not in the cards for me."

"What does that even mean? So, you're just gonna graduate from high school and do what? Stay here?"

Explaining my life to Helena wasn't worth the energy. Trust me, I've tried. She didn't understand then, and she wouldn't understand now.

Helena grabbed my face with both of her hands and turned it toward her.

"Jesus Christ, Helena!" I yelled. I tried to pull away, but she held on tight.

"You have to apply to college. Promise me."

"Okay. Jeez. Just let go of my face."

She didn't. "Promise me, Reed."

"I promise, you psycho."

Finally she let go, and I wiped off the sweat marks on my cheeks from her hands. I never expected Helena Shaw to have sweaty hands. I liked that she did.

"It would really suck if you didn't go to college," she told me. "You're like the smartest person I know."

"Seriously?"

"Well, besides me."

I laughed. Helena was back to herself. "Thanks."

"No problem. And I should also say thanks for listening to me vent. It's not something I can talk about with my parents, you know."

I did know. "Here, give me your phone."

"Why?"

"So that you don't keep checking it every five seconds. If something important pops up, I'll let you know."

Helena was hesitant, but she understood she'd drive herself crazy for the next hour, and she had all night to do that at home. She handed over her phone and disappeared back into the darkroom.

Earlier I'd been desperate to get out of the art room as soon as the IDs were in my backpack, but I no longer felt that way. I was a lot calmer now that I had a job to do—not cross-referencing the class lists for the yearbook, though I was doing that, too. But keeping Helena from losing her mind.

About forty minutes later, an email flashed on the screen of her phone. I didn't open it or read the one-line preview to see if it was good news or bad. I didn't even tell Helena it was there when she collected her phone before leaving because she didn't ask.

Maybe she'd accepted there was nothing she could do to change what would ultimately happen. Probably not, though. Helena was not that amenable. Either way, she deserved to be heartbroken or ecstatic by herself.

NINETEEN

"BEATRICE, you want pizza for dinner?" I asked as I walked into our apartment.

"Pizza?"

"Yeah. Whatever toppings you want. We can get it delivered."

I rummaged through one of the kitchen drawers that had take-out menus to find the one for the pizza place. Bea's eyes were glued to me, studying me like I was an alien.

"Oh, we can get Chinese food." I held up that menu.

"No," Beatrice answered.

"You're right. Too salty."

"No. I mean, what are you doing?"

"Ordering food. I just told you that."

"How? The other day you said we couldn't."

"Well, I found some money and now we can. What kind of pizza do you want?"

Beatrice shook me off. "How do you just find money? That doesn't make any sense."

I shrugged, not able to look up from the menu and at my

little sister. If I did, she'd see right into my soul and know I did something bad.

"Fine—I didn't *find* the money. Mom sent it." This was the lie I'd settled on during my walk home. I shouldn't have opened with the joke about finding the money; it had only made Beatrice suspicious.

Beatrice narrowed her eyes at me. "When?"

"Today," I said, still staring at the menu. "It was in the mailbox when I got home."

"Show me the envelope."

"What?"

"The envelope that the money came in. I want to see it."

"Why? It's just an envelope. I threw it in the trash."

"You're lying."

My face heated. "I'm not ly—"

"If Mom sent us a letter, you would've shown it to me right away. You would've wanted to open it together. There's no way she would've just sent cash and not written a letter. So where'd the money *really* come from?"

If my sister didn't make it as a white hat, she could probably have a great future as a detective. "You're right. It's not from Mom. I got a job," I told her.

"Where?"

"At school."

"Doing what?"

"Does it matter?"

"Yes."

"Why?"

"Because there's no job at school that pays you money."

"How do you know?"

"Because I know things."

I was stalling and she knew it.

"Reed, what's going on?" Beatrice asked.

The fact that she called me by my actual first name meant she was concerned, more concerned than I originally thought. No kid her age would ever think twice about the possibility of pizza or how we were going to pay for it. Of course, my sister couldn't just be a normal ten-year-old.

I sighed and plopped down next to her at the kitchen table. As much as I didn't want to tell her the truth, I also didn't like lying to her. Besides, she was smart enough that she'd eventually figure it out somehow.

I reluctantly let the words spill out of my mouth. "I sold some fake IDs."

"I don't understand."

I pulled out the one I made for myself and set it down in front of her. It needed no further explanation.

"Oh" was all Beatrice said.

Honestly, I couldn't tell if she was still confused or disappointed or maybe a little of both. Her eyes shifted from the card to me and then stared blankly at the table. It was the apartment door all over again.

"I don't know when Mom is coming back, but we need money to survive. I went back over to Cheap Check before school the other day," I told her. "I was going to apply for a part-time job there. I mean, I filled out the application and everything."

My sister looked up at me again. Well, actually, it was more like she looked through me. But I knew she was listening.

So I continued my babbling rationalization. "Poolio was about to give me the job until he realized I'm not eighteen. Then some guys from my school walked in and tried to buy a pack of cigarettes, but their ID was obviously fake and Poolio cut it up. They complained about how much they paid for the thing, which was pretty brainless since they were admitting it was a fake, but that gave me an idea."

Still no response. Not even a blink. It was worse than begging for forgiveness from a parent.

"I told them I could make one, Bea. And I did, and it's a lot of money." I flashed the wad of cash.

"We should call Mom," she finally spoke.

"What? Why? I'm not gonna tell her about the fake IDs."

"You need to call Mom. She needs to know how serious things are. She needs to come home."

I sighed, pulling out my phone. "Fine, I'll call her. But don't be surprised if she doesn't answer."

"Put it on speakerphone," Beatrice told me, and so I did.

The phone surprisingly only rang once before being picked up. "Reed, sweetie, I can't talk," our mom said. "I'm at the airport."

"Airport? I thought you guys drove to New York?"

"We did but now we're on our way to Miami."

"Miami!" I glanced at my sister. Her eyes were fixed on me like if they moved, it might just shatter her into a million pieces.

I knew calling our mom wouldn't lead to anything good.

"So you're not on your way home, then?" It was a ridiculous question. No one traveled to New Jersey from New York via Miami.

Mom sighed. "Not this again. Look, I haven't had a vacation since before you kids were born. That's *seventeen years*. Seventeen years without a break for myself! Is a couple of weeks too much to ask?"

Yes! I wanted to shout, but I knew it wouldn't do any good. All it would mean is that she probably wouldn't bother picking up the phone the next time we called.

"Mom?" Beatrice said, her voice unusually shaky.

Instantly, Mom's voice changed. "Beatrice, is that you? Aw, sweetheart, I miss you so much! Are you doing okay?"

Bea's chin quivered, which nearly broke me in half. "I miss you, too." She swallowed. "Mom, could you please send us some money? We really need food, and—"

An announcement at the airport interrupted Bea.

"Money's tight for me right now, sweetie," Mom told her. "But your brother is resourceful. I'm sure he'll figure something out. Listen, our flight is boarding—I've really got to go. I'll call you guys tomorrow, okay?"

Then she hung up.

Beatrice and I didn't say anything. We didn't need to say anything. Saying something could only make everything worse—and more real.

Finally, Bea let out a breath and examined the ID again. "It's very realistic."

"Thanks."

"What are they gonna do with the IDs you made them?"

I shrugged. "Probably try to buy another pack of cigarettes. Maybe some beers."

"What are you going to do with yours?"

"Nothing. This was just a test to see if it would work."

"You can use it to drive. It's like an actual driver's license."

"Except it's not. It's still fake and it would still be illegal for me to drive."

"So was making the ID in the first place. But you did it, anyway."

Now I was the one staring, mouth open. This conversation was going in a very different direction than I expected.

"Bea, if anyone finds out I did this, I'm going to jail," I said.

Her eyes got wide. "You'd really go to jail?"

"Probably. I broke the law."

That was the first time I really thought about the legal side of the situation, and the enormity of unknowns came crashing down. Like, I really had no clue if the IDs would work for Tucker and his friends as easily as mine did for me.

Would they rat on me if they got caught?

Probably. We weren't friends.

I had been so wrapped up in the chance to make some cash that I guess I never fully considered the consequences if I got caught— the biggest one being the fact that Beatrice would definitely get taken away. A brother with a record plus an M.I.A. mom was not a good equation.

"Are you going to make any more IDs?" Beatrice asked.

"I'm not sure. I guess it depends on how long Mom will be in Miami."

"You could just get a real job now that you can prove you're eighteen."

I nodded. "True. I don't know why I didn't think about that."

"That's why you have me." Beatrice smiled. "I think we should use it. The ID, I mean. For something fun. Or else you did this bad thing for no reason."

"I did it so we can have food."

"Yeah, but food doesn't come with the same freedom as a driver's license." Then Beatrice winked at me. God help me, my ten-year-old sister winked at me and rolled herself away from the table and toward the door. "We should go out to eat. Now you can drive us to a restaurant."

So much was running through my head that everything Beatrice said simultaneously made perfect sense and no sense at all. Either way, I knew exactly where we should have dinner. It'd either be remembered as a celebration or my last meal as a free man.

TWENTY

I AM TERRIFIED of driving, which I imagine is a pretty standard reaction when your dad gets killed in a car accident. But I do sort of know how to drive—enough to occasionally repark my mom's car, for example. And one time at a carnival, Dad and I drove bumper cars, but that was over a decade ago and probably nothing like driving a real car. He also died a few days later, making the bumper cars and whatever limited driving skills I attained the least memorable thing from that week.

Beatrice seemed to believe in me, though. At least I knew how to sit her in the middle row behind the passenger side and fold her wheelchair to stick it in the trunk. I've done that hundreds of times. But when I sat down in the driver's seat, it felt like I was in a different car—almost like a totally different universe and perception of everything around me.

I adjusted the side and rearview mirrors about half a dozen times and my seat belt, trying to get comfortable but also just delaying. It was like once we pulled away, there was no going back to who we were and what we could or couldn't do.

My nervous eyes shifted to my sister, who was smiling behind me. She gave a quick thumbs-up.

"Diet Soda Club goes on an adventure," she announced.

I took a deep breath, exhaled, nodded, and off we went on that adventure.

Despite running over the curb on the way out of the apartment's parking lot, I'd say I drove pretty decently. The place I wanted to eat at was a diner about five minutes down the road, and there were two left turns. But we got there, and I was alive and Beatrice was alive, and that was the most important thing.

In less than a minute, I had Bea's wheelchair set up and her proudly rolling up a winding ramp toward the door. The classic-looking diner hostess held it open, and beneath the surface of her bleached hair and obligatory smile, I could tell she was trying to figure out who we were and why we were there without parents.

"Just two?" the hostess asked.

"Yup. Can we sit in the back?"

She nodded and grabbed two of the oversize menus. Bea and I followed her to our table, and an overwhelming sense of nostalgia hit me so hard in the chest that I had to stop to catch my breath. Diners have a specific scent that's almost a proprietary mix of lingering cigarettes from when customers were allowed to smoke inside along with fryer grease and burnt toast. The diner industry could bottle and sell it. This particular one also came with the soft atmospheric tenor of an old-fashioned jukebox.

My dad used to tell me it was the only diner in New Jersey that still had a vintage jukebox and not some digitalized knockoff. I have no idea if that's true, but Beatrice and I were sitting right next to it.

"Does that still work?" I asked the hostess, pointing at the jukebox. "We haven't been here in a while."

She nodded and walked away.

"I've never been here," Beatrice told me.

"Yes, you have. You don't remember what happened?"

Her eyes narrowed. "Remember what?"

"Last time we were here, you got us kicked out."

"No way. For what?"

"Well, Mom had just finished giving you a bottle and was trying to get you to burp. Except you didn't burp. You barfed and it went *everywhere*. Then the kid at the table next to us barfed, which made his dad barf and their waitress barfed, too, and soon enough the whole diner was covered in vomit."

"That's disgusting, Yo-Yo. We're about to eat."

I leaned back in my seat. "I just can't believe you don't remember."

"I was a baby. How would I remember? Besides, I don't really think it happened."

"Oh, it happened." Just then our waitress showed up, showcasing a very professional scowl. "Do you remember Barf Baby from ten years ago? This is her all grown-up."

The waitress, whose name tag read CARMEN, glared at me and then at Beatrice and back down to the order pad in her hand. "What can I get you two?"

"We actually haven't looked at the menu yet," I said.

Carmen sighed and stomped away. I had a feeling we'd be getting kicked out again but for a different reason.

"See, it never happened," Beatrice told me.

"She's probably just sworn to some agreement to never talk about that incident. But she remembers. Trust me."

Beatrice shook her head. "You're ridiculous."

"Speaking of ridiculous, you wanna go check out the dessert case? They have like a hundred types of cupcakes and pies."

"Before we have dinner?"

"Yeah, why not? Diet Soda Club has no rules."

Beatrice twisted her head as far as it would go to get a good look at the desserts. It was overwhelming for both of us. Not just all the different baked goods, but the fact that we were at a restaurant with a ton of cash and the ability to order pretty much the entire menu.

"Let's get real food first," she told me.

I shrugged. "Whatever you want."

When the waitress returned, we went absolutely wild like we hadn't eaten in weeks because, well, we hadn't. I'm talking two orders of chocolate chip pancakes and a blueberry waffle and a side of bacon and, of course, a large western omelet. It wouldn't have been a diner trip without a western omelet, that's what our dad would've said.

"Is that all?" Carmen sneered, scribbling down our order.

I wasn't about to let her ruin our fun. "No, we'll also have two diet root beer floats."

Off Carmen went to the kitchen probably to complain that she had to deal with a couple of obnoxious kids.

"What are you looking at?" Beatrice asked.

"The jukebox. Dad really loved it."

"I wish he was here. I wish Mom was here, too."

"We're doing a pretty good job though, right? Just me and you?"

Beatrice shrugged.

"What's wrong? You sad about Mom?" I asked, a silly question.

"I'm sad about you."

"Why me? I'm right here."

"Yeah, but what if you're not? What if you do get in trouble and go to jail? Then I'll have nobody."

"What are you talking about? Earlier you were confident

116

that everything was going to be fine. I mean, it was your idea to drive here."

"I know, but I've been thinking about it, and I'm worried that if something happens to you, it'll be my fault. Just like how it's my fault Dad died, and it's my fault Mom left."

"How is Dad's death your fault?"

"Because he was driving to the hospital to be with me."

I grabbed on to one of Beatrice's hands. "None of that is your fault, okay?"

Bea wouldn't look at me.

"I mean it. The accident wasn't your fault. Mom leaving isn't your fault. Your disability is not your fault. And the choices I make are definitely not your fault."

"I know," she admitted reluctantly. "I'm just scared, Yo-Yo."

I grabbed a napkin out of the dispenser on the table and blotted the tears that were dripping down Beatrice's face. "Hey, listen, I'm not gonna get in trouble."

"How do you know?"

"I just know."

"Promise you won't make any more IDs," Beatrice begged.

"I promise."

I fully intended to keep that promise. As Beatrice had said, I could get a real job now that I had an ID saying I was eighteen— and I'd just proved I could drive when I needed to. But I still held out hope that Mom would be back from her "vacation" before it came to that; four hundred dollars should last us for a long while, assuming we didn't make diner splurges a regular habit.

Carmen still wasn't back with our root beer floats to double as a distraction, so I just held my sister's hand and told her all about the jukebox and our dad's favorite song and how one time he spent more money playing it over and over again than the cost of the food we ate.

By the time we'd eaten our reckless dinner and paid the bill, which I could tell Carmen was surprised and relieved that we had enough money to cover, Beatrice was her cheerful self once more. But I knew it wouldn't last. Nothing good ever does.

TWENTY-ONE

BETWEEN OUR MOM jetting off to Miami and my promise to not make any more IDs, I for sure had to find a job. So, I got Beatrice up early that weekend so we could go over to the grocery store. Since I had decided to start driving, that was now an option. Plus, we required food that wasn't from a convenience store.

I'd never been grocery shopping without a parent—and I'd stopped going altogether once Beatrice started being hospitalized so often and needed someone with her, so I wasn't sure how long an excursion like that would take. Considering I had a ton of home-work and an English paper due on Monday, I hoped it wouldn't waste too much of the day.

My sister was the only one out of the two of us with recent food-shopping experience when she went to buy the meat loaf ingredients with our mom before she left us. Beatrice told me we had to make a list. Our mom didn't have one that day, but she'd seen other people who did and they seemed more organized.

"We should get lobster," Beatrice said.

"I don't know how to cook lobster."

"You could look up a recipe."

"Will you eat it?"

Beatrice shrugged.

"Isn't lobster really expensive?"

Beatrice shrugged again.

"We're not getting it," I told her. "We have to buy things that are cost effective and that we'll actually eat."

"Well, I want ice cream. And those yogurts you squeeze out of a tube."

I added those to our shopping list, which brought the grand total of items to three: cereal, ice cream, and now yogurt.

"Let's just go and figure it out when we get there," I said.

"Good. I was getting bored of this list thing, anyway."

"It was your idea."

"I'm ten. I don't know how to shop for groceries."

"Well, neither do I."

Beatrice seemed to be feeling better, stronger. Each morning she coughed up less and less mucus, which I hoped was a sign that she'd recovered enough to have the surgery, although we still didn't know when that was even going to be.

I hadn't heard from the surgeon that Dr. David mentioned, and I wasn't sure if I was supposed to call or how any of that got arranged. And every time I thought about calling Dr. David's office, a deep pit carved into my stomach, so I never did. I wondered if our mom ever felt the same nauseating sensation.

"Sit tight for a sec," I told Bea. "I have to make a quick phone call."

"To who?"

I didn't answer her, walking into her bedroom to find the hospital paperwork with all the information, including the number for the surgeon's office. Keeping secrets from Bea wasn't something I was proud of or really wanted to do. I mean, I used to yell at our mom for doing the same thing. But if my stomach hurt from just thinking about the doctor, then how did Beatrice feel?

Maybe it was just easier to keep her out of the loop.

I found the number and dialed. The phone rang twice; meanwhile, my heart pumped a thousand times.

"Pediatric Spine and Orthopedic," a friendly sounding voice answered. It relaxed me a little.

"Uh, yes. I'm calling to make an appointment. I think."

"You think you need an appointment?"

"Well, we were told we need a surgery consultation."

"What's the patient's name?"

"Beatrice Beckett?" I said it like a question.

There was a moment of silence while I listened to the faint noise of nails typing. My mind raced and obsessed over all the small details of how I inflected my voice. I had blown it. I was convinced the person on the other side of the call knew I wasn't a parent and was calling the police.

"Oh, yes, I see we've left a few voice mails with the patient's mother," the person said.

"She's busy with work so she asked if I could call. Is that all right?"

"That's fine. Would you like to make an appointment now?"

I instantly broke out of panic mode. "Yes, please."

"I have Wednesday at twelve o'clock available. Does that work?"

"Can it be a little later? I have schoo—I mean, I have work that day."

"Unfortunately all presurgical consultations are done in the early afternoon. Dr. Jenson likes to schedule an hour, and that's when she has the most free time."

I hesitated, wondering if I could ditch school for a couple hours.

Maybe I could get an excused absence, if that was even a real thing? If it was, then all of my previous absences should've been excused, since most of that time was spent in a hospital, which was way more educational than school.

"Does that work?" the scheduling person asked again.

"Yes, sorry. I was just figuring out how to rearrange my day." That sounded like something a parent would say. "We'll be there."

The address was confirmed, which was the hospital, and then finally I hung up and collected my breath. I never knew a phone call could be so productive, nerve-racking, and give an incredible rush. It was too many emotions, too many *adult* emotions.

Riding that rush, I made another phone call.

"Hi, Reed. I'm at the beach," Mom said as if I'd care.

"Beatrice has an appointment with the surgeon on Wednesday. Will you be back by then?"

"I'm not sure."

"How do you not know?"

"My life is really unpredictable right now. But you can take her to the appointment, right? I left you the car keys."

I thought about reminding her that I couldn't legally drive, or that it wasn't my responsibility to take Bea to her appointments. But instead I said, "Can you call Beatrice tonight? She misses you."

"I'll see how late it is when Seth and I finish dinner."

"Okay, well, I have to go to the grocery store now."

"Okay, love you. Bye!"

And that was it.

I needed to stop pretending she'd start caring. That was the last time I'd call her, I decided.

"Who were you talking to?" Bea asked when I got back to the kitchen.

"The office for the doctor who's gonna do your surgery," I told her, which was true. "You have an appointment on Wednesday."

"Okay" was all she said.

"Are you nervous? We can talk about it."

"No, I'm fine. But we better add vegetables to our shopping list."

"Like what?"

"Like broccoli and carrots and whatever else is good for you."

"Okay, sure. And you'll eat all of that?"

"Dr. David said I have to be strong for the surgery."

I smiled. "You're right."

And then we left to drive to the grocery store to buy ice cream, cereal, yogurt, and now vegetables. A phone call to a doctor's office can help make a grocery list. Adult stuff is weird like that, apparently.

"What's that light mean?" Beatrice asked from her seat in the car.

"Where?"

"Behind the steering wheel."

My eyes had been glued to the road as soon as we pulled away from the apartment. I hadn't glanced down once or anywhere else except the mirrors, especially because the route was mostly left turns. I counted eight, and I couldn't tell if I was getting better or worse at them.

But we were at a red light, so I quickly looked at the dashboard and then back up. Of course the fuel tank symbol was lit, at least that's what I thought it was.

"How did you see that?" I asked.

"Because it's big and yellow. And the car is making a beeping noise."

Only then did I hear the beep. I must go into some kind of laser-focused driving zone.

"I think we need to stop for gas," I said.

"There's a gas station up ahead," Beatrice said.

She was a pretty decent backseat driver. I definitely would've missed spotting the station. Thankfully, it was on our side of the road, so I didn't have to make one of those death-trap U-turns. So far driving sucked as much as I thought it would.

"What side is the gas tank on?" I asked as we pulled in.

"Um, I don't know. The back?"

"No, it's either left or right."

"Oh, left, I think."

Either Beatrice paid more attention than I did when we drove with our mom, which very well could've been the case, or it was a lucky guess. An added bonus was that I didn't have to pump the gas; in New Jersey there are people to help with that.

After two more left turns, we were finally at the grocery store, which was swamped. We quickly shuffled through the automatic doors. Beatrice wanted to push the cart herself, which wasn't really possible since she also needs her hands to drive her wheelchair. But she insisted and held on to the cart, although she could barely reach, and I pushed her wheelchair from the back. We most definitely looked like the strangest conga line.

"Where should we start?" Beatrice asked.

I scanned the store, trying to get my bearings and a general idea of what to do, but everyone was going in different directions without any obvious reason. Then an older woman walked in, one hand clutching a bag of coupons and the other a hefty-looking list. She oozed the kind of confidence people have when they're experienced with buying groceries.

"Let's follow her," I said as the woman headed toward the fruit section.

First, she stopped at a bin filled with melons. I watched her squeeze and sniff each one, and then I did the same, even though I had no clue what I was supposed to be squeezing or sniffing for. I mean, some of the melons were softer than others, but overall they were the same to me. But I chose one that looked almost identical to the one the woman placed in her cart.

"I don't really like melon," Beatrice said.

"It's good for you."

I pushed her and our cart over to the wall of vegetables, where the woman stopped next. There were so many options of tomatoes, peppers, and carrots that it was overwhelming. And don't even get me started on the lettuce.

"A lot of options," I said to the woman.

"Yes. Too many options if you ask me. Organic over there and nonorganic over here."

"What's the difference?"

"Practically nothing except how much it costs."

I nodded. She was more opinionated than I would've guessed. I liked her.

"But always get organic bananas," she told me. "Best banana you'll ever have."

"Got it. Thanks."

I turned back to the wall of vegetables, feeling slightly more sure or at least confident not to fall for the organic trap.

"Let's get the rainbow carrots," Beatrice said. "They're pretty."

I grabbed a bag of those along with a few regular-looking toma- toes and some romaine, which apparently is a type of lettuce. Our cart was filling up, and that was surprisingly a good feeling.

"If we get bread and some bacon, we can make BLTs," I told Beatrice. "Will you eat that?"

"Sure, but do you know how to cook bacon?"

Our new friend chimed in. "Just throw it on a plate with some paper towels and put it in the microwave. Perfect bacon every time without the messy cleanup."

Beatrice and I were sold and decided that would be our dinner. Before leaving the produce aisles, I grabbed a few bell peppers, some celery, a head of broccoli, and a bag of radishes. I just selected whatever the woman was choosing, hoping it wasn't too obvious that I was copying all her decisions. But I think she was on to us; at one point she grabbed an avocado for herself and then handed me one.

I also circled back to the fruits to pick up some organic bananas and also some apples, because they seemed like something Beatrice and I should have. But we had to be quick. The woman was on the move, and I didn't want to miss where she was headed next.

The crowd was pretty dense, so I had to weave Beatrice and our cart in and out of people and families while also trying to keep an eye on our shopping partner, who was fast for someone her age.

"You're making me dizzy," Beatrice said.

"I'm trying to keep up."

"Why are we following her, anyway?"

"Because we both have no idea what we're doing."

When I turned the corner into the meat department, another cart crashed into us.

"Reed?" Ms. Gold said.

"Ms. Gold," I muttered, "wild seeing you here." That seemed like something an adult would say. "I'd love to chat but—"

She cut me off. "Who is this adorable ball of sunshine?"

"I'm Beatrice," my sister proudly answered. "Reed's sister."

"Well, hello there, Beatrice. That is a beautiful name. Did you know the meaning of Beatrice is 'she who brings happiness'?"

My sister shook her head, but I could tell she was figuring out how to use that info against me. I tried to move us along, but Ms. Gold held the edge of our cart.

"And you, sir." She looked at me. "You never told me you had a sister."

"I'm sure I've brought her up before."

"No, never." Ms. Gold firmly shot me down. "I would've remembered Beatrice. I used to have a lover with the same name."

While she gazed off into her past, I peeked down the aisle and all around in search of the woman we'd been following. She was gone, vanished into the mob of hungry shoppers.

My sister looked at me and I looked back at her, and I knew that was our cue to try to escape. "Ms. Gold, it was nice seeing you, but Beatrice and I really have to get going."

With some luck, we could catch up to the woman. Maybe we'd bump into her in the paper goods aisles so she could explain the different kinds of toilet paper.

In the meantime, we rolled up and down each aisle, scanning for things that we'd want to eat. It was similar to being at Cheap Check, except we didn't have a budget. Beatrice wanted more cereal, and I grabbed a few cans of chicken noodle soup, jars of peanut butter and jelly, a package of hot dogs, and, of course, bacon and bread.

"We need more soda?" Beatrice said.

"No, we should cut back on that. You need to start eating healthier to get ready for your surgery."

"Yo-Yo, we can't be Diet Soda Club without soda."

She was right. We looped back to the section of the store that housed all brands and sizes of soda, and without any parents to say no, it really is an amazing sight to take in. For kids, at least.

"What should we get?" I asked.

"Dr Pepper, obviously."

I grabbed a six-pack of that and hung it over the edge of the cart.

The cans of Diet Pepsi also caught my eye. I never really liked Pepsi, but I grabbed a six-pack anyway.

As we piled things into the cart, I read the instructions on the back of the items to see if we needed anything else. That wasn't an instinct. I saw other people doing it, so I decided to do it, too, which ended up being a good thing because the brownie mix Beatrice wanted said it required oil and eggs. And now that we had eggs, I guessed we could also make them for breakfast.

Food shopping spirals like that, or so I was learning.

"What else do you think we definitely need?" I asked my sister.

"Milk. And we still have to get yogurt and ice cream."

"True. I was also thinking we should check out the frozen section to get some chicken nuggets or fish sticks."

"I don't like fish sticks."

"Okay. Then just chicken nuggets."

"We could get frozen pizza instead of fish sticks."

I smiled. "You got it."

Unfortunately, we never saw the woman again, so Beatrice and I had to decide alone whether two-ply was worth it. We decided it definitely was.

While we were checking out, I noticed there was a hiring sign hanging behind the customer service counter. I grabbed an application on our way out.

TWENTY-TWO

"YOU DON'T WASH BACON," Beatrice told me.

I turned away from the sink, bacon strips in my hand. "Really? It's kinda slimy."

"The woman from the store didn't tell us to do that. She just said put it on a plate with paper towels and then into the microwave."

"How long do you think?"

She shrugged. "Ten minutes?"

"I'll do four."

While the bacon cooked, I grabbed the tomatoes and romaine, which we'd put in the fridge when we got home. We'd spent over an hour unpacking—well, I mean, I'd unpacked while Beatrice just told me where to stick everything and worked on one of those yogurts she wanted. On a positive note, it seemed like we'd bought enough food to last us a month. At least I hoped it would, considering the groceries cost almost two hundred bucks.

"Why don't you talk about me at school?" Beatrice asked.

"What are you talking about?" I finished cutting up the tomatoes for our BLT and gave her a piece to try.

"That strange lady we saw at the store said that she didn't know you had a sister."

"I mean, there's really never been a reason for me to bring it up."

"You don't think I'm cool enough? Is that why you don't talk about me?"

"No, Bea. Honestly, it's the opposite. You're too cool, and I'm afraid if I do talk about you, then the kids at my school won't think *I'm* cool."

"Well, you're not." She grinned.

"Ouch. You're cool *and* mean. You'd fit into high school perfectly."

That made my sister laugh, and she seemed to forget about how much of a jerk I was for never telling anyone about her. It's not that I'm ashamed of her or anything like that; Beatrice is amazing, obviously. In fact, it's because she's so amazing that I haven't told anyone about her. She doesn't deserve to be known as "Reed Beckett's disabled sister," which is all she'd be to the teachers and kids at my school.

Beatrice caught me spacing out. "What are you thinking about, Yo-Yo?"

"Nothing." I snapped myself back to reality. "Should we check on the bacon?"

Her face instantly lit up, a resounding *hell, yes.*

The mysterious woman from the supermarket was correct: microwave bacon was some of the best bacon I'd ever had. Maybe even better than the bacon we had at the diner. It was crispy but not so crispy that it felt like it was stabbing us in the throat. And there was no grease, which is practically the majority of what makes up diner bacon.

Anyway, I slapped a few strips on the whole-wheat bread we bought along with the lettuce and tomato. I sort of felt like a chef, or at least a chef who does the minimum amount of cooking possible.

"Tastes like it's missing something," Beatrice said.

"I agree." I spun the laptop to face me and did a quick Google search. "Apparently, we were supposed to buy mayonnaise. And toast the bread."

"I still like it, though. You did a good job."

I leaned over and kissed the top of her head. Whether the universe wanted us to or not, we were going to survive.

TWENTY-THREE

WHEN I OPENED my locker on Monday, there was five hundred dollars and five different pieces of paper with names and locker locations waiting for me. Word from Tucker must've spread over the weekend, which meant the IDs I made worked for whatever he and his friends needed them for.

At least it seemed I wouldn't have to worry about being arrested anytime soon. My new problem was that I needed to return the five hundred dollars in cash when everything in me screamed to keep the money. But I'd promised Beatrice I wouldn't make any more IDs. And, as of that moment, I didn't need to. We had plenty of food and I still had a little over a hundred bucks left. Plus, an application to work at the grocery store was waiting for me at home.

Anyway, before homeroom, I stopped by the main office to make sure I'd be okay to take Beatrice to her appointment. My favorite secretary was waiting for me.

"Hey, I was wondering if I could take a half day on Wednesday," I said.

"Take a half day? This isn't a job with vacation days."

"It's for a doctor's appointment. It's important."

"You just need a note from the doctor, dear."

"A note? What should it say?"

She sighed. "That you were at a doctor's appointment and that's why you were absent from school."

I nodded and started to leave, but then turned back. "Does the note have to say 'school' on it? I mean, can it just say I was at a doctor's appointment?" I was still planning to pass myself off as an adult when I brought Beatrice to see the surgeon.

She looked suspicious. "I don't know, dear. They have form letters for these sorts of things. Some of them say school, some of them don't. But they have to be on official letterhead."

I forced a laugh. Clearly she thought I was planning on forging a letter—and clearly I no longer was. "Heh. Yeah. Obviously. Okay, thanks for your help!"

The secretary nodded, already over our conversation.

"Good morning, students," Helena's voice rang out of the loud-speaker. "Today's going to be a magical Monday, but first some announcements."

Right on cue, everyone in homeroom groaned. Even the teacher made a face. I was the only person who stayed silent or didn't roll their eyes. Call it progress or just flat-out indifference.

"As some of you might've noticed," Helena continued, "I have placed suggestion boxes throughout the halls, bathrooms, and in various classes. Feel free to drop in a note with some improvements you'd like to see."

There was one directly next to me, and it was classic Helena Shaw: a shoebox with a slit cut into the top and decorated with colorful construction paper and glitter with the words SUGGESTION BOX written in puffy paint so everybody was aware it was indeed a suggestion box.

Sadly, this wasn't Helena's first attempt to "hear the voices of her peers." She'd also put out the boxes in the beginning of the year. I'm pretty sure she never received a serious suggestion.

It didn't look like she would this time, either, as everyone ignored the box while they left homeroom. I felt kind of bad for Helena. Although she was overbearing and a little too enthusiastic in the morning to actually connect with her peers, Helena did put a lot of effort into her duties as student council president.

I scribbled a note and folded it tightly. On my way to first period, I dropped it in the suggestion box. Hopefully, she'd take the hint.

The money and list of names were still in my locker at the end of the day. I knew I needed to return the cash, but it was proving to be much harder than I'd thought to give back so much money.

Thankfully, Helena showed up—a phrase I never thought I'd say—so I didn't have to deal with the money just yet. "You ready for Yearbook?" she asked.

"Always. I count down the minutes every day we have a meeting."

"I'm gonna pretend that wasn't sarcasm."

"Whatever."

"Unless it actually wasn't sarcasm and you really do love working on the yearbook."

I glared strong enough that she should've understood without me needing to say anything, but I clarified anyway for the record. "It was sarcasm, Helena."

"Right." She forced a smile. "Obviously."

We walked silently to the art room, and I thought about how Helena used to be more confident when we were kids. I mean, she was confident now but in a different way, a fake way. As kids, she'd never let me get away with roasting something she cared about.

One summer she was obsessed with some awful boy band, and she talked about them and listened to their music all day, every day. I hated it. Maybe I just hated how she gushed over them, but when you're seven, you really aren't that self-aware, so I flipped and told her how they were a bunch of poseurs and probably didn't even write their own songs.

The next day she pointed out that my favorite baseball player got in trouble for taking steroids, which made all his record-breaking stats fake. I started to think that maybe everything is fake, if most music isn't real and neither are athletes.

I stopped watching baseball. Helena never stopped listening to the boy band.

"Did you get any suggestions today?" I asked as we turned the corner to the art room hall.

Helena snorted. "No. Just a bunch of obnoxious comments like 'no homework' or that I should wear shorter skirts."

"People suck here."

"Seriously. There was even one note that said 'You try too hard. Remember second grade?' Like, what does that even mean?"

"No idea," I answered, head down.

"It came from the box in your homeroom," Helena added. "Did you see anybody put a suggestion in there?"

"No," I lied. "Maybe it was from one of the classes during the day."

"Maybe." Helena watched me for a second and then turned to Ms. Gold. "Can you take a look at the candids I shot today? They should be finished developing."

135

"I'm actually late for my meditative eating session," she said, "but Reed can take a look."

Both of them turned toward me. "Um, I guess," I answered, although I wasn't entirely sure I was qualified.

"Can I trust you two?" Ms. Gold asked. "No hanky-panky?"

"No!" I said, just as Helen asserted, "Definitely not!"

I'd never been in a darkroom, but it's exactly what I expected: dark, obviously, and covered with photos in various stages of development. Some were hanging from a string, and others were floating in a liquid. It was almost like a birthplace for memories.

And Helena had taken and developed more than I could count; there had to be hundreds. I could only make out a few that were close to the red bulb, which was the only source of light in the room. There were pictures of random kids at our school, eating lunch, laughing in the hallways, or playing sports. All the photos somehow captured what high school should feel like.

"I didn't know you took photos," I said.

"Then what do you think I do in here?"

I shrugged. "I mean, I know you take photos, but I didn't think like this. I've never seen you with a camera."

"Well, I'm not gonna wear it around my neck all day."

"So, when do you take these, then?"

"Reed, they're called candids. If I told you how I do it, then you'll always be looking and it wouldn't be authentic."

Helena fluttered her eyes at me. As kids, I'd seen that look a thousand times. But now it made my stomach flip in a way I wasn't expecting.

"You should go to photography camp instead of whatever you applied to," I said.

"No, this is just a hobby. I'm going to be a lawyer."

"Like your dad?"

"Yeah. He wants me to join the family business."

"What do *you* want?"

"Well, I mean, it's what we both want." Helena stumbled over her words. "I can't really make a living from taking photos."

"Who says?"

Helena didn't respond. We both knew the answer.

There wasn't much I remembered about her dad other than that he was a lawyer, and I think that's probably the reason I don't remember much; he was rarely around. And when he was around, he was either hiding in his home office or doing everything possible to stay clear of where we were. At least that's how it felt. The only time I saw Helena interact with her dad was when we were apparently making too much noise, and he'd yell at us for disrupting him.

After that happened, we'd usually go over to my house, and my dad would make us grilled cheese and chocolate milk. Helena would always cry halfway through our snack. I never understood why.

"What did you need help with in here?" I asked.

Helena pointed to a lineup of photos. "I can't decide what to use for the Most Memorable Moment."

"How many do you need?"

"Just one. Hence the name."

I stepped closer to the freshly developed film and studied each one. They each seemed pretty good, but she'd asked me to help her choose, so I randomly held up a picture.

"How about this?" I asked.

"Why that one?"

I shrugged.

"So, you just arbitrarily picked it?"

"No, not arbitrarily. It caught my eye."

"But why? What about it deserves to be featured in the year-book?" She grabbed the photo I was holding and shuffled it around the table with the rest. "Look, this one was taken when Katie Moore made her decision to play basketball at Princeton. And this one was when Eric Fox found out he was the lead in *Little Shop of Horrors*. This one I took at the robotics tournament, and this one is when Malcolm's dad came home early from his deployment and surprised everyone at Winter Wonderland."

Helena went on to describe each shot—where it was taken, and why she took it. It was like they were her memories just as much as those of the people on the other side of the camera.

"All of these photos have meaning and deserve to be carefully considered," she told me.

"Then use all of them. Just reformat the page so they all fit."

"No, that defeats the purpose of Most Memorable Moment. One of these has to be better than the others. We just need to figure out which one."

Helena planted both of her hands on the table and leaned down to examine each picture like she was searching for a clue, or maybe a blemish or a bad smile. Any reason to take it out of the running.

"Remember your sixth birthday?" I asked.

"Sort of. What about it?"

"Your mom took us to the store to pick out a birthday cake. You chose vanilla with chocolate frosting. And then when your mom was paying, you freaked out wondering if all your friends would like vanilla cake with chocolate frosting."

I paused, waiting for Helena to look up or say something, but she didn't. She just stared at the table, motionless.

"Then I saw there was a package of cupcakes that had a bunch of different flavors," I continued. "You got excited about that because everyone could choose their favorite."

Finally, Helena looked at me with her eyebrows scrunched as if she couldn't believe I remembered all of that. I was just as surprised as she was. I thought I'd wiped my brain of every memory from those years, but apparently a few good ones stuck around.

"What does that have to do with choosing a photo for the yearbook?" she asked.

"Everything," I told Helena, thinking she'd take the hint and let the students vote on their favorite picture. But her mind seemed to be somewhere else.

Helena sighed. "I didn't get accepted."

"What?"

"The other day when I was waiting to hear back from that summer college program. I didn't get in."

"Oh, I'm sorry." I realized I really meant it.

"I haven't told my dad yet."

"Maybe you don't have to."

"I wish. He knows I applied. He's been asking if I received their decision."

When Helena got upset as a kid, I always knew how to cheer her up, and she'd do the same for me because that's what friends do. But I had no idea how to make either of us feel better now.

"You know, your dad never ate any of the cupcakes at your birthday," I said.

Helena smiled. "This is kind of nice, hanging out again."

I nodded. I was afraid if I said anything, it might not sound how I'd want it to, and for the first time since I was seven years old, I didn't want to ruin a moment with Helena Shaw.

So, we both just stood there and stared at each other, soaked in the glow of the red light and surrounded by evidence of how Helena saw the world. In that moment, I saw her as she used to be—my best friend with pigtails and too many opinions. And I hoped she still saw me as a boy with parents and a future.

TWENTY-FOUR

FOR TEN YEARS I told myself I'd never be friends with Helena Shaw ever again or even look at her face, though that last one was unrealistic since we went to school together and she was far from the type of person who likes to stay hidden.

Honestly, Helena should have been the one trying to avoid *me*, and the fact that she went about her business like nothing happened made me hate her more.

But after a while you move on, even from really bad things. Younger me would never have believed that. But just like my dad's death, the incident with Helena slowly faded to the back of my mind until it stopped being something that was happening and became a thing that happened a long time ago.

I was thinking about all of this as I was walking home from spending the afternoon with Helena in the darkroom, when I realized my mom had called me and left a voice mail. I considered deleting it to not waste my time or ruin the decent day I was having with whatever she thought was worthy of being recorded, but then I had the naive hope that maybe she called to say she was on her way home.

She was not.

"Hey, sweetie, it's Mom. Listen, I don't think I'm going to make Bea's appointment. Seth thinks it's important for us to have this time together, just the two of us, before we take the next big step. I hope you understand. Anyway, things will be so much better once we're home, okay? Well, let me know how the appointment goes. Give Bea kisses for me. I love you!"

I had become so numb to her that the voice mail barely fazed me. In fact, I expected the last shoe to drop and it finally did. As soon as I got home and while Bea was finishing things up with Zigzag online, I got to work on the grocery store application. Most of it was identical to the one for Cheap Check except this one gave me options for preferred work hours. Obviously, I couldn't work days or evenings, especially during the week, so that left me with weekends.

I imagined it'd be pretty similar to when I was at school: my sister would stay home, and I'd check on her via email and during my lunch break.

The application also listed the hourly wage: sixteen bucks. If I worked two eight-hour shifts per weekend, I'd earn a little over two hundred and fifty dollars. And that was before taxes and didn't include money we'd need for food and gas.

But I didn't have much of a choice. Who knew when Mom (and Seth) would show up? And I promised Bea I'd stop making IDs. It would be enough money for the necessities. Plus, the application mentioned something about an employee discount.

It felt good to have a plan. In fact, I was about to tell Beatrice we were going to drive over to the grocery store so I could drop off the application and ask if I could start that weekend. But through the window of the front door, I noticed the mailman had just finished delivering.

Strangely, it was one of those moments when you get tunnel vision, and for some reason all I could think about was the mail. Usually I don't care. Sometimes I let it pile up for a few days, but my gut was telling me to collect it now.

I did, and I was sifting through the mail and most of it was junk.

Then I saw it, an envelope from the hospital.

I walked away from Beatrice to open it. She couldn't see it anyway from where I was standing, but my brain was telling me to put distance between her and whatever information was inside.

When I felt like I was far enough away, I opened the envelope. Inside was a bill covered in rows listing medications, procedures, room and board, and miscellaneous supplies, along with corresponding quantities and prices. Some were only a few dollars while most were hundreds or even thousands.

I flipped to the next page to continue scanning, my heart threatening to explode from my chest as I added up the numbers.

Finally, I got to the bottom, and there was a box titled WHAT YOU OWE. It was about two hundred bucks. I almost collapsed from relief. I guess insurance covered most of it.

While two hundred dollars was *definitely* better than the thousands of dollars I'd been expecting to see in that box, I didn't actually have enough to pay the bill.

To be totally certain, I pulled out the ball of cash that was stuffed into my pocket; I really needed to get a wallet. Just as I'd known, I was almost a full hundred short.

Next to the pile of junk mail was the fully completed application for the grocery store.

The job wouldn't be enough.

Could I just ignore the hospital bill? Maybe for a little while.

But how many times could Beatrice see a doctor or be in the hospital without paying before someone realized?

I didn't plan on finding out.

The plan was the same as before: get to the art room unseen, print the IDs, and get out. I had to make a detour to my locker to grab the list of names, though, and as I was rounding the corner, Mr. Milton, the custodian, was backing out of a closet with the floor-polishing machine. We collided, full-on, both of us falling down.

"Who the hell are you?" he shouted. "What are you doing here so early?"

I lay sprawled out on the floor, my life flashing in front of me.

"I—I'm here to finish a project?" It sounded like a question, which definitely didn't help my case.

"What kind of project needs to be worked on at six in the morning? How'd you even get into the building?" Then, miraculously, his concerned face cleared. "Oh, I know you. You're that boy who's always hanging around Helena."

I opened my mouth to protest but thought better of it. "Yup. I'm in Yearbook Club with her. That cart was a big help. Thanks again, Mr. Milton." I left out the part about the squeaky wheel and how it was almost impossible to steer.

"No problem. Helena's a nice girl. Is she here with you?"

It seemed like only one answer would let me freely walk away. "Yes. Actually, she's waiting for me in the art room."

Mr. Milton nodded. "Off you go, then. Try not to knock over anyone else on your way."

As soon as he was out of sight, I sprinted the rest of the way to my locker. That run-in delayed me almost five minutes, which is a lifetime when you're trying to do something you're not supposed to. I should've realized that was a sign.

When I got to the art room, though, I didn't think or freeze up; I went right to work. Everything was going pretty smoothly for the first three names. They were seniors—one girl and two guys—and easily passed as older than their age.

But the last two were freshmen and a big challenge. One of them had the same last name as the girl and must've been her younger brother. I could just imagine him catching wind of what she was doing and wanting in or he'd rat her out to their parents. There was no way this kid would ever in his right mind have thought about doing this himself.

First off, he had a mouth full of braces. Now, I'm pretty decent at Photoshop, but removing those braces wasn't working no matter what technique I used. Maybe I could do it if I had a few hours, but the clock was ticking and at one point Mr. Milton stopped by, and I had to make up a reason why Helena wasn't with me. I told him she went to the bathroom. But the pressure was clearly on.

I decided to move on to the last name on the list. He was also a freshman—probably friends with Braceface and wanted in on blackmailing the sister. Sadly for him, he looked younger than Beatrice and still had obvious baby fat and a mom haircut.

I had precisely five minutes before I expected any teachers to start arriving for the day, and in those five minutes, I needed to fig- ure out if I should make the last two IDs and jeopardize everything or say screw the extra two hundred bucks and move on.

Quickly, I came to the conclusion that it wasn't worth it. Three hundred dollars was enough to pay the bill and have plenty left for groceries and stuff when I added it to the hundred I already had. I thought about not giving the girl her ID—it was risky, since her brother and his friend weren't getting theirs—but decided to let her handle them. This was the last time I'd be making IDs, and I couldn't afford to say no to her hundred bucks.

Just as I was packing up, the lights in the art room flicked on, and it literally felt like my heart fell out of my body. Helena stood in the door, just as shocked to see me.

"What are you doing here?" I asked.

"I have some film I need to start developing so it's ready by lunch. What are *you* doing here?"

My mind went completely blank. Meanwhile, my eyes kept shifting over to the printer; I couldn't help it. Helena noticed and she slowly walked over to the printer.

"What the hell is this?" she asked, picking up the scrapped ID from when I'd attempted to erase that kid's braces.

"Helena, please let me explain," I said.

She waited but not long enough for me to think of a lie. The ID was right there in her hand, and there was no web I could spin to make it make sense.

"Is that why you joined Yearbook? So you could use the printer to make fake IDs?"

"I know it looks bad, but I had no choice. I really needed—"

Helena cut me off. "You used me, Reed. You took advantage of our past relationship and used it to—to, what? To make a few bucks?"

"It's not that simple. If you just let me explain—"

"Get out." Her voice was quiet but harsh.

There was no point in fighting with her—she obviously wasn't going to listen. Besides, she was right. I *had* used her. And once again, my future was in her hands.

"Helena, you can't tell anyone," I begged, standing by the door.

She didn't answer, barely even looking at me.

"Please promise me you won't tell. Don't do what you did last time, please."

"What are you talking about? What last time?" She shook her head like it didn't actually matter. "Just go."

On my way out, I dropped off the three completed IDs. When I got to the lockers of the two freshmen, I returned their money along with a personalized rejection note. One said "See me after you get your braces off" and the other "Maybe grow a beard."

TWENTY-FIVE

I WAS A paranoid mess after my run-in with Helena. Every time I saw an unfamiliar adult in the hallways or heard a car door shut outside our apartment, I was convinced it was the cops. People don't just stop being tattletales.

By the time Wednesday rolled around, I was practically shaking with anxiety.

"Do you think the doctor will be nice?" Beatrice asked on our way to her appointment.

"Probably. The people on the phone were. And Dr. David recommended her, so she must be good."

"Yeah, Dr. Jenson got impressive reviews."

"Oh, I didn't know there are reviews you can read online."

"Yup, for all doctors. But I also hacked into the hospital's HR system and read Dr. Jenson's employee evaluations."

I shook my head, upset with how nonchalant Bea spoke about hacking. But my brain was too distracted to reprimand her. I mean, I was losing my mind thinking about Helena. There was a two-mile span on the way to the doctor where I was convinced we were being followed by a cop. And I wasn't even concerned about the fact that I was breaking the law by driving. Thankfully, when I started to pull over, the cop passed right by. Beatrice didn't even notice; she was busy reciting the history of the doctor's evaluations.

"Just don't bring that up today," I said. "That you read her employee files, I mean."

"There's nothing to bring up. I said she got good reviews. The only negative was it said she smiles too much but, honestly, I think that's a positive."

We were pulling into the hospital parking lot, so I decided to drop the hacking conversation to concentrate on finding an available handicap spot. And, truthfully, I didn't have much of a leg to stand on when it came to reprimanding her about illegal activities.

"You feel good?" I asked Beatrice before getting her out of the car.

"Yes. I'll be brave."

"I know you will. But this is just a consultation for the doctor to get to know you and talk about the surgery. So, you can ask any questions you want if something doesn't make sense."

Bea nodded and wrapped her arms around my neck so I could pick her up and transfer her into her wheelchair. Then, before I could close the door, she raced toward the hospital entrance, steady and knowing that as soon as her tires crossed inside, her life would change; hopefully for the better.

The waiting room was huge and colorful and decorated to distract kids from whatever reason they had to be there. Beatrice didn't waste time with the games on the walls, the three TVs playing cartoons, or the fact that the floor lit up a trail of her tire tracks and my footsteps. I barely paid attention to any of it, too.

Side by side, we moved across the room directly toward the check-in desk.

"Beatrice Beckett here to see Dr. Jenson," I told the woman behind the desk, my voice steady and confident.

"Date of birth and address, please?" she asked. It was the same voice from the phone. DEBBIE her nameplate read. "Also, I'll need your insurance card."

I handed it over—thankfully, I had it since Mom kept it in a drawer and not in her wallet—and while Debbie entered the information on the computer, I glanced down at Bea, who was waiting and fidgeting with her hands and wheelchair brakes. The nerves were kicking in.

"This is your first time seeing Dr. Jenson?" Debbie asked.

"Yes," Beatrice answered before I could.

Debbie stood up so she could actually see Beatrice, whose head was barely even with the check-in counter. No matter where we went, the world towered over her, but Bea made up for that in other ways.

"Is it true Dr. Jenson went to Harvard?" she asked Debbie.

"Yup, she did."

"And did she really perform two hundred and seven surgeries last year?"

"That one I'm not sure about." Debbie chuckled. "You'll have to ask her."

"I'm sure it's true," I said. "Beatrice does her research."

Debbie sat back down and finished typing. "Okay, you're all checked in. Your co-pay for the visit is forty dollars."

I reached into my pocket for the wad of cash and turned my body a bit so Beatrice and Debbie couldn't see how much cash I was carrying around. I'm not sure how effective it was, though; Debbie raised one eyebrow and then suspiciously gazed at my hands fiddling and then at my face, which was starting to turn red.

Finally I got the wad organized and handed Debbie the exact amount.

"You're gonna pay with cash?" she asked.

"Yeah, is that a problem?"

"No," she said, but her expression told me it was an unusual payment method. "I'll print you a receipt."

"Thanks. Also, I received a bill from when she was in the hospital." I pulled the letter out of my other pocket.

"Bill? What bill?" Beatrice asked, trying to peer at the letter.

"Don't worry about it," I told her, smiling apologetically at Debbie.

Debbie smiled back. "You don't pay that here. Main hospital billing is downstairs. You can visit them after your appointment."

I nodded and made a mental note to stop there before leaving.

"They also accept cash," Debbie said, handing over the receipt.

Even though we waited for less than ten minutes to be called in to our appointment, it felt like an eternity because some random mom decided to sit right next to me in a nearly empty room. I wouldn't have cared if she hadn't brought up her support group for single parents and asked me if I wanted to join.

Honestly, I was tempted to get the info—I could pass it to my mom if she ever came back—until the lady admitted they mostly just drink at the meetings. When I asked what her kid does when she's at those meetings, she pretended she had to answer a phone call. I was grateful when the nurse called Bea's name.

"How much does Beatrice weigh?" the nurse asked once we were in the exam room.

I looked at my sister for the answer.

"Um, when I was in the hospital, I think someone said I was sixty pounds," Bea told her.

"And what were you in the hospital for?"

"Pneumonia," I answered. "Everything should be in her chart."

The nurse clicked around on her laptop. "Yup, I see. Okay, well, the doctor will be in shortly."

Then the door was shut, leaving Beatrice and me in a room that felt like it was getting smaller and smaller by the second. Everything was a lead-up: the hospital stay had led to more testing, which had led to the decision that Bea needed surgery, and that had led to Mom taking off. And now we were here, in the world's smallest exam room, taking the next step toward saving my sister.

"You're breathing really heavy," Beatrice told me.

"Sorry. I'm just a little nervous."

"I don't know why you're nervous. The appointment is about me."

"You're right. I guess I'm just excited—for you, I mean."

"Why would you be excited?"

"Because I think Dr. Jenson is really gonna help."

"Do you think the surgery will stop me from getting sick so much?"

"Hopefully. That's what Dr. David seemed to think. But you'll have to ask the surgeon."

Then there was a single knock on the door, and a woman in a lab coat walked in. Only doctors wear lab coats, so this had to be her.

"Hi, guys. I'm Dr. Phoebe Jenson," she announced. Her voice was soft and confident but so unassuming for a doctor. "It's so nice to meet you both, especially you, Beatrice. Dr. David has told me a lot about you."

"I've known Dr. David my whole life. Did he tell you about the time when I was really sick and I couldn't cough and he was trying to suction the mucus out and then I finally coughed and it went all over his shirt? It looked like vomit."

Dr. Jenson tried not to laugh. "He didn't tell me that one, no. But he did say you're precocious."

"What's precocious?"

"It means you're very smart."

Beatrice liked the sound of that. "I am smart, so you don't have to talk to me like I'm a baby. I can handle it."

"Okay. We'll talk like big girls, then."

Dr. Jenson looked at me for I guess some kind of approval to proceed. I just gave her a quick nod. Really this was Bea's show, and so far I was very proud of her.

"Do you mind if I feel your back?" Dr. Jenson asked.

"Sure, I'm used to it," Beatrice said.

"Okay, and can you take off your shirt, too? I just want to make sure I can see everything perfectly."

While I helped Beatrice take off her panda shirt, Dr. Jenson washed her hands and put on a pair of gloves. My sister sat there in her chair, half-undressed, seeming vulnerable in a way I've never seen. My eyes watched Dr. Jenson's hands as they followed the curve of my sister's spine, which forced a small hunch behind her left shoulder. That was the same side she leaned toward while sitting, and my eyes couldn't stop looking at the crease from where her rib cage was caving in, the reason we were there.

Dr. Jenson tossed her gloves in the trash. "The curve of your scoliosis is pretty significant. I reviewed your X-rays before coming in, and I think it might have changed since getting those taken."

"Better?" I asked.

"Worse, I'm afraid. But that's to be expected. It just means we'll need to figure out an earlier surgical time."

"When do you think?"

"Well, really it depends on how Beatrice is recovering from her last bout of pneumonia. It's only been a couple weeks out. I wouldn't want to put her under anesthesia if she still has junk rattling around in her lungs. Dr. David wouldn't approve that, either."

"I'm fine," Beatrice said. "We've been following the instructions Dr. David gave us, and I'm doing good with the cough-assist machine and nebulizers."

"It's true," I added. "She used to fill up one of those suction canisters just in the morning. Now it only gets, like, half-full."

Dr. Jenson unwrapped her stethoscope from around her neck and stuck it in her ears. "Let me take a quick listen." Beatrice took a dozen deep breaths. "You sound good. But it's really not my call. Dr. David is the pulmonologist, and he'll decide if Beatrice is healthy enough for surgery."

"So, we should make an appointment with him?" I asked.

"Yes, just for a quick follow-up."

Everything led to more stuff. It was a lot, but doable. When I looked at Beatrice, I could tell she wasn't afraid, just ready to do what needed to be done. We both were.

"Any questions?" Dr. Jenson asked.

Of course, Beatrice had one. "Is it true you performed two hundred and seven surgeries last year?"

"I'm not sure how you know that, but yes."

Beatrice was satisfied with that answer as if any more or less would've been a deal-breaker.

"Any other questions?"

"What actually happens during the surgery?" I asked. "Nobody's really explained it to us."

"Well, a couple different things. First, I'll place metal rods on

154

both sides of Beatrice's spine to make it as straight as possible to correct her scoliosis. Then little wires get tied across to hold everything together."

"That sounds intense."

"A little, at least for the person doing her surgery. But her X-rays will be pretty awesome after that. Beatrice's spine will kind of look like a railroad track."

"Cool!" Bea said.

"What about her ribs?"

Dr. Jenson nodded. "That part is trickier. We'll expand her ribs to provide space for her lungs and organs, but her rib cage will need support so it doesn't cave in again. Typically, we'll insert a rib bone from a baby cadaver that'll grow with Beatrice's body."

I didn't want Beatrice dwelling on *baby cadaver*, so I quickly moved on to my next question: "And what happens after the surgery?"

"The recovery will be long. Beatrice will be in the ICU for a few weeks to make sure she's healing and doesn't get an infection, not to mention there'll be a few drainage tubes. We'll cast her for a back brace to wear, and Beatrice will also be getting a decent amount of physical therapy."

I glanced at my sister, whose eyes were wide. Everything was starting to get too real.

The last thing Dr. Jenson had me do was put Beatrice on the exam table so she could stretch her arms and hips and check her contractures. Bea's hips were a little tight, but that's common for kids with SMA.

"All right, Beatrice, everything looks pretty good," Dr. Jenson said. "Why don't you go ahead and get dressed, and then you can check out at the front desk. It's been a pleasure meeting you."

"You, too," Bea said as I helped her to sit back up.

As Dr. Jenson was leaving, I remembered the note I needed.

"Are you able to give me a note for work?" I asked. "My boss is kind of a jerk about taking time off during the day."

If she knew I was lying, her expression gave nothing away. "I'll leave one at the front desk for when you check out," Dr. Jenson said.

The note was waiting for me, as promised. And as luck would have it, it didn't mention *work* or *school*—just confirmed that I had been attending a doctor's appointment. My luck held out when I visited the hospital billing department to pay off the two-hundred-dollar balance. The woman at the desk didn't count the cash out loud, so Beatrice didn't know how much it actually came to.

She also wasn't as concerned about the cash but still offered me a receipt, which I took as though I kept a careful file of such things. I waited till we were in the elevator to stuff the receipt in my pocket.

I really needed to get myself a wallet.

TWENTY-SIX

THE NEXT few days I kept looking over my back, waiting for that knock on the apartment door that would crumble my world or finding cops at my locker. Thankfully, none of that happened. What did happen was a morning announcement from Helena that the school would be starting random locker checks. It couldn't be a coincidence, and I felt like I should apologize to everyone in my homeroom. Obviously, I didn't.

I kept my head down the rest of that week. I focused on Beatrice, who seemed to be doing a good job of handling the afterthoughts of the appointment with Dr. Jenson and listening to me on the phone, making more appointments.

Then the weekend hit, and everything fell apart.

"That's not a fishtail braid!" Beatrice whined.

My hands twisted her hair, but it was just a tangled mess. "I don't know how to do that."

"She's showing you in the video." My sister pointed to the laptop, which was sitting next to the bathroom sink, replaying the same hairstyling tutorial over and over.

"Why can't I just do pigtails? You always love pigtails."

"Because today I want a fishtail braid."

We'd been going at this for over an hour. The tutorial repeated so many times, I'd memorized the script but somehow couldn't figure out that damn fishtail braid. But I kept trying as calmly as I possibly could because I knew Bea's sudden obsession over something she usually doesn't care about was just her way of trying not to think about everything else.

"How about this?" I asked my sister, moving my hands away from my twentieth attempt.

Beatrice intensely examined herself in the mirror, turning her head side to side and reaching her hand up to feel the braid. Then, like a spontaneous tsunami that devastates an entire city, she started crying big and loud and scary.

"I want Mom!" she sobbed.

"Mom's not here. I'm sorry. I'm really sorry. Do you want me to try again?"

Beatrice shook her head.

"Seriously, I'll try all day to get it right. I have nothing else to do."

My sister didn't answer; she just lowered her head and wept. And I couldn't stand looking at it happening, feeling like I could've prevented the meltdown if I knew how to braid hair. Or if our mom was around to be a mom. Or if Beatrice didn't need surgery. There were a lot of *ors*.

I grabbed my phone and headed out of the bathroom.

"Who are you calling?" Beatrice yelled to me.

"Someone who can help."

It doesn't matter what I said when the call was answered or what she said. All that matters is she said she would come.

*   *   *

"Who's coming over?" Beatrice asked. I finally got her to settle down and breathe after she nearly choked on her spit and I had to run an extra nebulizer treatment on her.

"A friend."

"I didn't know you had friends."

"You know, you could be nicer. I'm trying to help you with your annoying braid."

"I didn't mean it like that. I just didn't know you were friends with people. It's cool."

"Well, this is kind of a new-old friend."

"What does that mean?"

"Honestly, I don't know. But she can help. I know that for sure."

Exactly as I finished that sentence, there were three quick knocks on the door. The sound instantly reminded me of when I was a child; she still knocked the same. That both terrified and comforted me.

I opened the door and let Helena Shaw into my life for the first time in ten years.

"Thanks for coming," I said, wondering if I'd made a terrible mistake.

"No problem," she said, probably wondering the same thing.

I closed the door and led her into the living room where Beatrice was waiting.

Helena froze when she saw her.

"This is my sister, Beatrice," I said.

Beatrice smiled and waved. Helena did the same, with a look of utter confusion.

"Do you know how to do a fishtail braid?" Bea politely asked.

Helena looked at Beatrice, then me, before looking back at my sister. "Um, yes. I do."

"Great!" I shouted. "She's all yours. Have fun."

Beatrice happily spun around and waved Helena to follow her. "Everything is set up in the bathroom. By the way, you're really pretty."

Fifteen minutes later they came back out, and Beatrice had a fishtail braid that might have been better than the one in the tutorial. I mean, her hair was even decorated with butterfly clips and some colorful ribbon, which I knew we didn't have. Helena must carry around crap like that, I guess.

"Yo-Yo, isn't it beautiful?" Beatrice exclaimed.

"Yup. Your hair definitely looks like a fish's tail."

Bea turned to Helena. "Yo-Yo tried to do this all morning, but he was so bad, he almost pulled my hair out."

"Why do you call him Yo-Yo?" Helena asked Beatrice.

"Because he used to carry around a yo-yo all of the time," Bea answered.

"Oh my God, I'd forgotten about the yo-yo! That was, like, sixth grade, right?"

"Yeah," I said, "and according to my sister, it's my only memorable characteristic."

"Can I call you Yo-Yo?"

"Absolutely not."

A few seconds passed before they finally came down from busting on my childhood hobby. Then we kind of just stood there in the living room, the awkward tension almost tangible. Suddenly, I no longer wanted Helena there, mostly because I couldn't stop looking at her.

"Well, thanks for your help," I said. "Bea, can you thank Helena so she can go?"

"Thanks, Helena, but you can't leave. It'll be so boring the rest of the day without you!"

"Hey, I'm not boring," I said, defending myself.

"Um, yes, you are. Helena, you have to stay and save me from being the only girl."

"I guess I can stay." Helena glanced at me.

"Yay!" Beatrice yelled. She rolled her wheelchair over to me at the couch, and Helena sat next to her. "You have to tell me everything about how my brother is at school."

"What do you want to know?"

"Well, first, how do you know him? Yo-Yo said you're 'new-old friends,' whatever that means."

"I guess we are. But also I know your brother because we're in Yearbook Club together."

Beatrice's eyes widened. "We're in a club, too! It's called Diet Soda Club. Our dad started it."

Helena stared right at me, smirking. "Oh, really? And what does that entail?"

"Not much," my sister told her, "except for sometimes we drink soda when we're feeling sad."

"I get sad sometimes. Can I join?"

"Definitely. But the initiation is really tough."

"What's the initiation?"

"You have to chug a can of soda and then burp your name."

I shrugged when Helena looked at me for confirmation. Honestly, I was just surprised she was loosening up enough to consider doing it. But my sister tends to have that effect on people.

Helena stood up and followed Beatrice to the kitchen to grab a soda. Bea brought me a Diet Dr Pepper and one for herself.

"I'll demonstrate," Beatrice told Helena. She took a big gulp and then forced out a burp that sort of sounded like her name. Bea still thought it was the most hysterical thing.

Helena concentrated on her soda, one of the Diet Pepsis. "Okay, I think I got it."

If only I was ruthless enough to snap a pic of Helena Shaw sipping soda, the first thing she banned during her presidential reign. I could use it as blackmail if she threatened to tell anyone about the IDs.

But I ignored my phone, letting the opportunity slip past me. Beatrice wouldn't have wanted me to do that, anyway.

Watching Helena try to burp was everything I expected: dainty and painful-looking.

"That was the weakest burp ever," Beatrice said.

"Sorry, I haven't practiced in a long time."

"All right, you can try one more time. I'm just not sure you're Diet Soda Club material."

One thing I knew for sure about Helena was that she wasn't about to be denied entry into any club, fake or not. So, she tipped her head back and chugged that Diet Pepsi until the can crumpled in her hand. When she came up for air, there was a familiar gleam in her eyes.

Then she burped not just her first name, but her full name: first, middle, and last. As gross as it sounds, I knew she had it in her.

Beatrice sat stunned for a moment. "Wow, that was intense," she said at last.

"Thank you. So, am I in the club?"

"Definitely. You might even be better than my brother."

Helena gazed over to me, taunting me. "Let's see, then."

I had no desire to chug a Dr Pepper just to prove to Helena I could still do something as silly as burping. But if I didn't, I would've never heard the end of it from my sister.

I stood up from the couch just to make sure I had full flow of all my internal organs. In a move I'd perfected over the years, I popped the soda can tab with one hand and chugged. Unlike Helena, I didn't need to drink the whole thing to get the bubbles moving up my throat.

I reared back and belched, "Hi, I'm Reed Beckett!"

There was a brief moment of silence before Beatrice started laughing to the point of tears. Even Helena laughed and gave me a high five. And, I'll admit, I laughed at myself, too.

Helena stayed for probably another forty minutes and watched one of Bea's shows about cybersecurity. She obviously had no interest in it, and I debated pointing out that what she was feeling was exactly how I felt when she talked about yearbook crap. But every time I'd turn to say something, our eyes would meet and I'd forget what I wanted to say. It happened four times, and each time Helena would smile and I'd look away first.

Anyway, she was finally able to make an escape when Beatrice fell asleep. Instead of just letting her leave, I figured I'd walk her out to her car. Beatrice would've walked her out if she wasn't passed out; so would've our dad. But mostly I just wanted to know if she was planning on ratting on me.

"You know, it's crazy I've never met your sister before," Helena said. "Honestly, I forgot you had one."

"Well, that's her."

"What's wrong with her, anyway?"

"Nothing's *wrong* with her. You just saw she's like any other kid and smarter than both of us."

"Sorry. I just mean, why is she in a wheelchair?"

I paused to make sure Helena was genuinely interested. She was, of course.

"She has a disability called spinal muscular atrophy," I said. "She was born with it. Pretty much means she has weak muscles."

"Is she gonna get weaker?"

I shrugged. "Probably. At least that's what her doctors say. She's been fine besides getting pneumonia all the time. But Beatrice always fights back." For a wild moment, I was tempted to tell her about the surgery and how scared we all were and how it had sent our mom fleeing across the country and how I'd made the IDs to pay Bea's hospital bills. But I came to my senses and stayed quiet.

Helena nodded, playing with her car keys and staring at the ground. "I remember my mom talking to your mom about something when Beatrice was born, but we were so young. I didn't really understand."

"Neither did I at first, but now she's our whole world, mine and my mom's."

As soon as the words escaped my mouth, I knew I'd made a huge mistake. It wasn't the fact that Mom was hardly acting like Bea was her whole life. No, it was the fact that I'd mentioned Mom at all.

Just as I feared, I saw a thought pop into Helen's brain. "Reed, where's your mom?"

"Work."

"Really? Because Beatrice made it seem like there hasn't been another woman in your house in a long time."

I was backed into a corner, literally and figuratively. I mean,

Helena stepped a little closer, so I stepped back and into the front door.

"Actually, she's on vacation," I said.

"Alone?"

"Her boyfriend took her."

"And not you and Beatrice?" With each question, Helena appeared more and more confused.

"Well, I have school, you know."

"How long has she been gone?"

"A little while," I admitted. I knew that if I acted too secretive, Helena would become even more suspicious. I just hoped she was buying my everything-is-cool act.

I could practically hear Helena thinking, which was making me sweat.

"Look, it's not what you're thinking. Beatrice and I are doing just fine on our own. I'm taking care of us, and Mom'll be back soon, so there's no need for you to tell anyone about—"

"So that's why you were making fake IDs!" Helena said suddenly, like she'd just solved an annoying riddle.

I should've said no. I should've said that Mom left us plenty of money and I was just making the IDs for fun, or maybe for a dare or something. Instead, I said, "You can't tell anyone."

Helena sighed. "Reed, what's actually going on? Where's your mom, really?"

"I already told you, she's on vacation."

"Till when?"

I looked away. "Please, just promise you won't tell."

"Okay, I won't."

Helena backed away, giving me some room to breathe. That's

when I realized the last time I told her a big secret, it was almost the same weather. I remember because I spent a lot of time outside that evening, watching my mom plead with the cops.

I hoped that wasn't a sign. The fact that days had gone by since Helena caught me making the fake IDs and no form of authority got alerted must've meant she changed.

"So, for now it's just you and Beatrice?" Helena asked.

"For now," I reiterated. She needed to believe that. In a way I did, too.

"I guess that's why you always leave at lunch, huh? To check on your sister?"

"Yup."

Suddenly, Helena flipped to being President Shaw. "Then you're gonna have to meal prep."

"Meal prep?"

"Yes. I looked in your fridge, and there's no food prepared. You need to make your lunches in advance and get everything ready for dinners so you can just cook them when you get home from school. Otherwise you're going to get exhausted, quickly."

Little did she know I've never not been exhausted.

"By the way, the vegetables in your fridge are rotting." Helena added.

"What? I just bought them."

"And you have to use them, Reed. What are you doing tomorrow?"

"Nothing. Why?"

"Because I'm coming back to teach you how to meal prep. It's easy. I do it every day."

Obviously, there wasn't a possibility of saying no to her. "Okay.

Thanks," I said, and meant it the same as when she gave me that peanut butter and fluff sandwich.

"No problem."

Helena turned to walk toward her car—the same car her mom used to drive us in. When she got halfway there, she abruptly spun back around.

"You know, I am a little offended you told Beatrice that your dad invented Diet Soda Club," she said. "That was our thing."

"Sorry. At the time I was just trying to distract Beatrice and cheer her up. She didn't know you. She needed to think it was connected to our dad."

"I forgive you. The Pepsi in the fridge made up for it." Helena smiled, and everything felt right. "See you tomorrow, Yo-Yo."

Maybe once in a lifetime you get the opportunity to meet the same person twice. And the second time you meet them, your entire first impression of that person gets deleted from your memory.

Helena coming to my apartment, meeting Beatrice, doing her hair, and burping like she didn't care about anything was the second time I met her. Maybe there was hope for this new version of us.

TWENTY-SEVEN

TO ME AND HELENA, diet soda seemed like the adult version of soda. I mean, you rarely see a kid drinking diet, but some adults are obsessed. They think they're drinking something healthy when in reality it's probably worse or at least no different than regular soda.

Much like life, diet soda is a mind game. One minute you're buzzed from its sweet nectar and feeling pretty good for making what seemed to be a smart beverage choice. Slowly but surely, though, you're still poisoning your body.

The story I told Beatrice about how Diet Soda Club started isn't much different from the actual truth. There was a parent who banished soda, but it just wasn't my mom—it was Helena's dad. And I didn't hide under a blanket with my dad just to sip on Dr Pepper, I hid with Helena under a blanket fort in her bedroom, and we would drink soda and burp and talk about how annoying parents are.

That blanket fort is also where I got my first kiss, which led to me saying things I shouldn't have. But I was young and soda drunk, and a girl had just kissed me.

"Why are you cleaning again?" Beatrice asked me. "You did that last week."

"Because the apartment needs to be clean for you to stay healthy."

"I think you're cleaning because Helena is coming over again."

"It has nothing to do with that."

"Is she your girlfriend?"

"No," I told her, turning away to do some dusting—and so she wouldn't see I was blushing. "We're just friends. Sort of. We're sort-of friends."

"Helena and Yo-Yo sitting in a tree. K-I-S-S-I-N-G."

"Just leave me alone and play on the computer or something."

"Do you know how fast you got me ready this morning?" Bea asked, ignoring my request.

I rolled my eyes. "How fast?"

"Forty minutes!" If Beatrice could've jumped out of her wheelchair, she would've. "That's, like, a record. And you had a look on your face like you were dreaming about someone. It was weird."

I was at my limit of how much I could handle Beatrice teasing me. The problem was I couldn't get too angry because everything she said was true. I mean, my face was moving in ways it hadn't in a long time—it was like my mouth, cheeks, and eyes were trying to tell me something. But maybe it wasn't so much about Helena. Maybe I was just excited to have a friend again—or even a sort-of friend.

Either way, Beatrice would keep making fun of me if I didn't occupy her. So, I went into my bedroom, found some math homework I kept from ninth grade, and scribbled out the answers.

"Here, work on this while I finish cleaning," I said, placing the paper on the kitchen table.

My sister looked underwhelmed, but then she shrugged and picked up a pencil and got to work, which I was grateful for. Helena

169

was going to be at our apartment in a half hour, and I still had to take a shower.

When I walked out of the bathroom, showered and changed into something other than a black hoodie, Helena was already there, playing with Beatrice's hair and showing her a pile of rainbow hairclips she'd brought. My sister looked like she was having too much fun being the center of attention, so I just watched until they noticed me lurking.

"You smell funny," Beatrice finally said to me.

"That's because he has on cologne," Helena told her, and then smirked at me.

"Ew, why? You never wear that."

"It's just deodorant," I lied. I changed the subject before my face turned any more red. "So, I see you brought some stuff?" I asked Helena, nodding at a full bag on the kitchen counter.

"Ahh, yes." She started unpacking veggies and other random food. "I saw you guys have radishes and you can make a great salad with those, but I didn't remember if you had mozzarella."

"We don't, but you didn't have to buy us anything."

"Oh, no. These are ingredients I had at home. My mom will never notice they're gone."

A couple weeks before that I would've rejected the food, thinking that Helena was treating us as if we were a couple of charity cases. But when she gave me the sandwich for lunch, she didn't know Beatrice and I needed help. She gave me that sandwich because she saw what I was eating for lunch and the crap I was putting in my mouth just flat-out disgusted her, so she made me something that didn't.

And even now that Helena knew the whole story, I was

confident that she brought the food not because she felt obligated to but because that's just who she was and had always been. I hadn't stopped liking Helena because she was a bad person. I stopped liking her because she cared too much.

"Did you bring ice cream?" Beatrice asked.

"We have ice cream," I said.

"You can never have too much ice cream."

Helena laughed. "I didn't bring any ice cream, but I did bring Marshmallow Fluff." She pulled out a brand-new jar from her bag.

Bea almost started drooling, reaching for the jar. Helena pulled it away.

"It's for your brother's school lunch," Helena said. She sounded like a mom.

"Beatrice probably won't eat your salad," I said. "Might as well give her the fluff now."

"I'll eat it," Bea protested.

"Yeah, right. The other day you took the lettuce and tomato off your BLT and just ate the bacon and bread."

"That's because you didn't make it right."

"You told me you liked it."

"I was being nice."

"Don't worry, Beatrice," Helena said, jumping in. "One time your dad made Reed and me chocolate pudding with gummy worms sticking out, and Reed refused to eat it because he was convinced it was real mud."

"Okay, that's totally different," I argued.

I waited for Beatrice to join in on making fun of me, but she was quiet.

"You knew my dad?" she asked Helena.

"I did. He was a really nice guy. Everyone loved him."

The three of us were silent. Helena gazed at me to apologize, though she didn't need to. She had memories of my dad just like I did. And as much as I know Beatrice hates that she'll never have her own memories of him, maybe one day she'll understand how cool it is that she gets to learn about our dad from how other people saw him, from the impression he left on the world.

"You know what?" Helena said. "I can't start this cooking class until we officially commence a Diet Soda Club meeting."

She grabbed a Diet Dr Pepper for me and Beatrice and a Diet Pepsi for herself. One sip, one burp, and Helena reset the mood.

"Why'd you guys buy radishes, anyway?" she asked. "They're kind of random."

"Some lady we were following at the grocery store bought them, so we bought them, too," I said.

"Seriously?"

"Yeah," Beatrice confirmed. "We didn't know what we were doing."

"It's true," I added. "If we didn't copy what that lady was doing, then we probably would've left the store with only ice cream, yogurt, and frozen pizzas."

Helena rolled her eyes, amused by our incompetence. "Before you go to the grocery store, you're supposed to look up recipes and buy those ingredients. And if you buy something extra, then you come home and look up recipes for how to use that."

My sister and I nodded and listened as Helena floated around our tiny kitchen, pulling together everything she needed for her radish salad. She grabbed a knife, metal bowl, and the celery and tomatoes that were in the fridge, which were both copycat purchases.

She sliced the radishes thin, mentioning they'd be even better if we had something called a mandoline. Obviously, we didn't have that, but Helena managed and moved on to chopping up the celery and tomatoes into bite-size pieces. Everything was mixed together in the bowl with a drizzle of the olive oil she brought.

"Bon appétit," Helena said, serving us each a portion.

Beatrice dug into the salad.

"You'll eat this but not a BLT?" I asked.

"This actually tastes good," Beatrice said with a mouthful of radish.

I didn't love veggies and I'd also never tried a radish, but it would be pretty humiliating to get shown up by my little sister, especially after Helena told the story about the pudding incident.

"This is really good," I said after taking a bite. "How'd you learn to make this? From your mom?"

"Not really," Helena said. "My mom doesn't cook much anymore and you know my dad won't, so I had to teach myself easy things to make so I'd have something to eat besides takeout. And that's what I wanted to show you. It took me literally five minutes to make that salad, and it'll last a few days if you keep it in the fridge."

"So, you just make stuff like this at night?"

"Yeah. Whenever I'm done with my homework and have free time, I meal prep." Helena finally forked a mouthful of her creation. "That reminds me, next time you go to the store, you need to buy deli meat for sandwiches."

"Deli? Isn't that what old people eat?"

"No, it's what normal people eat who have to make their own lunch and realize they can't survive off of soda and Doritos."

I smirked, giving Helena a silent touché. It was like there hadn't been a decade of zero communication between us.

And just when we were in the middle of having a good time—

drinking soda and obnoxiously burping while eating a salad, which somehow made us seem more mature—there was a knock on the door, one that pounded loud and rattled the windows. We all froze.

When I caught my breath, my first instinct was to look at Helena. But she shook her head, silently telling me she had nothing to do with whoever was at the front door.

"I'll see who it is," I said, walking away from the kitchen.

Standing outside the front door was a large man. I mean, the dude was huge, towering over me. An unlit cigar hung out of his mouth, and as soon as I saw that, I recognized him as the owner of the apartment building.

"Can I help you?" I asked.

"Yeah, the rent's due. Actually, it's overdue. Again."

I stared at him, trying to think of a way out of the situation and not look too panicked.

"Your mother home?" he asked.

"No."

"Where is she?"

"Work," I lied. Apparently, I was only capable of one-word answers.

"When is she getting home?"

I shrugged.

"Listen, kid, I need the rent."

"Well, obviously I don't have it, so I'm not sure what you want from me." I was impressed by how unconcerned I sounded. I resisted the urge to wipe my sweaty palms on my pants and ruin the facade.

You know how guys who think they're tough will just stand there and nod? Well, he was doing that, which started to piss me off.

"You gonna stand here until she gets back?" I asked.

"Just tell your mother I stopped by. And tell her that she owes me for this month and half of last."

I kept my eyes on the buffoon as he walked away, but I hesitated before I closed the door. People always say don't ask questions you don't want the answer to, but I had to know if we were on the verge of getting evicted.

"How much?" I yelled.

"Eighteen hundred! I'll be back at the end of the week."

Once he was totally out of sight, I shut the door and triple-checked it was locked. Then I disappeared into the bathroom and did the thing I told myself I'd never do again: I called our mom.

"Reed! What a coincidence. I was planning on calling you and Beatrice tonight," she said as she picked up.

"You said you'd call Bea almost a week ago."

She laughed guiltily. "Was it that long ago? Vegas is an easy place to lose track of time."

"I thought you were in Miami? You know what, I don't care. I just need you to send money for the rent."

"The rent? Why?"

"Because it's overdue. The scary landlord just showed up and said you still owe him rent for this month and half of last month."

"Oh, don't worry about him. He's harmless. Just tell him I'll pay him when I get back."

"And when will that be? He said he's coming back on Friday."

There was a long, telling pause mixed with the sounds of slot machines. In that moment, I truly hated her.

"Never mind. Can you just send me the eighteen hundred dollars?" I asked.

"I'm still not sure how I'd do that. I didn't bring my checkbook, and you don't have a bank account, so I can't transfer anything to you. But I'll talk to Seth. Maybe he can figure out a way."

She'd said the same thing last time, and obviously nothing came of it. "Yeah, well, if he can't, maybe someone at the casino can help," I said as I hung up.

I took a moment to compose myself. And when I opened the bathroom door, Helena was standing right there.

I gasped. "Jesus, why are you always creeping up on me?"

"You were taking a long time. Beatrice was getting worried."

"Well, everything's fine. I just had to pee."

"Reed, I heard almost the whole conversation with your mom. What's actually going on?"

I stared at Helena, wondering how much I could really trust her. It was one thing for her to bring us food and teach us how to meal prep or whatever, but Helena got more dangerous with the more information she knew. On the other hand, it seemed like she'd already connected most of the dots.

I took a breath and plunged in. I told Helena about how Mom left without much of a warning and how Beatrice and I had virtually no food. I explained that I made the first few IDs so we could eat, and then I made more to pay a hospital bill.

"Hospital bill?"

"Yeah, it came after our mom left. I've been trying to get her to send us money, but she says she can't figure out how . . ." I didn't add that I suspected it was Seth who didn't want her sending money to us when they could use it to fund their vacation.

Helena raised her eyebrows at that. "So you don't know when she's coming back?"

I shrugged. "She keeps bouncing around. First she was in New

176

York, then Miami, and now Vegas. She said she deserves a break. Honestly, I think Bea's upcoming surgery has scared her." I tried to sound sympathetic, but it was hard. Bea's surgery was scary for all of us, but Mom was the only one running away and hiding.

"I'm really sorry, Reed. Should we tell someone? Do you have anybody who can help?"

"Oh my God, no, Helena! No one can know that my mom's not here. If the cops find out I'm alone with Beatrice, then they're going to separate us until our mom comes home."

"Would they really do that?"

"Probably. You can't tell anyone, Helena. I mean it."

"Okay, okay. I won't." She paused to let the tension settle. "So how are you going to pay the rent?"

"I'm not. I'll just have to hope Mom shows up by Friday— or that our landlord feels too guilty to evict a couple of kids."

Helena looked skeptical. "*Or* you could just pay it yourself."

"Sure. There's just one small problem: I don't have eighteen hundred bucks."

"There's an easy solution to that: just make more IDs."

Was Helena Shaw really suggesting that I engage in illegal activities? Or maybe this was some kind of twisted test. "I can't," I told her. "Beatrice made me promise to not make any more. She's worried I'll get arrested. Honestly, I am, too."

Helena frowned. "So, what are you going to do?"

I shook my head. "I don't know," I said. "Even if I *did* decide to make more, I can't distribute them now thanks to your new random locker-check rule."

"That wasn't even one of my rules! Miranda Gilsip got caught smoking weed under the football bleachers, and when the cops checked her locker, they found a bag of pills."

"Yikes. Well, either way I can't really distribute without a distribution system."

She put a hand on my shoulder. "We'll figure this out," she said. "I want to help."

I felt the warmth of her hand on me, and I realized something: if Helena didn't make that rule, then she wasn't trying to get me in trouble. And no cops had ever shown up, either. She really hadn't told anyone.

Still, ten years of not trusting someone doesn't disappear so quickly.

"Why?" I asked. "Why do you want to help?"

"Because you're my friend." She said it like it was obvious.

"We haven't been friends in ten years. Why suddenly do you care so much?"

"Well, that's your fault, not mine. But if you don't want me helping *you*, then I'll do it to help Beatrice."

She had me there. I knew in my gut that we'd gotten as far as we possibly could by ourselves. If Helena insisted on helping, I needed to let her. Besides, don't they say you should keep your enemies closer?

"Okay, if you really want to help, then you can figure out a new way to distribute IDs."

Before she could respond, Helena's phone dinged with a text. She looked at the screen and grimaced.

"I have to go," she said. "My parents want me home."

"Did you tell them we were hanging out?" I asked.

"No. They think I went to the library."

For some reason that offended me. I tried not to look like it did. "Classic teenager alibi."

"Yup. Anyway, I'll start brainstorming ideas and share them

with you at school tomorrow." Helena gathered her stuff. "Bye, Beatrice. Promise you'll put those rainbow barrettes to good use."

Still chowing on the salad, all Beatrice could do was nod and wave. And then Helena was out the door. I watched Bea enjoy her special meal. The salad definitely wasn't going to last as long as Helena said it would.

TWENTY-EIGHT

AFTER HELENA LEFT, I instantly felt the weight of everything crash down again. After I paid the hospital bill, I'd hoped that maybe life would start to calm down and even out a little. Like I could actually catch my breath or just simply breathe. But I couldn't.

Each day there was something new to handle, and the constant need to save the day began to feel like a cruel joke. It was almost as if somebody was controlling the pressure, and just when I'd get used to the environment, they'd crank it up.

Around one o'clock in the morning, when I'd finally fallen asleep, my phone rang. Thankfully, it was on silent so as not to disturb Beatrice, but the vibration from under my pillow was enough to wake me up. Instinctively, I answered without looking at the caller ID.

"Hello?" I mumbled.

"The suggestion boxes!" yelled the voice on the other end.

"What? Who is this?"

"Helena. And I figured out how to distribute the IDs. We use the suggestion boxes!"

"Hold on."

Her tone was way too chipper for the middle of the night. I

rolled out of the bed and headed to the living room so I could actually talk. On the way, I splashed some cold water on my face to get closer to Helena's level of insomnia.

"Why are you awake?" I asked.

"I do some of my best work at night. I'm sort of like a worker ant."

"Great. And you decided I should join you?"

"No. I told you I had an epiphany about how to distribute the IDs."

"Yeah, the suggestion boxes or whatever. It doesn't make any sense. Are you sure you're okay?"

"Yes, Reed, listen. I've spent the past two hours fixing my suggestion boxes and—"

"What do you mean fixing them? They get destroyed or something?"

"Yes, it happens all the time," Helena told me.

"People suck," I said.

"They really do. But that's why I'm calling you. The other day I asked a teacher if anyone had put suggestions in the room's box, and he looked at me like he had no idea what I was talking about. It's like the faculty doesn't even know they exist."

There was a long pause while Helena waited for me to figure out where she was going with the story, but I was completely lost.

"Helena, if there's a point you're trying to make, then I need you to spell it out," I said. "Unlike you, I am not at peak performance during the night."

"It's obvious! Instead of using lockers to pass the money and IDs, we'll use the boxes. People can drop their name and cash in there, and the teachers will never know because they don't pay attention. But if they do pay attention, they'll just think a student is dropping in a suggestion."

"But the boxes aren't secure. All the money could easily get stolen."

"I'll make new ones with locks." Helena said that as if it wasn't a hassle. "So, what do you think?"

My brain was still slow to connect the dots. "Okay, but how will everyone get their IDs if the boxes are locked?"

Helena chuckled. "You leave that part to me."

I had forgotten how Helena can be when you're her friend. Kids at school just think she's some uptight priss, and she one hundred percent is. But if you're around her long enough, you realize that Helena is also pretty wild and creative and loyal.

So I laughed along with her, confident that Helena would find a way.

The next day, on my way to first period, Helena grabbed my hand and directed me around the corner of the hallway before abruptly stopping in front of a water fountain. Next to it, sitting on a stool, was a suggestion box—a new and improved suggestion box. The box itself was no longer a shoebox and instead looked like Helena bought a fishing tackle box, cut a wide slit in the top, and secured it with a three-combination lock. It was still decorated with glitter and puffy paint, though.

"It's great, right?" she boasted. "I made three of them last night; apparently, at some point my dad liked to fish. But it was easy: I just had to remove the trays on the inside and—voilà!—a secure box with room for suggestions or anything else someone might want to slip inside."

"I mean, I guess it'll work. But it seems pretty easy for someone to steal it and then figure out how to break the lock later."

"Already ahead of you." Helena shook the box and it didn't budge. "It's bolted down."

"How'd you do that?"

She smirked. "Mr. Milton."

I probably should've been more excited, at least for Helena, who could barely contain herself. But my conscience wouldn't allow me to be all in.

"What's wrong?" Helena asked.

"I promised Beatrice I wouldn't make any more IDs. I mean, I know I need the money. But I don't want to disappoint my sister."

"I think that's really sweet, Reed. I also think that Beatrice would understand that you might have to do some things you don't want to do in order to keep yourselves safe. Life isn't always about right and wrong. Sometimes the two blend."

I raised my eyebrows. "That's a funny philosophy coming from you."

"I'm not a naive kid anymore. My dad always says that bad people do bad things, but I haven't believed that for a long time now. You're a good person, Reed, who has to do some bad things right now—but for a good reason."

I studied her, still trying to believe this was the same Helena Shaw who once felt she knew better than anyone what was right and what was wrong. "We still don't know how to distribute the IDs, though."

Helena's eyes narrowed and twinkled as she grinned. I'd seen that look before when she decided to sneak soda into her bedroom. It could only mean one thing: Helena had thought of something and it was genius.

She reached into her bag and pulled out a stack of envelopes. Each one of them was stamped with the school's official emblem.

"You know how our homeroom teachers pass out random paperwork?" Helena asked.

I shrugged. "Like the yearbook order forms?"

"Sort of. But sometimes it's just for a specific student, like if they need to get a physical to play a sport or the school needs to send something home to their parents. And they're always in these envelopes, sealed, with the student's name on it."

My brain was trying to catch up with hers. "Are you saying you want to distribute the IDs in the middle of homeroom?"

"Even better: *We* won't distribute them, the teachers will! Just like with the yearbook forms, we'll drop these off before anyone arrives. They'll already be sealed and labeled. The teachers won't even think twice about passing them out."

I smiled. "Hide in plain sight."

"Exactly."

"And you have access to find out everyone's homeroom?"

"Reed, I'm student council president. I have access to everything. How do you think I got these envelopes?"

Then Helena playfully touched my arm, which was something that never happened when we were kids. Or maybe it had and I just didn't think about it back then. But I was thinking about it now, for sure.

"I guess all we need to do now is figure out a way to spread the word," I said.

"How'd you originally get going?"

"I sold IDs to Tucker Walsh and his friends."

"Then, I'd start there."

TWENTY-NINE

EVER SINCE I'd sold him an ID, Tucker Walsh spent fifth period smoking cigarettes by the back door of the boys' locker room. So, five minutes into calculus, I faked stomach pain, asked if I could go to the nurse, and then booked it to the locker rooms.

"Reed, my man. Good to see you," Tucker said. A half-finished cigarette hung from the corner of his mouth, and another was ready to go in his shirt pocket. He offered it to me.

"No, I don't smoke. I came to talk to you about the IDs."

"Dude, that thing has been working like a charm. Too bad Helena Shaw implemented random locker checks. You could be making *bank*."

"It wasn't Helena," I said, defending her. "Miranda Gilsip got caught with pills."

His eyes got huge. "Shit. Didn't her friend just overdose or something?"

I shrugged, anxious to move things along. "Listen, I have a new plan to distribute the IDs. I just need you to spread the word—discreetly."

I must've sounded pretty serious because Tucker actually put out his cigarette and paid attention. Then, to the faint sounds of shouting and bathroom noises echoing out of the locker room, I filled him in on the plan. The only detail I skipped was Helena. I made Tucker believe the locked boxes were mine.

"Sounds great, man," Tucker said. "You can count on me." Then he winked at me. The whole situation was like one of those cheesy reenactment scenes in Beatrice's documentaries.

Cheesy or not, I was back in business.

The week was going by fast, and the suggestion boxes were surprisingly slow to bear anything other than useless suggestions or insults. Helena would check her suggestion boxes every day, and so far each one had been empty. We never considered that maybe nobody else wanted fake IDs.

I was out of ideas. If the landlord showed up, I'd dodge him again. All I could do was take care of Beatrice.

And I was doing pretty well at that. We got better at meal prepping, and I even stopped by the grocery store to get deli meat like Helena suggested, which was a surprisingly exciting activity considering there are, like, ten different types of ham. I left with four pounds of meat—the guy behind the counter said we could freeze what we didn't need right away—and I started making sandwiches for me and Beatrice when I went home each day for lunch.

Still, the looming threat of Friday was never very far from my consciousness.

But on Wednesday, something magical happened. Kids at school started talking about some local indie band that had been touring nationally and had just announced a few concerts in the area. I didn't know the band, but I'd hear people whispering about them at gym class or when I'd be grabbing crap from my locker.

Only thing I did know was that the shows were at a bar called Dirt Bags, which apparently checks IDs at the door.

By the end of the day Wednesday, the suggestion boxes were completely filled. I mean, Helena had to remove them just so they wouldn't overflow. But our plan had worked and that's all I cared about.

Helena insisted on helping me make the IDs. When we entered the school the next morning and passed Mr. Milton, he didn't even budge or question why I was back so early again. Having Helena around was like a free ticket to do anything because everyone trusted her. Nobody would ever expect the straitlaced, pencil-skirt-wearing, projected valedictorian, student council president to be pushing counterfeit driver's licenses out of the art room.

But I'd always known Helena had an edge. If you'd ever met her dad, then you'd understand just how covert the original Diet Soda Club had to be.

Anyway, she finally unlocked one of the suggestion boxes, and the thing practically burst open with pieces of notebook paper folded around cash; cold, hard cash. There easily had to be a hundred pieces in just one box, and there were two more boxes equally as full. I almost blacked out thinking I might've made thirty thousand bucks if every person on that list had a decent picture, or at least one that I could believably edit.

"Holy shit," Helena mumbled, eyeing the pieces of paper. I'd never heard her curse before, but she was good at it like everything else.

The excitement faded fast as we dug through the boxes and realized most of the papers were just more insults aimed at Helena. It's not even worth mentioning what they said, but they weren't complimenting her presidential administration.

"I'm sorry," I said, and I meant it.

"It's fine. I'm fine." She was stone-cold, eyes fixed on the opinions of people who don't really know her. "How should we start with the actual orders?"

Tossing out the hate mail, we had about thirty orders. That wasn't nearly as exciting as three hundred, but it was more than enough to cover the rent.

"I think we should go through all the names and look at their pictures to see if an ID is doable," I said. "I've been burned before."

"What does that mean?"

"Like, I'm sure some of these names are freshmen with braces or kids who look like they're still in middle school."

Helena scrunched her eyebrows. "So, you don't make IDs for those people?"

"No, or else I would for sure get caught or get someone in serious trouble."

"Hmm, that's actually kind of admirable."

One by one, Helena read me a name, and then I'd find the file with their picture and take a quick glance. The first person was a sophomore, but the way her hair was cut and how she did her makeup made her look ten years older, easy.

We were off to a good start, but then the reject pile quickly grew with a streak of five freshmen and a few unfortunate seniors who hadn't yet hit puberty. By the end, though, we had twenty legit buyers. Which meant we had two thousand dollars—enough to pay the rent and have some cash left over. Maybe Bea and I would hit up the diner again, this time getting dessert first.

"What do you do with the rejects?" Helena asked.

"Usually I write a note saying why they got rejected and stick it in their locker with the money."

"What about the locker checks?"

"I think it's okay. All that security will find is cash and an insult. They won't know what it means."

I didn't need to say more. After reading those other notes, Helena was understandably still heated, though she'd never admit that, and furiously wrote a reject for each name. They were surprisingly insulting. Like, for one kid she wrote, "Lose your virginity first." And on another: "You look like you still wet the bed."

"This is fun," Helena told me as she added another to the pile.

"Don't you think you're being kind of harsh?"

"Did you not just read what people wrote about me? No, I don't think I'm being harsh."

To me, Helena always seemed like someone who could handle herself, and maybe if someone told her off to her face, she might be able to. But words cut a lot deeper when you don't know who said them. You can't help but think it must be how everyone feels about you. But I knew the things people wrote about Helena weren't true; I've always known that, even when I'd tried to pretend otherwise. I just hoped Helena knew that I knew.

"Do you always use the same birthday for every ID?" Helena asked.

I shrugged, not having put much thought into it before she brought it up.

"You should change that—and the expiration date and driver's license number. All of the IDs should be different. If people enter the concert together, it's going to seem sketchy to security if they match."

Of course, Helena said this as though she was giving orders rather than suggestions. But I didn't argue. It was decent input and would make the IDs more believable. So far she was a valuable business partner.

The clock at the bottom of the computer screen told me we only had thirty minutes until teachers would start arriving for the day. I quickly finished up the IDs while Helena stuffed and labeled the envelopes. We were a machine.

"Here are the locker locations of the rejects," Helena said, handing me a hastily scribbled list. "I'll drop off the orders to the homerooms."

I nodded, and on my way toward the door, Helena reached out to touch my arm again. When I looked at her, I saw the same amount of anxiety I was feeling. Real empathy is the only way to feel less alone, and Helena had a huge capacity for empathy, which was another reason why I knew the things that were said about her weren't true. Most of those people were probably just jealous of her. I used to be, too.

THIRTY

WHEN I GOT to my homeroom, Helena had already been there, and two envelopes sat on the teacher's desk. It's sort of an invigorating feeling, walking past an object that's so unassuming but filled with a secret. To me, the envelopes glowed like hazardous material as my eyes kept glancing at them and every person who walked in.

And the more I looked at them, the more I started to freak out, questioning if Helena and I had thought this through enough. Were we being naive to think we could actually distribute the IDs in plain sight? What if Tucker forgot to mention the distribution method to some of the buyers and they opened their envelopes in front of a teacher—or a student narc?

Finally, one of the buyers entered my homeroom. "Malcolm, this is for you," the teacher said, handing him an envelope.

It was all very casual, but I still held my breath as Malcolm collected the envelope and sat down at his desk. He slid the envelope into his backpack without even opening it, and I exhaled in relief.

I prayed the other handoffs were just as smooth, and I didn't completely relax until the end of second period. If anybody had been caught, I would know by then.

No news was great news. It seemed we were in the clear.

Like clockwork, the landlord showed up after school on Friday. I handed him the money and slammed the door in his smug, cigar-smoking face. He mumbled something about not being late with next month's rent, but that would be next month's — and hopefully Mom's — problem.

On Monday, it seemed like everyone was talking about the concert. Since there weren't any angry customers at my locker, I assumed nobody got turned away — although I wasn't even sure people knew I was the one making the IDs. I mean, obviously Tucker and his friends knew, but they wouldn't really need to mention the person behind all of the IDs now that the orders came through the suggestion boxes. But I was pretty sure no one assumed Helena was involved; even I hadn't suspected she would dabble in criminal activities, so people must just figure someone was intercepting her suggestion boxes before she collected them, or creating counterfeit versions or something.

With the concert in the rearview, I figured the ID business would probably dry up, which I should've been okay with since it meant I could go back to keeping my word to Beatrice (and avoiding jail time). But I'd kind of enjoyed the thrill of creating the IDs with Helena. I'd still be hanging out with her for Yearbook Club stuff, but that didn't exactly have the same rush.

Case in point: my current assignment, which was to help Helena set up a photo shoot.

"Can you carry these lights over to the bleachers?" Helena asked, handing me a pair of seven-foot poles.

I didn't flinch, just like how I didn't protest when she asked me to be at school an hour early to help take pictures of the sports teams and other clubs. Believe it or not, I was actually looking forward to it.

I liked watching Helena direct everyone and contemplate where she wanted the bleachers in the gym and which way they should face for the best background. She even carried a clipboard with the list of teams and clubs and the names of everyone in them. If someone dared to enter the gym who wasn't on the list, they had the misfortune of dealing with Helena Shaw in her element.

It reminded me of when I first met her. She invited me over for a tea party, the kind of tea party kids have but there's no real tea served. When I showed up with my stuffed giraffe, which I was obsessed with carrying everywhere, Helena showed me a list she'd made of allowed attendees, and my giraffe was not one of them. This was very devastating news to accept, yet I left my giraffe outside her bedroom door while we sipped invisible tea. Even back then, Helena had been a master of taking charge and getting people to do what she wanted.

"Why weren't these group photos taken on picture day?" I asked.

"Because not all the teams and clubs were formed yet. Now move the school banner down an inch."

I did and it literally made zero difference. Helena was pleased, though, so I climbed down from the ladder and walked over to her playing with the settings on her camera.

"Hey, I never really thanked you for making that salad last week and teaching us how to meal prep," I said. "Beatrice loved it."

"That makes me so happy. No one in my house appreciates what I make."

"You should become a chef or something."

"Oh, no way. I don't actually like cooking."

I wanted to keep the conversation going, which I never wanted to do, but it felt like Helena and I had ten years of life to catch up on. Just when I was about to open my mouth, my phone rang. It was the hospital.

"Hello?" I answered, always half convinced that I was about to be told terrible news.

"Hi, this is Debbie from Dr. Jenson's office. We've been trying to reach Beatrice Beckett's mother."

"She's at work," I said, my go-to lie. "Is everything okay?"

"Oh, yes, everything is fine! I'm just calling to follow up on a few things from Beatrice's appointment, and this is the only other number we have on file."

I lowered my phone and walked away from Helena. She watched me, concerned, but groups were filing in, and she had to start snapping pictures before the homeroom bell.

"Okay, go ahead," I said.

"Great. Dr. Jenson wanted to know if you scheduled a visit with Dr. David."

"Yes, we're going on Friday."

"Perfect. Depending on what Dr. David says, we'll get you on the books for surgery and can always push the appointment back if we need to." There was a pause like maybe Debbie thought she said the wrong thing. "Hopefully not, though. Fingers crossed."

"Yeah. Thanks. Is that all?"

"Not exactly. We submitted a prior auth to Beatrice's insurance and didn't get the best news."

I stepped farther away from the photoshoot and under another set of bleachers. "Prior auth? What does that mean?"

"It's standard for all surgical procedures. The hospital submits a request to your insurance to see what's allowable and how much they'll cover."

"And what did her insurance say?"

"The plan covers a significant portion of the surgery but not the full amount. There will be a balance you're responsible for."

"How much?"

"You'll receive a full explanation from your insurance provider. But in order to schedule the surgery, the hospital needs a fifty-percent deposit."

"How much?" I asked again, more stern and angry than I intended. It wasn't Debbie's fault, I understood that, but she was still the person on the other side of the call.

"The deposit will be five thousand dollars," she told me. "With the remainder due after the surgery."

She might've said more, but my brain went numb along with the rest of my body. I hung up and stared at my phone in a daze. For Beatrice to get her surgery, a potentially lifesaving surgery, I somehow had to find five thousand dollars.

No, not *I*. This was definitely my mom's responsibility. Enough was enough; she needed to come home and face up to being a mom—and to the fact that Beatrice was going to have this surgery, however scary the idea of it was.

With shaking hands, I called my mom. She was sort of like a drug for me; nothing good or helpful came from the experience, but I kept going back for more.

The phone rang until her voice mail answered. I called again. And again.

And again.

Finally I took the hint that our mom wasn't there for us. I was no longer sure she would ever be again.

I slid to the floor, clutching my phone.

I don't know how much time passed till Helena found me. I was in the fetal position, tears still wet on my face.

"Oh my gosh, are you okay?" she asked, crouching beside me.

I shook my head, unable to put together the words to explain.

"Seriously, what is going on, Reed?" she asked again. "Is Beatrice okay?"

"No. I mean, yes, but she needs to have surgery." I forced the words out. "If she doesn't, she'll just keep getting sicker and sicker. That was the hospital. They need a deposit of five thousand dollars."

"Five thousand dollars? For the surgery? Do you guys have insurance?"

I nodded. "That's what we owe *after* insurance. Actually, we owe ten thousand; five is just the deposit."

"You should call your mom. You need to tell her to come back."

"I just did and she didn't answer. I don't think she's ever coming back."

"We'll figure this out." Then Helena grabbed my hand.

And just like that, I believed her.

THIRTY-ONE

THE REST OF the morning, I just went through the motions and didn't once look up at any of my teachers; staring at the desk was the only way I could continue functioning. If I turned my head or slightly shifted my eyes, it felt like I would explode.

When lunchtime rolled around, I seriously considered not coming back to school after going to the apartment. And I don't just mean for that day. There was zero chance I could come up with five grand, which meant Beatrice couldn't have the surgery, and if she didn't, then who knew what would happen to her. I needed to be there for her—now more than ever.

Helena found me headed toward my car. I assumed she was going to yell at me for not using the sign-out sheet.

"Are you coming back after lunch?" she asked.

"Yeah," I lied. "Why?"

She pointed at my backpack. "Because it looks like you packed up your entire locker just to go home for an hour."

I sighed. What did she want me to say?

"I'm coming with you," she said.

"What? No. No way."

"Yes. I'm coming with you because then you'll have to drive me back, and once you've driven all the way here again, then you might as well just go inside and finish the day."

"Or I could just make you walk. I only live, like, five blocks away."

"I can't walk back."

"Why not?"

"Because of street toughs."

"Street toughs?"

"Yes, street toughs who will try to steal my chemistry homework. I don't think you want that on your conscience."

"Helena, I'm pretty sure there aren't any street toughs lurking around to steal your homework."

"I can't risk it." She opened the passenger door of the car and climbed in.

As much as I hated to admit it, I was grateful to Helena for stopping me from bailing on school. Beatrice wouldn't have wanted that. It wouldn't have mattered to her that I would be doing it *for her*. She would've said I was giving up—and she would've been right.

I got in the car and began the short drive home.

"I guess your fake ID didn't come with driving lessons, huh?" Helena teased.

"I'm getting better. Still not a huge fan of left turns. Or driving in general."

"Because of your dad?"

I nodded.

Helena nodded too. After a moment she said, "We're going to figure out this surgery thing. I mean, we only need to sell fifty IDs. That's not too bad."

"Helena, we could barely sell twenty when the whole school apparently needed them for a concert."

"How about other high schools? I have connections."

"No. It's too risky."

She was quiet again. Then: "Did you call your mom again?"

"She still hasn't answered."

"Well, what if—"

"Helena, drop it, please. I've already thought through all of the scenarios."

Disappointed, she slouched down in her seat. We rode in silence until I pulled up to the apartment.

"Listen, I'm sorry I snapped at you," I said.

"It's okay. But if you're trying to get rid of me again, it's not gonna work. I'm in this for the long haul." Then she jumped out of the car and ran toward the apartment door yelling, "Race you!"

It wasn't until we got ready to eat that I realized Helena hadn't brought a bag or lunch box. She must've planned to tag along before she even saw me leaving.

THIRTY-TWO

ID ORDERS came in drips and drabs the rest of the week. I stashed the money in my underwear drawer, which is the last place Beatrice would go poking around in. And even though I would've felt rich if I'd had this much money only a few weeks ago, it was nowhere near enough.

The orders were so sporadic that it wasn't worth waking up at dawn just to make one ID. Helena had offered to make the one-offs. I trusted her . . . to an extent. I did make sure to reiterate that if the customer didn't pass the gut check, she needed to toss them.

"What would you like for lunch?" I asked Beatrice calmly, trying to hide my internal turmoil. Though my sister did have a sixth sense of sussing out my poker face. She would just stare at me, and I could practically see the wheels in her head spinning, but she never said anything.

"What are you gonna eat?" she asked.

"Probably a ham sandwich."

"Okay, I'll have a turkey sandwich with lettuce, tomato, and mustard but hold the lettuce, tomato, and mustard."

I had to pause to process what she just said. "So, you just want a plain turkey sandwich?"

"Yes."

"Then why didn't you just say that?"

Beatrice shrugged. "The other way just sounds fancier, like when you order a virgin rum and Coke. It's just Coke but way cooler."

"How do you even know about that?"

"What do you think I do all day? I watch TV."

I had no rebuttal and just made her the sandwich. At least she keeps my life interesting.

Halfway through our sandwiches, the doorbell rang. I had stopped thinking it would be our mom, which was actually worse than being disappointed each time.

Anyway, it was Helena, and when I opened the door, she handed me a wad of cash. "Here ya go, three hundred smackers."

"Smackers?"

"I don't know. That's what my grandma used to say."

I took the money and stuffed it in my pocket. "You printed three already?"

"Yup." Helena was proud of herself.

"How'd you have time?"

"I have a free period before lunch, so I headed over to the art room."

"Did Ms. Gold see you?"

"I mean, she was there but distracted by some yoga video."

"Cool. But you followed the rule, right? No baby faces."

"Yes, Reed." Then she frowned. "There is one thing, though."

My stomach dropped.

"What is it?"

"Well, Ms. Gold told me she was doing inventory of the room and asked why we were low on the blank ID cards."

"Because students lose their IDs?"

"That's what I told her."

"Okay, cool, so you handled it."

Helena nodded, though not as confidently as you'd expect. I couldn't tell if it was because Ms. Gold remained suspicious or because it was finally hitting her that doing this involved more than the thrill of popping out counterfeits at the crack of dawn. Sometimes you had to lie to the people you care about the most.

On cue, Beatrice yelled and broke the nervous energy. "Who's here?"

"It's Helena!" I answered.

Beatrice let out a shriek loud enough that our neighbors could probably hear. "Bring her in! I want to show her something!"

I gestured for Helena to enter, having no clue what my sister could possibly need to show her since it had only been a few days since the last time they saw each other. I mean, Beatrice doesn't go anywhere or do anything; not much can change that quickly.

But apparently the thing Beatrice wanted to show off was a big deal because Helena gasped as soon as she saw my sister. "The unicorn barrettes! They look beautiful on you."

Beatrice smiled so hard, I thought her face might split. That only made me feel like a terrible brother for not noticing.

"You put those in your hair all by yourself?" I asked.

"Well, you didn't do it and nobody else is here so, yes, obviously."

"Good for you."

Granted the barrettes were barely halfway up to her head and most of them were upside down or hanging on to the tip of a strand of hair, but still, it must've been a decent workout for her. It was yet

202

another sign that Beatrice was getting strong enough for the surgery. If only I was, mentally and financially.

"They really look great," Helena told Beatrice. "I wish I could still pull off that look."

"I found a hair in one of them."

"Gross. I know it's mine, but I would've puked."

For some reason, that was hysterical to the both of them. I chuckled just to feel like part of the conversation.

"You should tell Dr. David about putting the barrettes in your hair by yourself," I told Bea. "He'll be really impressed."

"Who's Dr. David?" Helena asked.

"My pulmonologist," Bea told her. "I have to see him to get approval for my surgery."

"Oh, are you nervous?"

"Not about seeing Dr. David. I'm just nervous about Yo-Yo driving us there."

"Hey!" I said, but they ignored me.

Helena nodded in sympathy. "Tell me about it. He drove me here the other day, and I'm still not fully recovered."

"We could walk to the appointment if you think my driving is so terrible," I said.

"When's the appointment?" Helena asked.

"Today after Yo-Yo gets home from school," Beatrice said.

"Darn. I was going to offer to drive you, but I have to do annoying errands with my mom. But I can maybe give your brother a quick driving lesson if you think it'll help."

Beatrice was obviously over the moon about this. Me, not so much.

"We have to get back to school," I said.

Helena chuckled. "Since when are you so eager to get to class?"

"Very funny. Anyway, I don't need a lesson," I insisted. "I'm really not that bad at driving."

"Yes, you are," Helena and Beatrice said in unison.

Helena slapped me on the back. "Grab your keys. I'll at least teach you how to turn left."

Beatrice was the first one out the door and to the car. Watching me get schooled by Helena would be the highlight of her week. Actually, we could've been doing anything with Helena and Bea would've been stoked.

"Just pull out of the parking lot, and we'll drive down to school and back," Helena said.

Grudgingly, I put the car in drive and stepped on the gas—a little too hard. All of our bodies jolted back, and I slammed on the brakes, which only sent our bodies flopping forward, hard. Maybe I did suck at driving.

"See what I mean?" Beatrice shouted from the back seat. "We didn't even go anywhere, and I already have a concussion."

"You don't have a concussion," I said.

"Well, I definitely have whiplash."

Helena placed her hand on my leg and gave me a look that said, *That was a bad start, but you'll do better.* I took a deep breath.

"Take your foot off the brake and slowly push on the accelerator," Helena told me.

"It's like that *SpongeBob* episode where he uses his big toe to drive," Bea added.

Helena laughed. "Exactly."

The car started to creep forward, and I gave it more and more gas until I was at a steady speed. Once the car was moving, I was fine. Driving down roads wasn't a problem because it's really not that hard to drive in a straight line. All the other components of driving were a pain, though, like stopping and going and other cars. And left turns.

"Put your turn signal on," Helena told me when we got to the end of the street.

"Why? Nobody's behind us."

"You still have to turn it on. That's the law."

The law also said I can't drive with a falsified driver's license, yet there I was. I didn't remind her of that and flipped on the blinker.

"No," Helena said. "The left blinker. I'm teaching you how to turn left."

I sighed.

"Turning left isn't that hard," she assured me. "It's just like crossing the street. You look left, right, and then left again."

"Don't be scared, Yo-Yo," Bea said. "I believe in you."

"There's nobody coming. Go for it," Helena added.

I won't lie, every muscle in my body clenched as I rounded the corner toward school. But once I was headed forward again, something changed. Maybe it was Helena's hand on my leg or maybe it was just the relief that came from doing something hard, but it felt as if I'd broken through some kind of wall and I just wanted to keep driving. So, I did.

I made another left and then a third left into a bank and then pulled out left from that bank to make another left back to my neighborhood. I owned the left turn, and maybe after the fifth time I didn't need Helena's hand on my leg to keep me calm, but I also didn't tell her to let go.

THIRTY-THREE

BEATRICE STOPPED teasing me about my driving after that. I think what made her feel better is that I wasn't terrified anymore. If the oldest person around—the one who's supposed to protect you—is terrified, then obviously you as a kid are going to be terrified. Kids pick up on that energy, the way dogs do.

"I'm excited to see Dr. David," Beatrice said. We were in the exam room, just waiting for Dr. David to come in.

"Yeah?"

"Yeah. I think it's gonna be good news."

"I hope so. You seem stronger to me."

"Should we tell him about that gross mucus you suctioned that looked like an alien?"

"No, I don't think he wants to hear about that."

"Why not? He's a doctor."

"True, but that happened right after you came home from the hospital." She looked disappointed. "Be sure to tell him about the barrettes, though. He'd probably like that."

Beatrice halfheartedly smiled. "What do you think Dad would do if he was here?"

Her question caught me by surprise. "I'm not sure," I answered honestly. "He'd probably be trying to stop Mom from yelling at the nurses for making us wait so long. Then he'd make up some random game to distract you."

"Like what?"

One of the walls in the room was covered in polka dots. I'd been staring at it since we walked in to prevent myself from passing out.

"Like he'd ask how many dots you think are on that wall," I told her.

"That's easy. You just need to measure the height and width of the wall and then the diameter of each circle. Then you can calculate how many could fit."

I nodded, laughed, and then once again prayed Dr. David would have good news so the rest of the world could eventually have conversations with Beatrice.

There was a knock on the door. "Beatrice Beckett," Dr. David announced as he entered the room. "I finally get to see my favorite patient again."

"You grew a beard," Beatrice said.

Dr. David rubbed the gray and black hair on his face. "Yes, I did. Do you like it?"

She nodded. "It makes you look distinguished."

Dr. David looked at me. "What do you think, Reed?"

"I agree," I said. "It's a good beard."

"Then, I guess I'll keep it." He laughed and walked over to the sink to wash his hands. "I hear you two visited my friend Dr. Jenson."

"We did," I answered.

"And how'd that go?"

"I think it went well. She pretty much just needs your sign-off that Beatrice is healthy enough for the surgery."

"Well, let's see if we can give you some good news." He winked at me.

Like Dr. Jenson, Dr. David listened to Bea's lungs but for a lot longer and more thoroughly than Dr. Jenson, which made sense since he is a pulmonologist. He made her breathe then cough and then do a few cycles of deep breaths and more hard coughs. Then he felt her neck and pushed on her sinuses. My sister adored the attention and made funny faces when Dr. David looked down her throat.

"You sound great," he said. "How have your secretions been? No color?"

"No, just big alien-looking things," Beatrice proudly told him.

"What?"

"It's been fine," I said, jumping in. "Her mucus isn't green or anything, and we've been following your discharge orders."

"My brother is very good at using the cough-assist machine," Bea added.

Dr. David nodded, jotted down some notes, and leaned against the counter in the room. Then it seemed like he realized something. "Where's your mom?"

"She's at work," I answered before my sister.

"Okay, well, tell her I think you're doing great. I just want to run a few tests to make sure you're fully over the pneumonia." He opened the door and, before stepping out, said, "A respiratory therapist will come get you."

The breathing tests were basically Beatrice breathing into a tube that was connected to a computer. She did it three times, a big breath in and then blowing out as hard and as long as she could. The respiratory therapist tried to guide each of the three tests along with the story of "The Three Little Pigs."

I thought it was pretty cringey, and I could tell Beatrice did too.

But she followed the directions, and soon enough we were out the door, met by Dr. David saying he'd send a message to Dr. Jenson with his approval to move forward with the surgery.

It was possibly the greatest day of my life.

On the way home, we stopped for ice cream, and I texted Helena the news. Both of those things were my idea.

That night I just sat on the couch and zoned out to the drone of the TV. I couldn't even tell you what I was watching. I didn't think about needing to make money or anything to do with the surgery. I was just thankful my sister was doing okay, maybe better than okay.

"Can I sit with you?" Beatrice asked, rolling up to the couch. She'd finally ended the three-hour computer bender she'd been on since we got home.

"Sure," I said. But Beatrice didn't turn to look at the TV; she kept staring at me. "Oh, did you mean on the couch?"

She nodded and I jumped up. I unbuckled her seat belt, lifted her, and plopped her down on the center cushion. Bea's body barely took up any space, and when I sat next to her, my weight tilted her cushion, and she tipped over on to my shoulder. I just wrapped my arm around my sister and held on.

"I've been thinking a lot about Dad recently," she said.

"Yeah? What've you been thinking about?"

"Just that I don't know much about him."

"And that makes you sad?"

"Sort of. I mean, you knew him and so did Mom and even Helena. I try to remember, but babies don't have memories."

If there was a way for me to transfer all my memories of the conversations I'd had and of the times I'd spent with our dad, I would've given them to Beatrice, no hesitation, even if it meant losing those memories for myself. I had heard the way he talked and seen how he smiled and knew silly things like how he couldn't start his day without eating a cinnamon Pop-Tart. My sister had none of that knowledge, and it wouldn't be the same no matter how much I told her. But I could share how he made me feel.

"I want you to close your eyes," I said.

She did, softly and without any questions.

"Dad used to call you his Honey Bea. He said you were named Beatrice for strength and called Bea to have the power to sting, to protect yourself."

"Like a bumblebee?"

"Exactly. But Dad would always put the word *honey* in front. He told everyone that you were going spread magic throughout this world. That it'll be sweet and pack a punch."

"But he was wrong. I don't do anything except stay home. You can't spread magic at home."

"That's not true," I told her. "Everybody you meet falls in love with you. Just think about all your doctors and nurses, and Helena, and even my teacher you met at the grocery store. Plus you're friends with Zigzag."

Beatrice didn't answer, but I knew what she meant. A ten-year-old should never be trapped while everyone else gets to grow up and experience life.

"Anyway, after your surgery, I'll make sure you get to see more of the world," I said.

"I don't even want to see the whole world, yet. I just want to go to school."

I kissed her head. "I know."

Beatrice smiled, probably dreaming about hanging out and

meeting people who are actually her age. "You only call me Bea. Why don't you call me Honey Bea?"

"Because that was Dad's connection to you. You said you don't know him, but you'll only ever be Honey Bea to Dad."

Beatrice kept her eyes closed as her breath slowly rose and fell and pushed into me. I gave her a gentle squeeze.

"Do you feel anything?" I asked.

"I feel Dad holding me. Is this how he would hold you?"

"Yes."

We sat there on the couch, still and silent and thinking about how dads hold their kids. I'm not sure how much time passed. At one point I thought Beatrice fell asleep, but then she opened her eyes and her innocent pupils looked right into mine.

"Yo-Yo, can you tell me a story?" she asked.

My mind didn't stutter; I knew exactly what to say. "Once upon a time, there was a prince who thought he was on his way to meet his future queen. But during his journey, he met a princess who was beautiful and kind and everything a princess should be."

"And what happened?"

"Well, the prince was so distracted by her beauty, he didn't continue his journey because he didn't need to. The prince was certain he had already found his real, true love."

"Do they live happily ever after?"

"I don't know," I said, the honest truth.

"Maybe keep telling the story and we'll find out."

So I did. I told her the story of our parents, exactly how I hope I'll always remember it.

THIRTY-FOUR

DR. JENSON'S OFFICE called first thing Monday morning. I was in the middle of getting Bea dressed when the doctor's name popped up on the screen of my phone and we both froze.

Beatrice locked eyes with me, and it was like we both understood that a new life—beginning, change, hope, or whatever you want to call it—was on the other side of the phone. But whatever amount of anxiousness Beatrice was feeling was double for me with the added concern of the looming deposit money.

I answered, stomach in knots, knowing for sure there'd be good and bad news. And there was.

Through all of it, I kept the phone pressed to my ear as tight as possible to prevent any noise from reaching Beatrice. Every couple of seconds, I'd speak one-word answers: "Okay." "Great." "Thanks."

When the call ended, I plastered on my best poker face. "Surgery is scheduled in four weeks," I told Bea.

Then she cheered and celebrated the way you do when you receive lifesaving news. I celebrated with her, keeping secret the other part of the phone call: the due date for the deposit.

The hospital needed the five thousand dollars in two weeks. Their exact words were "If the hospital doesn't receive the fifty-percent deposit in time, the procedure will be postponed."

I hate clichés but this was go time. Now or never. Do or die, literally.

Once Beatrice was all dressed and in her wheelchair, I rushed over to school as quickly as I could, sprinting through the hallways and trying to reach Helena before homeroom. I found her in the art room working on ID orders from Friday. I tried to speak but was out of breath.

"What's wrong with you?" Helena asked.

"We need to ramp up production," I panted. "The hospital just called, and they need the money in two weeks."

Helena gestured at the pathetic pile of orders next to her. "These are from all four suggestion boxes. Demand is way down. It seems like anyone who wanted to buy already did."

"What about all the baby faces?" I asked.

"You want to start making those now?"

"Helena, I need the money."

"I mean, we can do it. Though there's only a couple in this pile; our notes might've been scaring some people off. But I have some more bad news."

My heart spasmed. I swear I was on the cusp of a heart attack. There's only so much a body can handle, even a teenage body.

"What is it?"

Reluctantly, Helena exited the art room and I followed. She walked to the end of the hallway, and when I saw it—the *more bad news*—I felt my face turn pale.

One of the suggestion boxes was damaged. The metal box

was dented and half torn off from the bolted stand. It looked like somebody had taken a baseball bat to it. Even the steel lock was scuffed up.

"It was like this when I came in this morning," Helena said. "I checked all the boxes after lunch on Friday, so someone must've tried to break in after that."

I slammed my fist against the lockers next to us, sending out a loud noise.

"Reed, they didn't get in," Helena assured me.

"I know. But they're gonna come back. Whoever did this really wanted the money, and they're gonna come back."

I had reached my breaking point. I could deal with Beatrice's medical stuff and finding ways for us to survive every day. But now someone was trying to take money away from me, away from saving my sister.

"Reed, it's okay." Helena put her hand on my back. "I'll think of a new plan."

"I'm sure you will," I said, and I really meant it. "But that's not why I'm mad. It's just one thing after another. It never ends."

We both knew there was nothing else Helena could say to really make me feel better. So, she just stood there with me against the lockers. Maybe that's all I needed.

We stayed like that, silent, while other students slowly filed in for the day. Now that I knew someone tried to break into the suggestion box, each person who passed was my enemy. Each person was a suspect.

Eventually, Helena left me to go prep for morning announcements, and I remained pretty motionless until my hands did something without my brain's approval; they took out my phone and dialed my mom.

The call went straight to voice mail again.

As a last-ditch effort, I texted her and laid it all out: the scheduled surgery, the five thousand dollars, how Beatrice needs her mom. After a moment's hesitation, I added that I needed my mom, too.

THIRTY-FIVE

"GOOD MORNING, STUDENTS," our principal, Dr. Kenzing, said over the school's loudspeaker. "Before you hear from your student council president, I have an important announcement. During the school's locker checks, security has found an abundance of hateful notes. We do not know the culprit, but there will be an investigation and all students are encouraged to say something if they see something."

Although I couldn't see Helena, I knew she had to be sweating bullets after that. In fact, I could almost feel her nails digging into my arm as if she was sitting next to me. I don't think Helena had ever been in trouble, and even though I was pretty sure they wouldn't find us out, I knew that to Helena, Dr. Kenzing's indirect threat was enough.

"This school has zero tolerance for bullying in any form," Dr. Kenzing added. "Not to mention the level of cowardice it takes to distribute notes through student lockers."

That honestly made me chuckle. Like, if Helena and I said those things to the person's face, it would somehow be more moral and honorable. Sometimes I wonder if school administrators ever hear their strange messaging.

Dr. Kenzing paused dramatically to let her lecture sink in. "Now over to your student council president, Helena Shaw, with your Monday-morning message."

"Um, midterms are coming up," Helena nervously stumbled over her words, "which means the tutoring center in the library will have extended after-school hours. Visit them for help with papers or test prep."

Then I overheard the most amazing thing. A thing that I knew on the spot would solve all my problems.

Right after Helena finished her spiel about the tutoring center, some kid in front of me turned to his friend and said, "They should just write our papers for us."

That's not what caught my attention. What did was that his friend responded, "Seriously, I'd pay good money for that."

I have no idea where teenagers get all their money. Maybe they steal from their parents, have charitable grandparents, or do high-priced chores. It didn't matter, though, because the IDs proved they had it and wanted to spend it. And now I knew what they'd be willing to spend more of it on.

THIRTY-SIX

IN MOVIES, they always cut right to the scene where the crew is magically together and working on their elaborate plan as if they have nowhere else to be. Real life unfortunately isn't like that.

I texted Helena to meet me at my apartment during lunch, but she first had to meet with Dr. Kenzing to discuss some kind of school fundraiser. Although a bit anticlimactic, her delay did give me time to assist Beatrice in the bathroom, do her breathing treatment, feed us both lunch, and then get Bea situated on the laptop in the kitchen.

With about twenty minutes remaining in our lunch break, Helena uncharacteristically banged on the door. "Reed, I've been freaking out all morning," she said the moment I opened the door. "The school is going to figure out I wrote those notes."

"Is that Helena?" Beatrice called from the kitchen.

"Yeah!" I shouted back. "We'll be there in a minute—I just need to talk to her about a school project."

Luckily, Beatrice was too involved in whatever she was doing with Zigzag to wonder why I couldn't talk about a school project in front of her.

"Keep it down." The last thing I wanted was my sister joining the conversation. "Anyway, forget about that," I said, eager to spill my genius idea.

"How can I forget about it?" she whispered angrily. "I'll probably get expelled!"

"If they do figure out it's you, which they won't, then just show them the notes you get in your suggestion boxes. Tell them you were just giving kids a taste of their own medicine."

Helena froze. She knew I was right.

"But, seriously, forget about that for a second," I said. "I have a new way to make money."

"How?"

I glanced over my shoulder to be sure Beatrice hadn't snuck up on us. "During your morning announcements, when you were talking about the tutoring center, these two guys in my homeroom said they'd pay good money for someone to write their papers."

"So?"

"So just imagine how many kids are willing to cheat."

Helena nodded, pondering my proposition. "Not to mention the potential for repeat customers. I mean, you only need one fake ID, but we have papers due every week."

"Exactly."

I expected Helena to perk up, but she was still frowning.

"What's wrong?" I asked.

Helena sighed. "I mean, it's a good idea in theory, but who's writing these essays? You and me?"

"Yeah." I shrugged. "Probably."

"Reed, I barely have time to do my own homework. And you have *your* own homework and taking caring of Beatrice. I just don't see how this would be sustainable."

I deflated like a punctured balloon. "Damn. I guess you're right."

"Also, you're going to have people trying to negotiate price depending on length and whether it's for an honors class or not. I'm sorry, but—"

"I got it, I got it." I dragged my hands down my face, unable to believe I was back at square one. "I just really felt like this was the answer."

Helena didn't respond, probably because she felt guilty for bursting my bubble.

"What about midterms?" I blurted.

"What about them?"

"I'm just thinking that everyone would kill for midterm answers."

Helena raised her eyebrows at the thing we both knew I was implying. "Are you saying you want to steal and sell midterm answers?"

"Is that possible?"

"Not really. That's what Thomas Beatty got expelled for last year."

"I thought his family moved to Florida?"

"They did move, but only after Tom got expelled for stealing midterms."

"How'd he get caught?"

Helena was visibly over the conversation but humored me. "Apparently, he stole the AP bio midterm straight from his teacher's computer, which was right in front of a security camera."

I was quiet for a moment, which Helena clearly didn't like.

"There's no way to *not* get caught, Reed. There are cameras in almost every classroom—not the art room, though," she added, probably seeing the panic on my face.

I could hear Beatrice typing away on the laptop. I lowered my voice even further.

"What if I told you I might have a way to get the test answers from the outside," I said.

Helena narrowed her eyes, but I could tell she was intrigued. "How?"

"Beatrice knows how to hack."

This clearly wasn't what she'd expected me to say. "Excuse me?"

"It's true. She practices all day. Someone named Zigzag on the dark web teaches her."

"You let your sister go on the dark web? What is wrong with you?"

"You've met Beatrice; she's gonna do it no matter what I tell her. But she's safe, I think."

Helena shook her head. "We shouldn't do this, Reed."

"You've been making fake IDs no problem but draw the line at stealing high school midterms?"

"What I mean is we shouldn't involve Beatrice in committing a crime. She's a kid."

"We're all kids! Look, I'm not doing this for fun. This could save my sister. I just need your help to think of some explanation for why we need her to do it."

"No, I'm not manipulating your sister."

"Not manipulate. Just . . . influence."

Helena paced around the entryway, watching me watch her. Funny how if you know someone long enough, your problems start with secretly drinking soda and morph into something much larger, like selling fake IDs and figuring out how to hack into a high school's network.

Morality, much like age, is never constant.

"I think you need to tell her, Reed," Helena said at last. "I think you need to come clean to your sister and tell her about the IDs and the real reason why you want the test answers. The money is more about her than you, and she deserves the truth."

I knew she was right. I really had no desire to lie to Beatrice; doing so would make me exactly like our mom. I only wanted to protect her. But maybe that was exactly like Mom, too.

"All right, I'll tell her," I said. "But not till after school." I wanted Beatrice to have one more afternoon of being an innocent, law-abiding kid.

Helena smiled, which gave me goose bumps. Not scary goose bumps; the kind you get when you watch a stream of fireworks explode.

THIRTY-SEVEN

I SORT OF forced Helena to come home with me to face my sister and act as mediator. Bea couldn't be too mad if Helena was there. And if Helena was there, then it had to mean the things we were doing—and the things I had done—weren't that bad, right?

When we entered the apartment, Beatrice wasn't waiting by the living room couch like usual. She was still in the kitchen in the same spot at the table just staring at the computer. I made a mental note to talk to her later about her personal record-breaking computer session.

For now, though, I had more important issues to focus on. "We have to tell you something," I said. Helena elbowed my arm. "I mean, I have to tell you something."

"Oh, no. Are you two getting married?" Bea asked.

"What? No way!"

"Hey, why do you have to say it like I'm repulsive?" Helena asked me.

"No, I—that's not what I mean," I stammered. My face got warm. "I just don't know why she would even think that."

"Because your sister knows I'm a catch. Right, Beatrice?"

"Is this some kind of couple's fight?" Bea asked, getting annoyed. "Should I leave the room?"

I sighed. The conversation had derailed in record time. "No, I haven't said what I needed to tell you."

"Then say it already."

"I'm still making fake IDs," I blurted.

The room got eerily silent. For a second I thought what I said had made time stop or the universe collapse, but then Helena gave me a supportive tap on the back of my arm and I knew I was alive.

"Yeah, I know," Beatrice said at last. "And I know about the midterms, too."

"You do?"

"I heard you and Helena talking earlier. Our apartment isn't very big, you know. I just don't understand why you didn't tell me about the money stuff sooner."

"Because I made a promise that I wouldn't make any more IDs. I guess I was afraid you'd think I betrayed you if you found out I was still making them."

"Well, you did."

I lowered myself into the kitchen chair next to her. "I know, and I'm really sorry, but we really *do* need the money, Bea. We need it for food and your doctor appointments and rent and gas for the car."

"I know you're older and you think you're supposed to protect me and make all the decisions, but it's my life, too. You never ask what I want to do or care about my opinion, and that makes me really angry."

"You're right. I'm sorry."

"Like, nobody ever asked if I wanted to have surgery."

"That's because there's no other choice. You need to have it."

224

"I know that. And I want to have the surgery, but I would've liked being asked. You yell at Mom all the time that she doesn't involve me, but you do the same thing, and it's worse because you're supposed to know better."

"I just want to keep you safe." I looked down at my hands. "I think that's all that Mom wants, too. But you're right. I shouldn't keep you in the dark about your own life."

Beatrice studied me for a moment. "I mean, it makes perfect sense. You've always been a gray hat."

"What's that?"

"You know how I always tell you that I want to be a white hat? The kind of hacker who gets permission to do bad things to solve problems? Well, there are also black hats, of course—the real evil hackers. But you're a gray hat. You don't wait around for someone to give you permission, but you also don't do bad things just for fun. You do bad things for a good reason."

"I do them because I love you."

"Gross, Yo-Yo." But her cheeks turned rosy. Then Beatrice pointed to a stack of papers on the table.

"What are those?"

"Your midterm answers."

Her response was so calm and confident, I hardly believed the words. Not the fact that she could accomplish something like hacking into a high school and stealing test answers, but that she had decided to do it alone. It was like Beatrice didn't need me. After all I'd done to try to save her, here she was saving herself.

Helena and I flipped through the pages of midterms all organized by class type and grade level. Touching those was close to the feeling of holding the stack of cash from the first ID orders, maybe better.

"I didn't know what classes you wanted so I took everything," Bea told us.

"You didn't have to do this," I said. "Involving you was going to be a last resort."

"Yo-Yo, do you know why I love being on the computer?"

I shook my head.

"It's my only freedom. I have access to the entire world, and I don't have to think about being sick or surgery or my disability. Hacking is my superpower. I might as well use it."

"And you were safe? I mean, you think we'll be okay?"

"The high school uses a really basic proxy server. It took me about two minutes to get in. I can't wait to tell Zigzag."

"No, you're not telling anyone about this."

Beatrice grunted. "Fine."

Finally Helena spoke. "Won't the school eventually realize they were hacked?"

"Probably," Beatrice said. "That's why I took more than the tests. I also scrapped the lunch menu, maintenance schedule, and fire drill dates for the next month. I've learned from Zigzag and from watching movies that all good hacks look like accidents so they can't be connected to anyone."

Helena chuckled. "You're such a little genius."

Adults might be quick to judge us—that it was the wrong choice. That I really should've exhausted all possibilities. That we should've waited for our mom to come home and sort everything out, even if it meant postponing the surgery. But hindsight isn't alone with its twenty-twenty vision. Point of view also has its own clarity, and at that time my point of view was that my sister needed this surgery. It seemed like she had the same point of view, too.

"How are you guys going to sell these, anyway?" Beatrice asked.

"No idea," I told her.

"We could still use homeroom to distribute the answers," Helena said. "We just need a new way to collect the money and orders."

"I don't even think we can use homeroom anymore. Midterm answers are going to be popular, and too many random envelopes will look really suspicious."

"They're not suspicious when sports start and permission slips need to be passed out."

"Obviously, because it's school sponsored and all the teachers know it's happening."

Helena, exhausted like the rest of us, plopped down at the table. "If only we could get the school to sponsor *our* extracurricular activity."

I understood Helena was being sarcastic, and at first I ignored the comment, racking my brain to find a logical solution. But then I was stuck on it. The idea of the school somehow sponsoring the sale of stolen midterms was so outrageous that the more I thought about it, the more sense it made.

"Didn't you say you're trying to do a fundraiser?" I asked Helena.

"Yeah, for the spring dance after midterms."

"What do you usually do?"

"We sell baked goods like every other school fundraiser."

"And kids just come up to the table and give you cash right in front of teachers, right?"

"They do, but I don't understand what that has to do with this. You can't hide test answers in a cupcake, Reed."

"I'm not thinking about selling cupcakes."

"Then what are you thinking about?"

227

I grinned. "We sell bottles of soda."

"Diet soda," Beatrice added.

I laughed. "Yeah, sure—*diet* soda."

"But I banned selling soda in school, remember?" Helena said.

"So just think about how thrilled your constituents will be." I sounded like a real sleazeball campaign manager.

Helena looked unconvinced. "Okay, so, what? We stick the answers in empty soda bottles? How long before someone notices there's no soda in the bottles a lot of the students are carrying around?"

"But there *will* be soda in them." I reached into my backpack and pulled out the bottle of Diet Dr Pepper I bought at Cheap Check that morning. I smiled at Helena. "We don't stick the answers inside." I turned the bottle so that the nutrition facts and ingredients list was facing her. There was so much information crammed into the smallest amount of space. "We print them right on the bottle."

THIRTY-EIGHT

HELENA AND I planned to meet in the art room early to test my idea. Considering there wasn't a template like we had for the IDs, this was going to take both of our Photoshop skills to accomplish.

"One of the key parts in pulling this off is the paper type," I told Helena as I ransacked the drawers of the art room again. "It needs to match a standard soda bottle label."

"Reed, I think you're getting a little ahead of yourself. We haven't even figured out how many midterms we're going to sell answers for or what classes go with which soda."

"I thought all of them. Beatrice did get the answers to every class."

"There are over twenty different classes. Are there even twenty different kinds of sodas?"

"I have no idea. Honestly, I'm not even sure how we'll get *any* sodas. I really don't want to dip into my savings to buy a bunch of soda, even if we do make a profit. Does school give you a budget for supplies for the fundraiser?"

"They let me have access to art supplies for flyers and stuff, but that's about it. Anything more would sort of defeat the purpose of a fundraiser, wouldn't it?" she asked. "Anyway, there's a storage room in the basement with cases of leftover soda from when we still had vending machines. Sometimes I go down there and take a Diet Pepsi."

"Hypocrite."

"Whatever. The point is I have a plan. I've been thinking about it since I left your apartment yesterday."

I sighed. She couldn't have mentioned this sooner? "What's your plan?"

Helena's face lit up. She lived off of feeling needed.

"I calculated that five classes should be more than enough for you to make the five thousand dollars."

"Only five? That doesn't seem right."

"Are you questioning my math?"

"No," I tried to back off, knowing exactly what was coming next.

"I'll break it down for you." Helena pulled out a notebook and pen from her backpack and started scribbling. "First, we can automatically eliminate all English midterms since those are essay-based. That leaves us with math, science, history, French, and Spanish. Almost all of those have a college prep, honors, and AP class. Not to mention the different areas of math, science, and history. So, how do we choose?"

I shrugged, rolling my eyes. It was very sarcastic, but Helena ignored me and moved on.

"Statistically speaking, eighty-three percent of the cheaters that were caught last year were AP math and science students. They hit a learning wall, have an existential meltdown, and cheat. The only AP math and science classes this school offers are calc and biology."

"Great, so that's two."

"Wanna hear how I figured out the rest?"

I sighed again. "You know, somehow you've managed to take an exhilarating experience of stealing midterms and turn it into its own midterm."

"I know, I'm having a great time, too." Helena took a deep breath and continued. "AP and honors language tests are oral so that leaves only college prep. And then history was the most difficult to pick. I sort of came to the idea that the college prep students won't care enough, and the AP students are history nerds who don't need to cheat."

"That seems like a stereotype."

"Either way, the only honors history class is one that Mr. Bavroe teaches, and I hear he's a huge jerk."

Hearing Helena explain how she'd come up with her solution made me really hate that I'd stopped talking to her for ten years. I wasn't worried because she wasn't worried. I wished I hadn't missed so much of that.

"Okay, so you figured out the five classes," I said. "How am I going to make five thousand dollars from just five classes of people?"

"Because it's not just five classes. Each class is repeated four times a day with roughly twenty-five students in each class. That's five hundred people. Assuming we're charging one hundred dollars for exam answers, you'd only need ten percent of them to be too lazy to study."

"Or just classic ol' flunkies." I smiled. "Based on the number of ID orders we got, I like our odds."

Before Ms. Gold arrived, we found the perfect paper type and whipped up a rough draft of a label for AP bio, using Diet Dr Pepper as the test. It looked great to me. Better yet, it looked believable and the answers unnoticeable to a passing eye. Helena flashed a smirk when it printed that oozed an amount of rebellion I didn't know she had.

Finally, making the money for the surgery deposit seemed possible, and I could breathe a little.

THIRTY-NINE

IN THE STORAGE ROOM Helena had told me about, there were eleven different types of soda: Coke, Diet Coke, and Coke Zero, Pepsi and Diet Pepsi, Dr Pepper and Diet Dr Pepper, Sprite and Sprite Zero, Sunkist Orange, and ginger ale. Nobody really wants ginger ale unless they're puking, so we focused on the remaining varieties.

The plan was that regular soda would be displayed on the table as the legit fundraiser items—the part of the fundraiser where the money would actually go toward the school dance. Diet versions would be hidden and reserved for our cheating customers.

"How much are you selling them for?" Beatrice asked, lying in bed and breathing in her evening nebulizer treatment.

"A hundred dollars."

"That's expensive."

"It's the same price I sold the IDs for and nobody complained."

"But you were actually doing something. Like, you had to make the IDs, and there wasn't anybody else who was doing that, right?"

"Yeah. But I'm also the only one with the midterm answers."

"For one hundred dollars, people will just study instead. At least the IDs could be used more than once and for fun stuff. You need to lower the price."

The rest of the night, I thought about what my sister said, and she had a good point. *I* wouldn't spend a hundred bucks for test answers—but on the other hand, I wouldn't need to, so I really wasn't sure what somebody who actually needed the test answers would think.

I had to get a second opinion.

"I'm working on the labels right now," Helena said when she answered the phone. "Diet Dr Pepper for AP bio, Sprite Zero for AP calc, Diet Coke for honors ancient history, Diet Pepsi for French, and Coke Zero for Spanish."

"Okay, cool."

"And I made a couple different versions for each class. I thought it might draw attention if too many people get perfect grades, so there are a few wrong answers. But we still promise an A."

"Smart. But, listen, I need to talk to you about the price."

"Okay. What about it?"

"I think we should lower it."

"Interesting. By how much?"

"Half?"

"Fifty bucks?" she shouted. I had to pull the phone away from my ear. "Reed, we'll have to sell double what we originally thought."

"Yes, I'm aware."

"And you're okay with that? Like, you honestly think that'll happen?"

"I've given it a lot of thought. I just think a hundred is too expensive and not worth it, especially if someone wants to buy multiple tests."

There was a long pause where all I could hear was Helena's breathing. I like moments like that; the in-between moments when you kind of hope the other person stays silent forever because maybe that means time isn't moving.

"All right," Helena said, interrupting the moment. "I agree we should lower the price. Oh, and I talked to Dr. Kenzing, and she's all for our fundraiser idea."

"Thank God. Imagine if she said no."

"I knew she'd be down. Dr. Kenzing is a Diet Coke fiend. She already promised to stop by and purchase a few bottles."

I chuckled nervously. "Just be sure you give her one of the *real* bottles." We'd already figured we'd have to keep a stash of legitimate diet sodas — carefully separated from the ones for cheaters — just in case anyone ordered one after seeing someone else with one.

"Obviously." I could practically hear Helena's eyeroll.

"I can't believe we're about to sell midterm answers in the open, in front of the entire school."

"Don't get scared now, Reed Beckett."

"I'm not scared," I told us both. "But I just wish we could start selling this week."

"I know, but we talked about this. It has to be during midterms so everyone can bring the bottles with them to class without it looking suspicious."

"I know, I know. I'm just worried about not making enough in time for the deposit."

"Doing it like this is our best chance of not getting caught."

As always, she was right.

Over the next few days, Helena and I met in the art room in the morning to print the labels and then take turns in the storage room during free periods to swap the real diet soda labels with the ones concealing the midterm answers. We made a hundred ten labels in total, twenty-two for each class, and they were pretty mind-blowing. I mean, the answers were there but not there. They really just looked like ingredients.

This might have been the slyest operation in the history of crime. I felt both proud and ashamed but also like a TV show should've been documenting our genius.

Midterms began on Monday, so on Friday morning Helena made her most celebrated announcement. "Afraid of midterm burnout?" she spoke over the loudspeaker. "Don't worry, school has you covered. Stop by the cafeteria and find a refreshing soda table stocked with your favorite caffeinated beverage. All proceeds go toward the Spring Fling Dance."

My homeroom literally erupted with applause. Even the teacher clapped, since their lounge vending machine was also shut down. For the moment, all was forgiven, and Helena was the hero of every student, teacher, and office receptionist.

After that, I found Tucker in his normal fifth-period spot behind the locker rooms and filled him in on everything. Well, not every-thing; I didn't tell him how I got the answers, just that I had them.

"All people need to do is ask for the right kind of diet soda, and I'll handle the rest," I said, giving him a list of the classes and their corresponding sodas.

Tucker took a long drag on a cigarette and then stomped it out. "How are you going to get this past Helena? I wouldn't let someone like her within thirty feet of those answers. She'll snitch as fast as her skirt lets her run to Dr. Kenzing."

I wanted so badly to defend Helena, but I knew I couldn't let anyone believe she was involved. "She won't suspect a thing. She thinks I'm helping because I'm in Yearbook Club and actually care about the stupid dance. If someone wants a test answer, tell them to get on my side of the soda table line."

Tucker nodded slowly. "Seems like you thought of everything. Or almost everything."

The bell rang but I held back, needing to know what hole he'd spotted in our plan.

"What do you mean? What didn't we—I—think of?"

"What's in it for me? Why should I help you out with this?"

I had to think fast. "You've got midterms next week, right?"

"Yeah."

"Well, your answers are on me. Just let me know your order the day of."

He seemed appeased by that, so I hurried off to class.

FORTY

ALL WEEKEND I paced around the apartment while Beatrice messed around on the computer, until the anxiety of waiting for Monday became so overwhelming, I had to get out of the apartment. So, I packed Beatrice into the car and drove to the place where I knew I could talk to someone who would listen. He wouldn't answer, but unlike my mom, at least he had an excuse.

"I remember the day when Dad bought this plot," I said to Bea. "He told Mom he was driving past the cemetery and saw the maple tree and decided this would be the best place to eternally rest."

"I love it," Beatrice said. "It's nice and shady so Dad doesn't get hot."

I knelt down to touch our dad's headstone. It sickened me that I'd forgotten what it looked like. Below his name it said *Father. Husband. Teller of love stories.*

"We don't come here enough to visit," I said.

"We should visit him every Sunday. That would be nice."

I nodded. "Hey, why don't you zoom over to those flowers and pick some to give to Dad?"

Beatrice agreed and drove down a path lined with wildflowers. I waited until she was far enough away to not hear me speaking.

"Hey, Dad," I spoke softly. "I'm sorry we don't visit as much as we should, but I do miss you a lot and I think about you every day. Beatrice does, too, and I wish you could see how amazing she is, Dad. You were right—she brings so much joy to the world, and she really does pack a punch. She's the greatest kid I've ever met, which is saying something because I think I was also a pretty great kid. Anyway, I just wanted you to know that I'm trying my hardest to save her, to keep Beatrice around so the whole world has the privilege of meeting her." I took a deep breath and watched my sister stretch her tiny arms as far as they could to pick daisies and buttercups and gently place them in her lap. "You told me there'd always be a net if I jump. I just hope you're holding that net right now. I love you."

When Bea returned, I stood up and planted a kiss hard on to the top of her head. She squirmed and yelled that my lips were too wet. I just laughed and then sat back and listened as Beatrice filled our dad in on all of our shenanigans from the past month.

By the first day of midterms, I wasn't anxious or nervous or angry or any other emotion that had been plaguing me almost my entire life. There was an overwhelming sense of calm and confidence as I helped Helena organize the table by the cafeteria, unloading the sodas Mr. Milton wheeled up from the storage room.

"Just try not to pay too much attention to the people on my side of the table," I told Helena.

"You know, you didn't have to cover for me. I told you I was all in."

"It wasn't about protecting you. Tucker needed to believe you aren't a part of this."

Helena smiled and nodded, although it was obvious she was

slightly disappointed that her good-girl persona would remain untarnished.

The school only allowed the table to be open for sales two times each day: during homeroom and during lunch. As soon as the school doors unlocked for the day, there was a rush of students wanting to get their hands on a bottle of soda. It's a little funny how wild people get over something that was once banned. I mean, we could still bring our own soda from home, but the idea of purchasing it in school was so taboo that there was literally a line that stretched down the hallway and curved into the next.

The first twenty students or so ordered regular sodas, happily paying the five bucks for a Coke or Sprite. Nobody asked about diet or looked anxious to cheat, which was hugely discouraging.

But then I saw a guy I recognized from my French class. He was acting jumpy, fidgeting with the money in his hand and sometimes looking like he was thinking about walking away.

When it was finally his turn to order he mumbled, "Can I have a Diet Pepsi?"

Suddenly I was nervous. What if he legit wanted a Diet Pepsi? His anxiety could've been entirely about midterms and have nothing to do with being moments away from buying test answers.

"You said a Diet Pepsi, right?" I asked, feeling him out.

He leaned closer. "That's right." Then he slid some bills across the table. I spotted at least one twenty.

Before anyone else could see it, I grabbed the money. "You have French today, right?"

"Yeah, that's right."

"Great. I think a Diet Pepsi will help you crush that French midterm."

When I gave him the bottle, he stared at it for a moment like he was confused about why he was holding an actual soda. Apparently, Tucker didn't explain the full process.

"Diet Pepsi doesn't have any calories, if that's what you're worried about," I said. "You can check out the nutrition facts to confirm."

Still confused, he spun the bottle around to read the label. Relieved, he nodded and then finally walked away. Handling her own customers, Helena gave me a pat on the leg.

By the time homeroom ended, I had made around five hundred bucks. It was nowhere near what I needed for the deposit, but we still had lunch-period sales, and maybe word would spread more by then. All I could do now was wait and see.

FORTY-ONE

FROM WHAT I could tell, the soda bottles were working like a charm.

In my first three periods, there were at least two kids in each class with diet sodas on their desk. But almost everyone had some kind of soda on their desk, so the teachers never batted an eye. It was just as Helena predicted, and I watched my customers nonchalantly take sips while scanning the label for the next answer. It was surprisingly satisfying to watch our plan in action.

During lunch, customer volume amped up significantly on both sides of the table. Even Dr. Kenzing, a woman of many pantsuits, stopped by to purchase two Diet Cokes, just like Helena said she would.

"This is quite the enterprise you have going," she told us.

"Isn't it great?" Helena said. "I was thinking we might be able to raise enough funds to rent the photo booth I was telling you about," she added, really driving home that everything we were doing was on the up-and-up.

Dr. Kenzing was still chatting with Helena while I handled more diet purchases. It seriously was some achievement to pull off distribution right in front of the school's principal—not to mention what it said about the students' desperation if they were willing to purchase test answers in front of Dr. Kenzing.

Just then, some girl I'd never seen before came up and ordered a Sprite from Helena. "Thanks!" she said in a high, chipper voice. "I can't wait for the dance! You always make them so amazing!"

Helena blushed, clearly happy to finally receive a compliment from someone at our school. I realized that in between all the plotting and the money exchanges, I hadn't really thought about the actual dance at all. A dance was typically something I stayed away from, but obviously it meant something to some people, including Helena. I mean, she cared about a lot of things, including the things nobody else really did, like our school and the yearbook. I always thought she did it for the attention, but I knew better now.

Helena also cared about me and my sister enough that she was willing to sacrifice her position as student council president and her reputation for us. She'd even volunteered to take care of Bea's afternoon routine after the big rush, so I could man the soda table and not miss any potential diet soda customers. She was doing so much for me. It was time I did something for her in return.

I waited till there was no one in line, then I asked, "Are people bringing dates to the dance?"

"Yeah, most people. Or they go with friends. Not me, though. I'll just stand by the snack table like I always do and chat with the chaperones. It's not as bad as it sounds."

"Well, I have a suit at home" was my awkward way of propositioning her.

"The dress code is semi-formal," Helena answered automatically. Then her eyes got huge. "Oh, are you asking me to the dance?"

"Yes. Maybe. If you want."

Helena smirked and my brain went fuzzier than it already was.

"Reed Beckett is asking me to a school dance, in public, in front of everyone. I can't believe it."

"There's no one around us right now," I pointed out.

She rolled her eyes.

"Well?" I asked, suddenly nervous.

"Well, what?"

Now *I* rolled *my* eyes. "You know."

"All I know is that you own a suit."

I scowled at her. She always made everything weird. "Will you go to the dance with me, pretty please, Helena Jaqueline Shaw?"

"Hmm, I'll think about it." She stood up from the table. "I'm gonna go check on Beatrice now." She started walking down the hallway, leaving me feeling like a complete reject. But eventually she spun back around. "I've thought about it and, yes, I'll go with you."

Then she was gone, which was a good thing because I couldn't stop myself from smiling and fist pumping. For the first time, I actually felt like a teenager.

That feeling lasted through the next day, as more kids showed up to buy answers during homeroom. They showed up in droves at lunch, too. I was more than happy to provide the solution to all of our problems.

FORTY-TWO

FIVE THOUSAND eight hundred and fifty dollars. I counted it four times, Helena counted it twice, and Beatrice got halfway through before giving up and agreeing we made a lot of money.

"I want to make the deposit first thing tomorrow morning," I told Bea and Helena.

"With a wad of cash?" Helena asked.

"I've done it before. Why, do you think that's suspicious?"

"A little bit."

Helena's hesitation made me nervous. The deposit for the surgery was important, obviously. I wanted to get it right. No, I *had* to get it right. No eyebrow raises or funny glances; nothing to raise suspicions. Everything had to go smoothly.

"Well, what do you suggest instead?" I asked.

"I assume you don't have a checkbook?"

"I don't even have a bank account. That's why I've been using cash for everything."

"So no cashier's check, then, either," Helena said, whatever that was. She leaned against the cabinets in the kitchen, thinking. Only a second passed before she had another idea. "You could get a money order. I've heard my dad talk about that with clients. I think you can go to, like, a grocery store and get one."

Beatrice was doing something on her computer, half paying attention to the conversation. But then her typing sped up and a moment later she said, "It says you need to show ID for a money order over one thousand dollars."

"Reed has an ID!" Helena exclaimed. "Sort of."

"Exactly," I said. "I sort of have an ID, which I've only had checked once in a dimly lit liquor store. The cash has been working fine, and the hospital doesn't seem to care. I just get a receipt."

Helena giggled.

"What's so funny?"

"You talking about receipts."

It was decided I'd use the cash. Honestly, the fewer steps and fewer people I had to deal with could only be a good thing.

"After the hospital, can we do something fun tomorrow?" Bea asked. "I'm so bored just sitting home all day. I never go anywhere."

"We can definitely do something," I said. I also felt like this momentous occasion needed to be celebrated, but silently. I wasn't trying to shout our achievement from the rooftops and get Helena and me expelled.

"What do you want to do if you could do anything?"

Beatrice thought about it for a second. "Go to Hawai'i."

"I meant something that doesn't involve an airplane."

"Oh, then I don't know."

"It's supposed to be really nice this weekend," Helena said. "Maybe we could do a picnic at the park."

"Sure, that sounds all right," I said, picturing Helena with a wicker picnic basket and plaid blanket. I had no doubt she owned the whole set. Honestly, she might have had one when we were kids.

"Or did you just want it to be you and Beatrice? I didn't mean to invite myself."

"No!" Bea shouted. "You have to come with us. It won't be fun without you."

"Hey, I'm fun," I said, defending myself.

"No, you're not. You barely considered Hawaiʻi before saying no."

Helena walked over to Beatrice and started playing with her hair, separating strands in different directions and loosely braiding them. "Since you think I'm fun, and literally nobody else does, I'll come over early to make your hair super pretty before we go out."

Nothing else had to be said. Beatrice was hooked just on a picnic and pretty hair, and I had two pockets full of lifesaving cash. I really had to buy a wallet.

As I watched Beatrice and Helena, I regretted ever sending that panicked text to our mom. We didn't need her. We could be just fine on our own. With Helena's help, we would figure out a way to survive.

That night, I slept like a baby for the first time since, well, since I was a baby.

Beatrice woke up early with that giddy energy kids have on Christmas morning. I felt it, too.

Helena let herself in the apartment with the spare key I'd given her on Monday. I liked that she felt so comfortable here.

She found us in Beatrice's bedroom while I was in the middle of Bea's morning routine. For a moment, Helena just stood in the doorway and watched as I held the mask for the cough-assist machine over my sister's face and then suctioned everything she coughed up.

"Do you need help with anything?"

I pointed to Bea's nightstand that held all of her medical equipment. "You can fill up that cup of water, if you want."

Helena didn't hesitate. She grabbed the cup, left the room, and quickly returned with more water.

"Thanks," I said, sticking the suction tube in the water to flush down Beatrice's morning mucus.

"Isn't it gross?" Bea asked.

"A little," Helena said. "Though not as gross as the time your brother wet the bed during a sleepover."

"I was a kid and it wasn't that bad," I said. I felt like I was constantly defending myself around them, but I loved it.

"I had to get new bedsheets. And a mattress."

Helena of course told Bea the entire story about how I chugged two juice boxes before bedtime and refused to use the bathroom when her mom asked me. I had an irrational fear of other people's bathrooms, and when I'd play at Helena's, I'd just run home if I needed to use the toilet. But I never considered that factor when I begged my mom to let me sleep over.

I've moved past my bathroom issues now, obviously. Partially because of that bedwetting incident, but mostly because I'd spent so much time in a hospital and had no choice but to use public bathrooms.

Anyway, Helena waited in the living room while I got Beatrice bathed and dressed in the outfit they'd chosen, which turned out to be slightly aggravating to get on her. Normally it was an easy pair of sweatpants and a T-shirt, but Helena had convinced my sister to be more "fashion forward."

"I didn't even know you owned a romper," I said to Beatrice, trying to wiggle her body into the one-piece.

Dressing someone who can't really move their body on their own is not easy, to say the least. It's also the main reason why I don't need to hit the gym. But when it's a shirt that's for some reason also a pair of pants; it's a whole other ball game. I mean, I probably rolled her back and forth three dozen times. *I* was dizzy so I couldn't imagine how she felt.

But once I got Beatrice in her chair and she looked in the mirror and I saw her look at herself, finally realizing how beautiful she is, the fifteen-minute workout was totally worth it.

"So, what do you want today?" Helena asked Bea, standing behind her in the bathroom mirror. "Another fishtail braid?"

"Can you do the braid where it, like, goes around the sides of my head and then there's a bun in the back?"

"Oh, like a crown braid?"

"I guess. I don't know what it's called."

Helena showed Bea a picture on her phone. "It's very fancy. But you have the perfect hair, it's so long."

"It's too long," I said. "We need to get it cut before your surgery."

"No," Beatrice insisted. "You can cut it after."

I smiled, knowing she'd keep finding excuses not to get a haircut. Besides her hacking skills, her hair was her only pride and joy. Eventually, it would be long enough to get tangled in her wheels, and I figured she'd probably beg me to take her to get it cut at that point. But who knows with Beatrice.

For a few minutes, I leaned against the bathroom doorframe and watched Helena brush and style my sister's hair. They talked about the picnic we'd have later and the food Helena brought. As strange as it sounds, we felt like a family. And I recognized every familiar sensation of just being completely happy and comfortable, and the feeling was so overwhelming that I had to back away.

"I'm gonna go make the payment while you two finish up," I said.

"Okay, don't be too long." Helena smiled. "The sandwiches will get soggy."

It was a perfectly Helena Shaw thing to say but also exactly what a wife or mom might say, and I wanted to scream and cry but also kiss and hug both of them because I've experienced that exact moment and loved every second.

One of the greatest moments of my life was slapping the stack of cash down on the desk at the hospital's financial office. The older man working there thankfully had no reaction. When I politely asked for a receipt, he collected the money, counted it, and never asked any questions. He knew I meant business.

FORTY-THREE

THE PARK Helena suggested was on the other side of town, closer to where she lived and my old home. My parents had taken me to that park a few times. Maybe Helena had even come with us. I wasn't sure.

Other families and couples were there, lounging on blankets. A young girl was sitting alone on a bench on top of the hill that overlooked the entire park and the pond that was surrounded by geese. Seeing her solitary figure made me even more aware of how lucky I was to have Beatrice and Helena there with me. We found a table far enough away from everyone for privacy but close enough so we still felt a part of things.

Helena unpacked our basket. "I brought cucumber and cream cheese finger sandwiches, the melon that was in your fridge, a bag of chips, and, of course, diet soda."

"Should we toast?" I asked, holding up my Diet Dr Pepper.

Helena joined. "To Diet Soda Club."

"And easy-to-crack proxy servers," Beatrice added.

Helena and I rolled our eyes. "Cheers," we said.

I didn't immediately grab a sandwich and start eating. For a second, I just watched my sister, who was taking tiny nibbles and mostly just looking at the world around her: the trees and grass and how the wind made them sway and all the animals that were hunting for leftover crumbs.

"So, what are you going to do with the rest of the money?" Helena asked.

I shrugged. "Probably just save it. If things go well"—I hesitated for a second, unsure if I meant *If our mom comes home* or if I meant *If I can keep finding ways to make money*—"maybe buy Beatrice her own laptop."

"Seriously?" Bea asked. "I'll have to do some research and talk to Zigzag."

"Okay, you do that." I laughed.

Beatrice gasped.

"What?"

"I just realized that I'll be using my new laptop at school next year."

My sister was definitely the only kid in history who'd be excited about that. Actually, that's not true. There's one other person who would have the same reaction, and she was sitting with us.

"You're going to have so much fun at school," Helena said. "You'll meet new people and make friends and learn cool stuff."

"Yo-Yo, what's your favorite part of school?"

"Don't ask him," Helena told Beatrice. "He hates school."

"I don't hate school. There are parts I like now." I glanced at Helena and then severely blushed, not believing I actually dropped that not-so-subtle hint.

Beatrice noticed. "Gross, get a room."

The thing about being with people you love is that you don't always have to talk to have a good time. Mostly we just enjoyed the finger sandwiches and fruit and laughed at people who walked past with grass stains on their butts.

Eventually, Beatrice finished her soda and let out a final burp. "Can I go over by the pond?"

"Sure," I said. "Just don't drive into it. And watch out for geese poop."

Then she was off, rolling fast down the sidewalk but totally free and in control. Bea wasn't scared of anything, pulling right up to a goose who had been harassing other people all afternoon. The goose backed down from Beatrice.

"I'm glad we're friends again," Helena said.

"Yeah, me too."

"Although I'm not really sure why we stopped being friends in the first place."

I chuckled, not believing her. "You know why."

"No, I don't. I mean, one day you're my best friend, and the next you're moving and refuse to even talk to me."

"You seriously don't know?"

Helena shook her head.

"Do you remember that time under your blanket fort, when we kissed?"

Her eyes widened. "Is *that* why you stopped talking to me? I remember you immediately wiped off your lips because you swore I had cooties, but I never thought you were serious." She stared into my eyes. "Reed, I promise I don't have cooties."

I frowned, frustrated that she was making light of this. "Do you remember what happened after that?"

"Not really. I think you just went home."

"My stomach growled so loud that it practically echoed inside the blanket fort. You asked if I was hungry and I trusted you, and so I said that I hadn't eaten anything in a couple days. You asked why, and I told you it was because my mom slept a lot and sometimes forgot to feed us."

Helena stared at me, and I could almost see her brain trying to replay the conversation.

"That night the police showed up at my house," I told her. "And they interrogated my mom and me. I was terrified and I didn't know what to say other than the truth, which was that my dad died and my mom sometimes forgot to make food. I was just a kid."

I looked away back to Beatrice. She was talking to some kids who were throwing rocks into the pond. She tried to toss one, but it barely made it past her tires at the edge of the water.

I wanted her to have so many more moments like that.

A second later, I felt Helena's hand on top of mine.

"Reed, I am so sorry you went through that," Helena said. "I understand there's nothing I can say that'll change how terrified you and your mom felt, but you have to know I would never knowingly betray you."

"I'm not saying you called the police. Maybe you told your parents, though, and they called the police."

"Maybe I did. I honestly don't remember. But you were my friend, and I wouldn't intentionally hurt you. If I did say anything to my parents, I probably was also scared and just wanted to help."

My mind was racing. I stood up from the picnic, needing some space. When they say your life flashes before your eyes, it doesn't only happen at the precipice of death. It also occurs during great epiphanies, when your brain forces you to relive all the moments that have led you to the place you are right now.

And, in that split second, I saw me and Helena under the

blanket fort, drinking diet soda, running around, and doing everything kids do. I was happy, not because it was before I thought she betrayed me, but simply because I was with my best friend.

Helena was a real best friend, the type of friend who would risk everything for the people they love. I know this because I'd experienced it firsthand. She risked everything to save my sister, jeopardizing her future. That's not the same person who tattled on my mom because it was never the same person.

"You know you're not the only one whose life changed that day, Reed," Helena said softly, coming to stand next to me. "And unlike you, I had no idea why, which hurt more than you probably think."

Then there we were, crying in the middle of the park. Everything I thought I knew about her and me and my life for the last ten years was a lie, a lie I created.

All that time I'd been mad at Helena, I should've been mad at myself.

Whatever happened that day when we were seven years old happened, whether Helena spilled the secret to her parents because she was worried about me or whether her parents overheard us talking or for some other reason altogether. All I knew for sure was that it was time I moved on.

I hugged her and she hugged me back. Suddenly ten years was replaced by a simple embrace. Nothing more needed to be said.

FORTY-FOUR

HELENA TEXTED ME the next morning saying her parents were concerned about who she'd been spending so much time with. Apparently, they had to meet that person face-to-face, so they invited me to dinner. Don't ask why she couldn't just tell them it was me instead of making a big deal about it.

Beatrice didn't want to come, even though I practically begged. There was nothing I dreaded more than spending the evening with the Shaws, even though I hadn't seen them in ten years. But adults don't change the way kids growing up do. They were insufferable then and I was sure not much better now. The only reason Helena and I hung out at her house so much as kids was because she had the cooler bedroom.

The thought of her parents was temporarily chased away when I pulled up and saw my old house. It was exactly the same: green front door, rosebushes, and a dent in the picket fence from when my dad backed the car into it. The only difference was the people who lived there, and they were outside with their two kids. They were my parallel family, the ones who actually got to have a life in that home.

I must've been sitting in the car for a long time because eventually Helena scared the crap out of me by opening the passenger-side door. I hadn't even noticed her approaching.

"I probably should've told you to come from the other street," she said, slipping into the front seat.

"It's fine. I would've looked anyway."

"You know, they're not very friendly neighbors. At least not like your family."

A few more moments of vicariously staring and I was over it. "Let's just go inside."

When we walked into her house, it seemed empty. Nobody was waiting for us in the foyer, which made me wonder if Helena's parents were as eager to meet the mystery man as she said they were. But then I heard quiet arguing coming from the back of the house, and Helena headed in that direction.

Her parents hovered near the kitchen island and looked exactly like the image I had in my head. Helena's mom was her twin just with makeup and pearls, and her dad still had the same navy business suit plastered to his body.

"Sorry, dear," her mom said. "Dinner's going to be a little late. Your father forgot to order it."

"I didn't forget. You never told me," he alleged.

Helena didn't respond. There was an awkward pause where her parents just stared at me like they weren't sure why I was there.

"You guys remember Reed Beckett, right?" Helena eventually broke the silence.

Mrs. Shaw gasped. "Oh my gosh! You're a man now. I hardly recognized you."

She gave me a hug, and the smell of stale alcohol lingered. I don't remember that being her normal scent.

257

"You look just like your father," she added. "How's your mom? I haven't seen her in, gosh, it must be more than ten years now."

"Don't overwhelm him." Helena stepped in to save me.

"I'm not overwhelming him. Am I overwhelming you, Reed? We're practically family."

It was a strange thing to say considering we hadn't seen each other for a decade, and I don't remember my mom receiving a phone call from them to see how we were doing or even if we were still alive. I took a deep breath and glanced at Helena's dad, who hadn't walked out from behind the island. I wasn't sure if his form of greeting was better or worse. Either way, it was classic Mr. Shaw.

"My mom's okay. She's been working a lot," I told her. Or at least she would've been if she'd actually been working every time I'd told someone she was.

"Well, tell her I said hi and that we should catch up sometime soon!" Then she forced a very toothy smile. "I can't believe you're the one who's been stealing our Helena."

"Mom, he's not stealing me," Helena said. "We're in Yearbook Club together and we're friends. We hang out."

Her mom waved her off and shuffled back over to the kitchen island to grab her half-empty martini. "You haven't hung out with anyone in years. God forgive me for being a concerned parent and making sure you're not doing drugs or getting pregnant." She chugged the rest of her drink. "Are you two having sex?"

"Jeez, Mom, no! What is wrong with you?"

"I'm gonna go pick up the food," her dad interrupted. When he walked past me, he said, "I hope you like lo mein."

* * *

258

Our Chinese food takeout was accompanied by deafening silence and utensils clanking on plates. It was uncomfortable to say the least, not to mention Mr. Shaw eyeballed me the entire time.

Finally, Helena's mom spoke. "How's your sister, Reed? Is she still ill?"

"She's not ill. Beatrice has a disability and that doesn't just go away."

"Reed actually just raised a bunch of money to help pay for a surgery she needs," Helena announced for some reason.

"How'd you do that?" Mrs. Shaw asked.

"Um, a fundraiser at school," I told her.

Helena giggled.

"Make sure you find a good doctor," her mom said in between sips of her third martini since I arrived. "There are so many quacks out there. Peter just finished a negligence case."

"Settled out of court. Seventy-five thousand" was all he said.

"You know, Helena's going to study prelaw," her mother said. "Like father, like daughter!"

"If she can get accepted anywhere," her dad added, not looking up from his plate.

I looked over at Helena, who had an expression on her face like she was trying really hard not to scream and throw her food across the room. I put my hand on her leg because that seemed like something she would do if I was on the verge of flipping out.

"Have you ever seen Helena's photographs?" I asked. "She's super talented."

Mr. Shaw sighed. "We bought her that camera for Christmas two years ago. I've regretted it ever since. Taking photos is a hobby, not a career."

"Helena can make it a career. She's also good at hair and putting

259

together outfits, so maybe she can do something in fashion. I mean, it's better than brownnosing judges."

Helena shot up from her seat. "You know what, I'm full and it's late on a school night, and Reed should really be getting back home."

I barely had time to say thank you to her parents for having me over before Helena dragged me all the way to the front door. I had no idea she was that strong.

"What are you doing?" she angrily whispered.

"Sticking up for you."

"I appreciate that, but I can handle my dad myself."

"Really? Because he belittled you right to your face, and you just sat there. You don't deserve that, Helena."

She sighed. "I know my dad is a lot, but there's no point in wasting your breath arguing with him. He'll never see your side. He's a lawyer."

"Then make him see your side," I told her. "Make him see the real you, his daughter."

Even though I've always known her dad was a huge jerk, I was still jealous of Helena's family. At least a dumpster fire keeps you warm.

FORTY-FIVE

"**THIS IS THE** coolest thing you've ever done," Beatrice told me.

"Going to a high school dance? Most people would think the complete opposite."

My sister had been following me all around the apartment while I got ready, asking me questions I didn't know the answer to, like was there a theme, do people really spike the punch bowl, and will there be a DJ or a band? During that interrogation, I was mostly trying to figure out what to wear; Helena had said semi-formal, but I wasn't entirely sure what that meant.

Honestly, I should've just asked her to pick out my outfit. But I wanted to feel like I was putting effort into this myself. Eventually, Bea and I decided on the pants that went to my suit and the only nice shirt I owned, which was hanging in my closet with the suit jacket.

The last time I wore a shirt with buttons and a collar, I was watching my dad get buried. I tried not to think about that while I ironed out the wrinkles.

"I wish I could go," Bea said.

"Helena tried to get you a ticket, but our principal said the dance is only for students."

She sighed. "Did you tell her I can do ninth-grade math? That's, like, the same thing."

I kissed her and then headed for the door, actually excited to go do something. Even the spring air felt refreshing and not how it usually feels to me: overhyped.

Helena had asked me if I could pick her up, and though I wanted to avoid her house at all costs, especially after that dinner, her parents had some rule about her not driving past ten o'clock. I wondered if they had any rules about her getting in the car with an unlicensed driver.

When I knocked on her door, her dad opened it before I could even finish the third knock. It was like he was waiting right there, anticipating when I'd show so he could beat the crap out of me for calling him a kiss-ass. Thankfully, Helena was right behind him and pushed her way past.

Unfortunately, our escape was disrupted by Mrs. Shaw. "Helena, don't you dare think you're leaving without taking photos."

"Mom, we don't need photos." Helena turned to me. "Do you want photos?"

I kind of did, surprisingly, but I shook my head.

With one hand, Mrs. Shaw pulled out her phone and started snapping pictures. In the other hand, she held a full cocktail. The multitasking was undoubtedly impressive.

"I can't believe how grown-up you two look," she said. "Put your arms around each other."

We listened and did all the cringey poses while Mr. Shaw observed from the door. His expression was inscrutable, and as much as I didn't care what he thought about me, I still wanted to melt into my dress shoes, which were already killing my feet.

"Okay, now put on your corsage," Mrs. Shaw ordered.

"Mom, we're not going to prom. There's no corsage."

"If it's a school dance, then you always get a corsage. Reed, didn't you get her a corsage?"

"I didn't know I was supposed to," I said.

"It's fine," Helena told me. "Mom, we're leaving now." She grabbed my hand and pulled me the rest of the way to the car.

Although it seemed like her dad hated my guts and her mom was, well, her mom, I actually didn't hate the whole charade of pictures. I was all in on this dance thing. Maybe I still hadn't come down from the high of making five grand or the fact that I made another four hundred from selling IDs that week, but I wanted to do this dance thing right. By which I meant, I should've gotten Helena a corsage; she deserved it. I imagined her with a wrist full of flowers, and I liked that aesthetic for Helena. Somehow that was a detail Bea forgot in her endless questions.

"Sorry about that," Helena said once we were buckled in. Her mom was still watching from the driveway, now holding her drink in both hands.

"No worries. I'm sorry I didn't buy you a corsage."

"I really don't care. The flowers would've made me itchy, and I probably would have taken the thing off and lost it."

I was pretty sure Helena was lying, but I appreciated her trying to make me feel better.

"Well, I like your dress," I said. "It's very bright."

"It's chartreuse. Do you think it's too flashy?"

Helena looked down to examine herself. The dress was a bright greenish yellow with ruffled sleeves and a puffy skirt. Nobody but Helena could've pulled it off.

"Nope," I told her. "You look like a highlighter but in a super-awesome way."

Helena smiled and for a second I forgot we had somewhere else to be. Then her eyebrows shot up. "Oh, I almost forgot, I got you a gift. Close your eyes."

When people tell you to close your eyes, the surprise typically isn't worth the anticipation. This time was one of those few exceptions. As soon as she put the object in my hand and I felt the leather, I couldn't stop myself from opening my eyes before she told me to.

"It's a wallet," she said. "I figured you could really use one now."

I was pretty speechless. I ran my fingers over the top and the letters that were engraved in the leather.

"'President of DSC'?" I asked.

"Yeah, Diet Soda Club."

"Shouldn't that be you? You're the founder."

"I'm president of enough clubs. You deserve this one."

The wallet was special, kind of like when Helena gave me that peanut butter and fluff sandwich but also so much more than that. I really had no clue how to thank her for it and everything else she had done to help. I guessed one way would be to use the wallet, so I pulled out the cash from my pocket and stuck it inside the pouch. I kept the fake ID away from the gift, though.

"Thanks, but now I really feel like a jerk for not getting you a corsage," I said.

"Well, you can make it up to me at the dance."

"How?"

"By dancing with me, duh."

"I was going to do that anyway," I said.

She laughed. "Then let's go!"

I stepped on the gas, and during the short drive to school, I tried to remember if I've ever danced. That was another question Beatrice didn't ask, and if she had, I might've practiced.

There was a DJ, not a great one but I guess not bad, either. They played all the expected high school dance music, and soon enough the floor of the gym was covered in discarded heels and dress shoes so people could dance easier. I was the first to take mine off, mostly because I definitely had blisters.

I tried my best to act like a comfortable, normal teenager who wasn't at all overwhelmed. I joined the sweaty mosh pit and took cues from Helena, although I was convinced she didn't totally fit in, either, but she waved at people and chatted and so did I.

Then the dreaded slow dance happened. The DJ got everyone warmed up and then said, "It's time to take it down a notch." I thought they only said cheesy crap like that in movies.

Obviously, the dance floor quickly cleared. Surprisingly, Helena also started to walk away.

"Where are you going?" I asked her, partially out of breath.

"We've been dancing for like an hour straight. I'm going to take a break."

"Are you kidding me? You said I had to dance with you, and I think that should include a slow dance."

Helena looked at me like she didn't recognize the person in front of her, which was fair considering I didn't recognize the words coming out of my own mouth. But then she smiled, not a full grin but one side of her lip curled, and her eyes did this strange twinkle that let me know she was in.

She put her arms around my neck, and I placed my hands on her waist. We swayed.

"I'm proud of you, Reed," Helena said.

"For what?"

"For being a kid."

I laughed. "I could say the same thing about you."

"Well, unlike you, I actually come to these things."

"That's because you planned everything. It's practically your party."

"True. Nobody sees it like that, though."

"Do you ever get tired of it? Trying to act so mature?"

"Not really. School is the only thing in my life I can somewhat control. Besides, I'm really good at it. Why, do you?"

"Sometimes," I told her. "Like, sometimes I wish I could experience one week of what it's like to only have to think about school or what Saturday party I'm going to or how many friends I have."

"Nobody our age thinks about school."

"You know what I mean. Just being free to worry about the crap I should be worrying about in high school."

Our gazes shifted around the room. I spotted Tucker and his friends huddled in the back and taking sips from a flask. Helena saw them, too, and I knew we both couldn't help but feel like that mess waiting to happen was partially our fault.

"Being a normal teenager is overrated," Helena said. "Think about how many people felt like they had to pay you a hundred bucks just so they could have a good time."

"And they probably had a good time."

"Maybe. But it wasn't real."

I wasn't sure I agreed. Sure, I fabricated the IDs that gave kids access to a bar, but that bar was real and so was the band and so were the other people at the concert. Their experiences and their memories of them were real, too.

As the throwback slow jam played on and we continued swaying, I looked into Helena's eyes and they were just as real as the drunken weekend I gave my classmates. Beatrice was real, too — the most real thing in my life. The more I thought about it, the more I realized that she was my reality, which was maybe the point Helena was trying to make.

You can't change reality, although people sometimes try to pretend to be someone they're not to mask how much their reality sucks. But no matter how much you might try to pretend you're someone you're not, you can't escape who you really are.

I was someone who knew how to take care of another living human, and I knew the difference between a fishtail braid and a crown braid. I was someone who drank diet soda instead of beer and would do anything for my little sister. I was a gray hat.

Helena liked that someone. Beatrice liked that someone. I liked that someone.

"Why'd you do it?" I asked.

"Do what?"

"Help me make the fake IDs and pass out midterm answers. I mean, it's pretty much the world's biggest favor."

"I told you, I did it for Beatrice."

"You barely knew my sister when you agreed to help, and we hadn't talked in a decade. You risked everything for us."

Helena shrugged. "Whether you knew it or not, I never stopped caring about you. I was just waiting for you to let me back in."

Finally, the music turned back up, and the dance floor was mobbed again. For a moment, though, Helena and I still held on to each other, staring. I really hoped she wasn't reading my mind, because I was having all kinds of complicated and embarrassing thoughts.

"I have to use the bathroom," I said, and backed away.

Since everyone was dancing again, it was actually a good time to be alone for a second. I splashed some water on my face and collected my thoughts. I was pretty sure I was falling for Helena Shaw. It's possible I started falling the day I kissed her under a blanket fort, and maybe the descent paused for a decade, but now it was a fast and uncontrollable drop.

"We need to talk," a loud voice slurred behind me. In the mirror I saw Tucker.

"About what?"

"About how you owe me a cut of the money."

"What are you talking about? I offered to give you free test answers; it's not my problem that you never showed."

"I wasn't sure your plan would work," he said. "Anyway, I want in."

"Tucker, you barely did anything. I'm the one who made all the IDs and got the test answers and figured out how to get them to people." I felt guilty for taking the credit for Beatrice's and Helena's brilliant contributions, but obviously now was not the time to highlight their achievements.

"I told people. You wouldn't even have customers if it wasn't for me."

"So you think drug dealers pass out bonuses to the druggies who tell their druggie friends to go buy drugs from that drug dealer? No way."

Tucker, mouth open, just stared at me. That sentence might have been too complicated even for his sober brain to follow.

"I could beat the shit out of you right now," he threatened.

"Dude, you're drunk and holding on to the wall for balance."

I pushed past him and confidently went back out to the dance. I tried not to think about Tucker the rest of the night, but deep in the pit of my stomach, I knew that conversation wasn't over.

FORTY-SIX

WHILE MOST people are either an optimist or pessimist, I've always considered myself to be more of a realist. I can usually keep my expectations neutral and then be pleasantly surprised when something good actually happens or not endlessly depressed if a situation turns out to be a steaming pile of dog crap.

But the cops standing at my locker the morning after the dance reminded me of why the glass is neither half-empty nor half-full.

"Are you Reed Beckett?" one of them asked.

I had no choice but to say yes. Dr. Kenzing stood behind the two officers, and there was already a crowd of students forming. I felt like I was going to hurl.

"We got a tip that you've been bringing contraband on to school campus," the other cop said.

"Contraband?" I played coy.

"Falsified driver's licenses with the intent to sell. Can you open your locker for us?"

I did what they said, although the school had their locker-check rule so I wasn't sure why they bothered asking. All the while I was panicking, wondering what the hell would happen to Beatrice.

Once I got my locker open, the cops tore it to shreds. Of course they didn't find anything.

Then they turned to me and checked my backpack and made me put my hands on the wall of lockers while they patted me down. In my right pocket, they found my new wallet virtually empty, since the bulk of my money was safely tucked in my underwear drawer. I kept pretty cool until they reached for my left pocket, and my heartbeat sped up about a thousand times faster.

After that, the world went silent. Handcuffs got slapped around my wrists, and the two officers escorted me toward the door. Through the crowd and blurriness, I spotted Helena. She looked just as petrified as I felt, but when our eyes met, she nodded and I understood that she'd look after Beatrice. But looking out for someone and taking care of them are two different things, and although I appreciated what Helena was trying to communicate, it didn't make me feel that much better.

It had to be Tucker. It had to be Tucker.

That's what I kept telling myself while I was locked up for hours. Well, actually, I don't know how long I was locked up because I couldn't see a clock, but it felt like hours, maybe even days, and the whole time I just replayed every moment of my life and, unlike the flashback I had at the park, each one made me feel more disgusted than the last.

What should I have done differently?

That's the question that kept tormenting me because the truth is I didn't have an answer. Adults like saying that life is all about choices. Well, I chose the path that could get Beatrice her surgery. I guess I could've dropped out of school and gotten a real job. But quitting school would've hurt my ability to help support Beatrice as we both got older. Plus, it would've devastated my sister if I'd dropped out.

Should I have tried to track down our mom and force her to come home?

That would've required a cross-country manhunt, and before we made it halfway to Vegas, we probably would have spent all our money on gas and then starved to death in the middle of Kansas. And if by some miracle we could have made it to Vegas, who knew if our mom would still be there. For all we knew, she and Seth could be in Europe by now.

Who was to blame, though?

That was the question that made me the angriest to the point where I couldn't stop my hand from pounding the metal bench I was sitting on. Tucker, my mom, and life in general were all easy scapegoats. But mostly I blamed myself, which inevitably brought me back to the first question and the vicious cycle of scary unknowns and *what-ifs* would start again.

I just wanted to know if Beatrice would be okay.

Was all of this for nothing?

Would they take her away?

Could they stop her from getting the surgery?

Were our lives over?

Eventually, an officer came to the cell door. "You can make a phone call."

"I don't have anyone to call," I said, which was an awful truth to admit.

A few more rounds of self-hate later and the same officer returned, this time to unlock the cell.

"You made bail," he announced.

I looked up to find Mr. Shaw standing behind him—visibly pissed—but still, he was there.

"How'd you know I was here?" I asked.

"My wonderful daughter," Mr. Shaw said.

"So, that's it? I'm good?" I asked on my way to freedom.

"You're a first-time offender, and they only got you on possession. Lucky for you, none of the alleged buyers would come forward."

"It's Tucker Walsh. I know he ratted on me."

Mr. Shaw wouldn't look at me. "Whatever beef you have with him, you can handle yourself. Just don't get arrested again."

As much as I wanted to find Tucker and beat the crap out of him for almost ruining my sister's life and mine, I knew I'd keep my distance. I wasn't about to do anything that put Beatrice at risk again.

As soon as Mr. Shaw and I were out of sight of the station, he grabbed my arm and stared directly into my eyes. He didn't blink once. "I want you to stay away from my daughter. You hear me?"

The intensity on his face scared me.

"I'm sure she's involved in this mess, and I don't need you screwing up her future with all your issues. You hear me?" he repeated.

I nodded and he let go.

Mr. Shaw adjusted his suit and then walked away, leaving me stranded on the opposite side of town from my apartment. For the first time, I agreed with the man. Helena was going somewhere, or at least had the potential to, unlike me. I'd be a terrible person to ever get in the way of that. My problems shouldn't become hers and, whether I wanted to accept it a second time or not, our universes split the moment after I kissed her underneath the blanket fort. No amount of peanut butter and fluff sandwiches, radish salads, fishtail braids, or diet soda could change that.

FORTY-SEVEN

I WALKED THE entire way back to the apartment in the dark, through neighborhoods and along the narrow shoulder of the highway, barely missing getting clipped by eighteen-wheelers. It was probably a good time to think, but I'd done enough reflecting when I was in that tiny jail cell, so I just locked my eyes on the pavement, erased my mind, and walked.

The only minute anything passed through my mind was when I reached the street the apartment was on and saw Helena's car. I decided it'd probably be a good idea to think of some reason why she and I couldn't be friends anymore. I suppose I could've just told her the truth so she'd at least be mad at her dad instead of me, but for some reason I felt like protecting Mr. Shaw. I mean, he did bail me out of jail.

When I got to the door, I had no solid plan of what to say or do. Maybe I'd just stop talking to Helena till she got the hint. That seemed to work the first time, though I didn't love resorting to the tactics of my seven-year-old self.

Before I could decide, she met me outside and greeted me with a tight hug. "Are you okay?"

"Yeah. Your dad handled everything. Thanks for calling him."

"No problem. By the way, I didn't tell them anything. They just think you had to stay late at school."

I nodded and took in a deep breath, relieved about that, at least. But something clicked in my head. "Who do you mean by 'them'?"

Helena didn't need to answer because I saw her then, our mom, sitting on the couch in the spot where I saw her hooking up with Seth, and it was like I was seeing some kind of mirage. Or, actually, it was more like seeing a ghost. My mom had seemed just as dead to me as my dad lately.

I walked inside without even acknowledging her, stepping over to Beatrice to give her my usual after-school hug and kiss.

"You're not going to say hello to me?" Mom asked.

"I'm sorry. I didn't realize we were on speaking terms."

She frowned. "I knew you'd be upset that I didn't call you back. But, listen, Reed, I—"

"Upset that you didn't call me back?" I yelled. I was getting hot fast, but I didn't care. "That's the least of it! It's been over *a month* since you left Beatrice and me to fend for ourselves!"

She looked at her hands, which were twisted together in her lap. "I understand why you're mad. But I just felt so overwhelmed by everything. I wasn't any good to you guys here, anyway, and I thought that maybe if I could get away for a while, clear my head and get some perspective . . ." She trailed off, then glanced up at me and Beatrice. "If I'd thought the two of you were in any danger, I would've come back in a second."

"Are you serious with this shit? You left us no money! You never checked in! You practically left us for dead!"

My mom opened her mouth, but I wasn't done yet.

"While you were out with Seth and living your life as if we don't exist, I was keeping us alive! I was feeding your daughter and doing her medicine and getting her better and taking her to doctors and making sure she can have that surgery. Oh, and I was paying the rent *and* the hospital bills because—again—*you left us without any money!*" I was breathing so hard, I felt dizzy. "But you want to know what the worst part of all this was? You'd been gone long before you took off with Seth. You haven't been a real mom to us since the day Dad died. That part of you got buried in the ground when he did. And any hope there ever was of you being that person again disappeared when you walked out that door."

Tears began to drip down my mom's face, but she remained perfectly still, her hands still twisted together in her lap.

She stood up. "Reed, sweetie, I am so, so sorry. But I'm back now and I want to make things right—" She reached to hug me, but I turned away.

"Get the hell away from me." I moved to stand over by Beatrice. "Why did you bother to come back, anyway? Let me guess: Seth dumped you."

She shook her head. "No, it wasn't like that. *I* dumped *him*. I couldn't sleep worrying about you and Beatrice, and Seth kept trying to reassure me that you were fine and distract me with new trips and new things to do, but I finally realized that everything I needed—everything I *wanted*—was back here with the two of you."

I was so tempted to believe her. But the thing about being a realist is that you know that if something seems too good to be true, it is.

I pointed toward the door. "I want you out of this apartment. You don't deserve us. And Beatrice deserves better than a mom like you."

Each word crushed me but it was the truth, and I stood there strong in the middle of the room, not breaking my stare with our mom. Eventually, she took the hint, kissed Beatrice on the head, and walked toward the door, grabbing the car keys on her way out—another thoughtless and selfish move.

"Mom!" Beatrice cried as the door closed behind her.

"It's fine," I said. "She doesn't really care about us, Beatrice, no matter what she says. I mean, she just took the car keys. How am I supposed to drive you to the doctor or go to the grocery store? Mom only thinks about herself."

"I can drive you guys."

It was Helena. I'd forgotten she was there. All of the rage I felt toward my mom was now coupled with humiliation at there having been a witness to our family drama.

Helena's face looked so open and sympathetic that it actually hurt to look at her. I remembered her dad's warning to stay away from her, that I was no good for her. If I'd had any doubts before that he was right, they were gone now.

"No," I told her. "You need to leave, too."

"What? Why?"

"You told me you'd look after Beatrice, but you allowed my mom to be around her, after everything I told you."

Helena's mouth gaped. "She's your *mom*."

"No, she's not. And if you were really my friend, you'd know that."

We stood there staring at each other for a moment. Helena's eyebrows dipped in concern. "What are you trying to say, Reed?"

I forced myself to hold her gaze. "I'm saying I was wrong to think I could ever trust you. I'm saying I want you to leave me and my sister alone."

"What?" Beatrice interrupted, her voice in hysterics. "Reed, no! What are you even talking about! Helena *did* look after me!

She was here the whole time Mom was here! Nothing bad happened to me!"

But Beatrice was wrong. So much damage had already been done, even if she didn't realize it yet.

Helena looked at me like she didn't recognize me. Then, with eyes filled with tears, she dug around in her pocket for our spare key, slapped it on the coffee table, and stormed out, slamming the door behind her.

Helena's exit destroyed Beatrice more than our mom's. "Why are you so mean?" she screamed, barely getting the words out between gasps for air. The top of her shirt was soaking wet from crying.

"We don't need them," I said, my heart twisting. "We'll be fine on our own like always."

"We *weren't* on our own! We had Helena! She was my friend and now I have nobody because of you. Everybody leaves us because you hate everyone!"

"I only hate the people who don't care about us."

"Helena cared about us. She loved us!"

I couldn't argue with her—and not just because she was having a meltdown, but also because she was right. Anyway, if I said anything then, I might've broken down, and there can't be two people in pieces during a catastrophe. One person needs to pick up the other; I learned that after my dad died when there was nobody else—and that was precisely the reason we were in this mess.

I was too young then and probably too young now, but when had that ever mattered? So, I tried to blot Bea's wet cheeks with a tissue.

"I hate you." She wouldn't let me see her face. "I want Mom. I hate you." Beatrice repeated those two sentences all evening until

I put her in bed. Just as I pulled her blanket up, she opened her eyes. They looked at me, brand-new and sad. "You can't sleep in here," she told me.

So I turned off the lights, closed the door, and collapsed onto the hallway floor between our rooms. I lay there all night, facing my bed, which hadn't been touched in months.

FORTY-EIGHT

I WAS SUSPENDED two weeks from school, which would've sucked under normal circumstances, but my circumstances were far from normal. In addition to the expected boredom that kicked in after the first day, I also had to deal with the fact that Beatrice wouldn't talk to me. She wouldn't look at me, smile, sniff, or acknowledge my presence in any way. Although it was awkward, I still got her dressed and bathed.

That must've meant I reached peak parenthood.

And it wasn't like I didn't try to smooth things over with Beatrice. I turned on her favorite shows and asked her questions about cybersecurity crap, but received no response other than the same dirty side-eye. She wouldn't even take a sip of soda. At least she stopped chanting how much she hated me out loud.

By the second day of suspension and utter silence, I couldn't take it anymore. I had to get fresh air, so I asked Bea if she wanted to come with me to Cheap Check, but she just grunted, which I counted as progress.

Poolio was working, which made me wonder if he'd ever hired anyone to help out. I hadn't seen him since he cut up Tucker's first fake ID, which in hindsight ended up being the beginning of my downfall. For a second I thought maybe Poolio should be blamed, but the guy was eating the store's sushi again.

"Where's the girl?" he asked me.

"We're kind of fighting right now."

"I get that. My dad and I fight, too, sometimes."

"Dude, I'm not her dad," I told him. "She's ten and you know I'm not even eighteen."

Poolio stared off, his mental calculator working overtime. "Yeah, I guess that makes sense. Unless you, like, adopted her or something."

I just walked away toward the back of the store. I didn't have the energy to deal with Poolio being Poolio.

"Is that why you're being such a Grumpy Gus?" Poolio asked. "Because you're fighting with your sister?"

"I'm not a Grumpy Gus, whatever that is."

"Yes, you are. You're walking around all slouched and depressed—classic Grumpy Gus. You're bumming me out."

"Whatever."

I headed over to the far side of the store, away from the refrigerator with the drinks. I couldn't even look at the rows of Diet Dr Pepper. But opposite the drinks was the slushie machine, which also wasn't great for my mental health, so then I just stood in the middle of the store, flipping my head side to side and unsure if I could bear going down the chip aisle and past the Doritos.

Poolio wouldn't leave me alone. "You wanna talk about it?"

Despite my urge to ignore Poolio and leave Cheap Check, there was nowhere else for me to go. Mom took the car and the only other place in walking distance was a nail salon. The thought of a stranger clipping my nails repulsed me more than using Poolio as a shrink.

"Sure, what the hell," I mumbled, stepping back over to the front counter.

Poolio was trying hard to not act too excited. "So, what's on your mind, partner?"

"Partner?"

"That's how my therapist starts all my sessions. He's originally from Texas."

"You see a therapist?"

"Of course. You have to care for your body and mind, bro. I also do yoga but only during months with less than thirty-one days."

I sighed, regretting my decision to talk to him. "Interesting."

But Poolio was eager to help. His eyes were wide and he leaned forward. He even removed the magazine he was gawking at so there weren't any distractions.

"So, partner, what's on your mind?"

"Have you ever made all the wrong choices for all the right reasons?" I asked.

"Like when I eat the store's sushi to clear out my bowels?"

"Surprisingly, yes. Sort of like that. And I'm sure your stomach hates you for doing it."

"I mostly just hate myself for eating it. Like, after I'm done with this pack, do you know how long I'll spend in the bathroom? Hours. And then I gotta figure out a way to get more toilet paper before another round starts. Thank God we always have that in stock."

I shook my head. "I think we're getting away from the point here."

"You brought it up."

"Well, just forget I brought it up."

I was about to walk out, but my body wouldn't move. As much as Poolio was annoying, he was the only person I had who was willing to listen.

"The two people in my life who were supposed to protect me left me." The words rushed out of my mouth. "They left me and my sister, and for a long time I thought I was responsible to handle everything alone. I did some bad things, Poolio, but it was our only way to survive. And then when one of them came back, I rejected them."

Tears poured down my face. Somehow it seemed appropriate that I would lose my shit standing next to the wall of cigarettes where it all started.

The bells above the door jangled as a customer walked in. "Get out. We're closed!" Poolio yelled, and the person ran away.

"Sorry, man," I said. "I didn't mean to take up your time with my issues."

"You know, a lot of people think I'm stupid" was Poolio's response.

"What?" I hoped I sounded surprised and not guilty.

"But I remember things, a lot of things. I remember you coming in here with your dad. I was about your age at the time. I know all my regulars' favorite drinks and snacks and what brand of smokes they buy. Most of the time I already have the register rung up before they're even finished shopping."

He turned the screen of the cash register so I could read it. The items listed were two packs of Diet Dr Pepper, a bag of Doritos, and a slushie.

"I didn't know you did that," I said.

"It's just easier to pretend I don't care because it seems like nobody else does. But most of the time that makes me really lonely. You know?"

And the thing was I did know. Out of all people, Jared Poolio at the Cheap Check was the one to make sense of everything. It really did begin and end with him.

* * *

When I got back from Cheap Check, I noticed our car in the apartment's parking lot. Our mom was sitting inside. I thought about ignoring her, but Poolio's words were still ringing in my ears. So eventually I walked over and climbed into the passenger seat.

I didn't really know what to say, but I probably wasn't the one who needed to speak first.

"I'm sorry, Reed," Mom told me, staring out the windshield. "I'm so, *so* sorry."

I stayed quiet, wanting her to say more but also dreading it at the same time.

"There's no excuse for what I did," she continued. "I never should've left you and your sister like that, never should've placed so much pressure on you. You're just a kid and you deserve to be a kid. So does Beatrice."

"Sometimes you feel really distant, like you don't care," I said. "Like, when Beatrice is in the hospital and needs you the most, you disappear."

"Most of the time I just sit in the car and cry," she said quietly.

"Why? I mean, I get that it's all really scary, but we're scared, too. Why not cry with us? That's what moms do. Moms stick around, even when things get hard. *Especially* when things get hard."

"I know." She traced the logo on the steering wheel. "I used to be like that, before your dad died. But after that, I just felt afraid all the time. I was afraid I wasn't enough for you and Beatrice. I was afraid something would happen to me, too, and you kids would be all alone. And then, when Bea started getting sick more often, I was afraid something would happen to *her*. And then when Dr. David

284

told us about the surgery . . ." Mom brushed a tear from her cheek. "You kids are my whole world. If anything were to happen to one of you, I don't know how'd I survive it."

Even though I'd known that she was scared about Beatrice's surgery—known it because Beatrice and I were scared about it, too—it still surprised me to hear the full measure of pain and fear in her voice.

We sat in silence for a long time. It felt like we were standing on a precipice and it was up to me to decide if we jumped. I couldn't see what lay on the other side, but I knew all too well what was on *this* side.

"You really came back to be a mom—a *real* mom? You think you can handle that?"

She looked at me. Her eyes were clear and earnest. "I don't know, Reed. I'm scared that I'm going to fail, or that I'm going to want to run again the next time things get hard. But I know that I want to try. More than anything, I want to try to be the type of mom you and Beatrice deserve."

I sat with her words for a while. "And Seth is really out of the picture?"

"Seth is really out of the picture. Anyone who can't see why you and Bea should be my priorities has no place in our lives. Besides, I need to focus on being a mom before I worry about being someone's girlfriend or . . . anything else."

"I don't think I'll ever fully forgive you," I said. The words were cold and harsh, but it was the truth.

Mom nodded. "I understand."

"But I'll do everything I can to help you be a good mom to Beatrice. She deserves that."

Mom patted my hand, but I pulled away. I wasn't ready yet.

"You know, this week it'll be ten years since your dad died," she said.

"I know."

"After you sent the message about needing the money for the surgery, I was terrified. I hated what I'd done to our family but I had no idea how to help or what to do. I kept hoping that if I just ignored the problem, it would go away on its own somehow. Then one night I was sitting in the hotel room, and I looked over at the nightstand and saw the earrings, the ones your dad gave me." Mom reached up and touched the gold hearts that dangled there. "I didn't even realize I took them with me, but I realized I had to get back to you and Beatrice."

I hated that it took a pair of earrings and a desperate text to make her come back. But I guessed that didn't really matter. All that mattered was that our mom did come back, and it was time for me to try to move on for Beatrice's sake.

"You know," I said into the quiet, "I could've told you Seth was a loser just by looking at his ridiculous mustache."

We both laughed, which felt pretty good. Then we sat in silence as mother and son, as a semi-repaired family.

FORTY-NINE

MY MOM didn't flip a switch and suddenly become a new person. But her desire to step up and take on more responsibility seemed real, since one of the first things she asked was how to do Beatrice's bedtime routine.

"Beatrice's medicine has to be kept in her bedroom in case she needs it," I told her. "And she needs to take them exactly as Dr. David prescribed. No skipping."

Mom listened carefully while I got Bea ready for bed. Occasionally, she would nod or ask a simple question like "Why does she need this?" or "Remind me, how many times a day does she take it?" In general, though, she stayed pretty silent that first night and helped in small ways, like filling cups of water or choosing Bea's pajamas.

Each time Mom did those things, each time she took the initiative to be Beatrice's mom, I forgave her slightly more. I think Beatrice did, too. But I saw how Bea's eyes remained wide and anxious the entire evening.

"Mom, are you going to be here in the morning?" Beatrice asked just as our mom was about to turn off her bedroom lights.

"Of course. Is that okay?"

Bea nodded enthusiastically. "You forgot to give me a good-night kiss."

"Oh, right. I'm sorry, baby." She stepped back over to Beatrice and gave her a kiss on her head.

I couldn't help but observe and analyze every move our mom made and everything she said. Like, it irritated me how she implied we had no reason to suspect she'd be anywhere else after she'd disappeared on us for more than a month. Or how she asked Beatrice if she wanted her to stay. The fact was it didn't matter what Bea wanted. I mean, Mom needed to stay because that's what she was supposed to do, plain and simple. And when she said that and forgot to kiss Beatrice good night, I deducted a point as if I was keeping some kind of motherly point system. As if after a few days, I'd add up all of those points to determine whether or not our mom was worthy enough to stay.

Maybe I would. Maybe I wouldn't. At least for now I slept in my own bed.

Anyway, the next morning I had to wake up our mom, who forgot to set an alarm and would've delayed Beatrice's morning medications if I wasn't home on suspension. I gave her the benefit of the doubt and didn't yell or chastise her for already being careless. I simply handed her a cup of coffee and the list for her to review while she came to her senses of what needed to be done.

"You're gonna do great," Beatrice told her when she finally got in her room. "The morning is fun because you get to suction gross boogers."

Mom smiled and played along, half-asleep and still studying the list. Eventually, she began digging through Bea's bedside cabinet, looking for her breathing treatment medicine.

"I think Yo-Yo organized all my stuff by when I take it. Right?" She looked over to me.

Leaning against the doorway, I nodded.

"Yes, I see your brother was very organized," Mom said, finally finding the vial of medicine. Her voice was tired but still proud.

"Now you squeeze that stuff into the mask thingy and put it over my face," Bea directed.

It seemed my sister had everything under control, so I disappeared into the kitchen to make breakfast. I thought if anyone should be giving step-by-step directions, it was probably best that person be Beatrice. She knew her routine and understood its importance. If I were in there micromanaging, I'd just make our mom feel more guilty, which, whether I liked it or not, was a feeling she needed to move on from.

By the time I finished cooking enough pancakes, bacon, and eggs for all three of us, Bea and Mom emerged from her bedroom ready for the day. Only three or four times did I hear my sister giving directions, and our mom knew how to give her a bath, so I'd say it was a relatively successful first morning.

But Mom didn't join us in the kitchen. She flopped down on the couch with an unmoving zombie stare.

As much as I still resented her, I wanted our mom to do a good job. More importantly, I wanted her to not give up.

I served Beatrice a plate of food and joined Mom in the living room.

"You did it" was all I said, small words of encouragement.

"Beatrice told me she's been timing you in the morning. I think I came in last place."

"Just ignore that. I think timing her morning routine just keeps her entertained."

"I'm sorry."

"I heard there are support groups for parents who have children with disabilities," I said. "Maybe something like that can help."

She nodded, still looking a bit dazed.

"Mom, you already know how to do most of the stuff, like giving Beatrice a bath and getting her dressed. It's just a few new things to learn. I had to learn all of that, too, at first. And believe me, I was terrified."

My mom didn't respond. She was fading.

"There's a great mom inside of you," I told her. "I know because I've seen her before. You're going to get better."

She gave me a weak smile. "Yeah, I know," she muttered, which I know was followed silently in her head by *I hope so.*

I was thinking the same thing.

FIFTY

MOM HAD good and bad moments over those next few days, but she didn't walk out, which was what really mattered. The worst moment came when Dr. Jenson's office called to schedule Beatrice's final X-rays before her surgery the next week, and Mom had a total meltdown. I guess life got a little too real again, but it was real for all of us and at least she stayed to cry.

Either way, I had to settle her down and Beatrice, too, who started crying just because our mom was crying. And then I was alone and had to be strong for both of them.

But who would be strong for me?

Recently that person had been Helena, and out of habit I picked up my phone to give her a call before stopping myself. My problems were for sure not her problems anymore after the way I treated her. Mr. Shaw was correct about me being a distraction.

But maybe that wasn't all I was to Helena. I thought about how for the past two months I only saw my mom as the world's worst human. I'm not denying she made mistakes, but there's always two sides to every story. Mr. Shaw's side was that I was a boy who broke the law and might lead his daughter down the wrong path, spoiling all his careful plans for her future.

My side of the story, though, was that I was a boy who'd pretty much lost everything but still found a way to survive. A boy who cared for his sister and protected her, even if that meant making some bad choices. But I was proud of that boy, and I know that my dad would have been, too.

That boy also deserved a friend. And so did Helena.

So, that evening, while Bea worked on the computer and our mom took a nap, I snuck out to Helena's house. Since I had no desire to risk being caught driving without a license (not even a fake one, since my ID had been confiscated by the cops), I took a bus across town, which also gave me some time to concentrate on what I should say.

I've rung the Shaws' doorbell hundreds of times in my life, but this was the first time my hand shook while doing so. Best-case scenario, Helena's mom opened the door. Worst case, Helena tells me to leave before I can say anything. Next-worse case, Mr. Shaw answers and beats the crap out of me.

Of course, he answered the door. "I thought I told you to stay away."

"I'd like to speak with your daughter, please."

Mr. Shaw didn't flinch. "Not happening."

"Why?"

"Because this is my house, I make the rules, and I already told you to leave." He stepped out onto the porch, arms folded. "We had a deal," he said.

"We did, Mr. Shaw, but the thing is I don't like that deal. And I don't think Helena would like it, either."

"It's time for you to go, Reed."

"No. No, it's not time for me to go because I took a bus all the way here and I practiced in my head what I wanted to say and you're not giving me the chance to say it." I stepped back, took a deep breath, and regained my composure. "Helena's an amazing person, Mr. Shaw. She's smart and caring and talented in so many things."

"You're right—and that's precisely why I want you to stay away from her."

"I know that you think I'm a bad influence on Helena, but did it occur to you that Helena is a good influence on *me*? Your daughter makes me a better person—someone who I think could actually be worthy of an amazing friend like her. Nobody has ever cared about me as much as she has, which I didn't always appreciate. But now I do, and I just want her to know that."

A shadow moved a curtain in one of the windows. I got excited thinking it was Helena, but I noticed the person was holding a martini glass. Maybe her mom was sober enough to remember to tell her everything I was saying.

"Helena and I need each other," I told Mr. Shaw, point-blank. "We're better together, and I think somewhere deep down you might know it, too. Haven't you noticed how happy she's been lately—truly, genuinely happy? Haven't you seen the way she smiles these days—a real, genuine smile and not her usual presidential smile. The way she smiled when we were kids. Like it or not, I make Helena happy. And she definitely makes *me* happy, too. And my sister."

I'd done it. I'd said everything I'd come there to say. I don't know what reaction I was expecting, but stone silence wasn't it.

For what felt like an eternity, Mr. Shaw stood there expressionless. Eventually, he said, "Reed, it's really time for you to go."

So, I left, hoping that something I'd said had gotten through to him.

FIFTY-ONE

I COULDN'T concern myself too much with the fact that I didn't receive one phone call or text from Helena. Toward the end of my suspension, all my attention was focused on Beatrice and her surgery. Our mom was locked in, too, doing things I've never seen her do before like making a list of things to bring to the hospital and calling them to double-check the surgery time. I just occupied Beatrice, who was unsurprisingly brave through all of it, and helped when Mom asked me to bring her something, but obviously it was nice to finally play more of a supporting role.

The only awkward moment was when Debbie at Dr. Jenson's office was giving us the final surgical details and Mom asked, "Don't we still have to pay the five-thousand-dollar deposit?"

She looked confused. "Nope. That's already been taken care of."

Mom shot me a look. Thankfully, I didn't need to say anything since Beatrice was ready to move to her next series of tests.

And when we got home, after everything was packed and ready to go for the next day, I handed Mom a grocery list. "I wrote down some snacks Beatrice might want once she's feeling better. Can you pick those up from Cheap Check while I make lunch for me and Beatrice?"

She nodded, but it was obvious the day had gotten to her. Still, she held on to the list and left on her mission to buy Doritos.

When Mom returned, Beatrice and I had eaten our sandwiches, and I had moved on to my homework. Apparently, you still have to do homework even during a suspension.

My mom peeked into my bedroom and watched me type on my laptop. "What are you working on, hon?" she asked.

Her question took me by surprise. She hasn't taken an interest in my schoolwork since I was in second grade. I mean, she didn't even care that I was suspended for two weeks—although Beatrice was pretty pissed.

"Just an English paper," I told her. "We started reading *The Catcher in the Rye.*"

Mom grinned and walked over to stand beside me. "Your dad loved that book."

"Really?"

"Oh, yeah. I used to call him my Catcher, you know. He saved me once, protected me." She placed her hand on top of my hair, combing messy strands with her fingers. "You do that, too, for a lot of people."

I shrugged. So far I'd found no similarities between me and Holden. He was a spoiled brat with the privilege to make reckless decisions.

"What's the assignment?" my mom asked.

"We're supposed to write about a room."

"What kind of room?"

"Any kind of room. It just has to be descriptive."

"Well, you've visited plenty of hospital rooms, but I'm guessing you don't want to write about those."

I shook my head in agreement, staring at the screen, blank except for my name and the date. Truthfully, though, I had considered writing about a hospital room, maybe the one where Beatrice fought her first bout of pneumonia and our dad never left her. But I decided against that for the same reason my sister hates having her picture taken when she's sick; no one wants to be remembered at their worst.

Mom wandered over to a shelf that held all the random crap I'd collected over the years. It was mostly junk that I refused to throw away, and she lifted and slid around each thing, looking for God knows what. Hidden in the back, she found a mug I bought on a sixth-grade field trip to the Natural History Museum, and from inside she pulled out my old yo-yo.

The yo-yo my dad gave me was purple, glittery, and lit up when you spun it, and it was hands down the coolest thing a seven-year-old could own, but for some reason I never played with it until years later. Dad would show me videos on how to do tricks, and I'd watch them and then just stare at the toy like it was a precious jewel.

When I finally gave the thing a whirl, I couldn't put it down. Beatrice and Helena were right; I brought it everywhere until one of my mom's boyfriends told me it was a baby toy. They broke up, but I never played with the yo-yo again.

"I thought I threw that away," I said.

"You did, but I saved it. Look what else is in here."

She handed me the mug, and lying on the bottom was a tiny folded piece of paper. I opened it up. It was a picture, one of me and Helena under the blanket fort.

"I had no idea this was in here," I said. "I don't even remember taking this photo."

"Your dad took it. He had a way of capturing moments." Then she paused, thinking. "I was really happy when I saw Helena. You two used to be so close. It broke my heart when you stopped being friends."

"Yeah, well, I'm pretty sure her parents were relieved."

"From what I remember, they just want the best for Helena. I admire that."

"Do you not want the best for me?"

"I do. Oh my gosh, Reed, I want the absolute world for you and Beatrice, but I have no idea how to give that to you two."

"You can start by just being here with us."

She nodded, her eyes filling with tears. "Today was rough. I felt scared and also like I had no idea what I was doing."

"But you got through it." For the first time since I was seven years old, I reached for my mom's hand. "You were there for Beatrice. You made her feel safe and loved."

"I know, and I'm sorry it's all still so hard for me. But I'm trying, and I promise I'll *keep* trying. And in the meantime, I really am happy you have Helena back in your life."

My eyes rested on the photo of me and Helena in the blanket fort. I couldn't bring myself to tell my mom that Helena once again wasn't in my life.

Mom gave me a kiss on the cheek. "I'll leave you to it, then."

"Leave me to what?"

She smiled faintly, though her eyes were still sad. "I think you're ready to write that essay," she said.

She tapped the photo and left. She must've still had her mom intuition because she was right; as soon as my fingers touched the laptop keyboard, the words came:

*In the bedroom of my best friend's house, there is another
room, a room inside of a room. It's hidden by blankets and old
sheets and can only be found by those with an imagination and
a love for diet soda.*

I went on to tell the origins of the original Diet Soda Club. It
was a love story that was a lot like my parents' story, except ours
didn't start in a bar—though it did involve drinks.

FIFTY-TWO

I WENT TO SLEEP that night feeling like things were really and truly looking up. Maybe Helena hadn't reached out to me yet, but in revisiting our early days in that blanket fort, I had renewed confidence that we'd find our way back to each other somehow. My mom was still around and still making an effort, even though things were scary and hard. And I had emailed Mrs. Kapoor a final draft of what I felt like was the best English paper I'd ever written.

But the next morning, the day of Beatrice's surgery, our mom wasn't in the apartment. I hadn't seen her since she handed me my old yo-yo and kissed me good night.

I wanted to believe that she wasn't really gone. That she'd just slipped out to get something she thought Bea needed before her surgery. But it was four o'clock in the morning and even Cheap Check was closed. There was no denying it: she'd left us again.

It was my worst nightmare come true. We got all the way here, kept Beatrice healthy, even figured out a way to make five grand, just to get turned away because there wasn't an adult present to sign some forms.

I swear, if people just observed my life for two days, they'd realize I *am* the adult. But now, thanks to Tucker, I couldn't flash a convincing counterfeit ID to those smug hospital administrators.

"Where's Mom?" Beatrice asked as soon as I woke her up.

I thought about lying to her, but after everything we'd been through, she deserved honesty, however brutal it might be.

"Mom's not coming with us today," I told her, grown-up to grown-up.

"What? Why? She was doing a good job! Did suctioning my gross boogers scare her?"

"No. Nothing you did scared her. I just think Mom isn't ready. But I'm here and we're gonna get through the day together."

She took a few seconds to come to grips with her new-yet-familiar reality, then she nodded confidently. "Okay," she said.

Beatrice's confidence gave me confidence. Whatever happened, we'd figure it out—together—just as we'd been doing.

Once I had Beatrice dressed and ready to go, our hospital bags lined up neatly by the door, I realized we were faced with our first major obstacle: how to get to the hospital since Mom had taken the car again.

I stared at my phone, wondering if I should call Helena. The cab company in town was out of the question since the driver had been a jerk about Beatrice's disability, sighing dramatically when Mom asked him if we could store her wheelchair in his trunk and acting all impatient as I got her in and out of the car. But maybe a jerk was better than asking a favor of someone who has good reason to hate your guts—and who might not even answer her phone at four in the morning?

I was still debating what to do when I heard a familiar sound: our car's engine. I looked out the window and saw our mom pulling into the parking lot. She hopped out and rushed to the front door without even bothering to turn off the car or close the driver's door.

"Sorry, sorry, sorry!" she said in a rush as she burst inside. "I know I'm late! I was driving around, trying to clear my head—it's a big day, you know? I mean, of course you know. But I'm here! I'm ready! Let's get going!"

Beatrice and I just stared at her, both of us trying to believe that she was really there, that we hadn't just imagined her. Then we snapped out of it and followed Mom to the car before we could wake up from this dream.

We arrived at the hospital so early, it was still dark outside. Beatrice insisted on wearing her unicorn pajamas for the occasion and the barrettes Helena had given her.

After Mom checked her in, Bea zoomed to an elevator we hadn't used before; its sole purpose was to bring people down to the pre-op waiting room. She was ready.

Mom and I trailed behind, and on our way over, she said, "I'm sorry if I had you and Beatrice worried this morning. This is all really hard on me."

My mom's face was pale and there were dark shadows under her eyes. I wondered if she'd slept at all last night, or if she'd just been driving around aimlessly for hours, contemplating the enormity of today.

I thought about telling her that this was really hard on me and Beatrice, too—especially Beatrice, as much as she played it cool— but I hoped she knew that. And I didn't really feel like fighting. The important thing was that she was here, like she said.

Inside the elevator, plastered on the mirrored doors, was a sticker that said "Inhale courage. Exhale fear." Bea followed the directions, loudly breathing in and out. I joined, too, for solidarity and not at all because I was definitely terrified.

During every step of the process, from when the elevator doors opened to when she was called into triage, I literally gulped and gripped tighter to the handles on the back of Bea's wheelchair. Time moved slowly and quickly, and altogether everything seemed much too real.

And still, Mom was right there.

"Hi, there, Beatrice." Dr. Jenson walked into our little waiting cubicle. By then, my sister was out of her pajamas, in a hospital gown, and lying on a cot with an IV in her arm. "How are you feeling?"

"Pretty okay. Do I really have to wear this hairnet?" She touched the ugly mesh the nurse had stuck on her head.

"Well, you have such beautiful hair. I wouldn't want it to get ruined or in the way of the surgery."

Beatrice moaned but didn't argue.

"My mom told me the surgery takes fourteen hours?" I asked. "That's a long time."

"Yeah, give or take. We'll keep you updated throughout, but Beatrice will be in good hands. Dr. David will also be in the OR to monitor her breathing."

"She's gonna do perfect," Mom said, holding on to my sister's hand.

"Yes, she will," Dr. Jenson agreed. She addressed Beatrice next: "I reviewed your X-rays from the other day and not much has changed, so I'm hoping the procedure is straightforward. Do you have any questions before we begin?"

"Do you know who the baby was?" Bea asked.

"Excuse me?"

"You said I'm getting a baby cadaver bone for my ribs. That's from a dead baby. Do you know who they were?"

During the entire conversation, Dr. Jenson had been scribbling on a clipboard, but as soon as Beatrice asked her that, she put it down and took in a deep breath. I could tell nobody had ever asked her that question, a question that destroys your heart if you think about it too long.

"I don't know the baby," Dr. Jenson told her. "But I know their family donated their body to save someone like you, so that you can keep living. You think you can do that?"

Bea nodded. "I will. For me and my family and the baby."

"Good girl."

Then, with the quick close of a curtain, the three of us were alone. There was an eerie feeling during those moments while we waited for the nurses to come get Beatrice and bring her to the operating room. It was like everything was about to change. Better or worse, as soon as Bea got pushed down the long hallway, our lives would suddenly be different. We all felt it, the anxiety. No amount of small talk would fix that, so we just stayed silent until it was time.

Mom kissed Beatrice.

I kissed Beatrice and whispered, "I love you, Honey Bea."

Every couple of hours, a nurse would visit us in the waiting room and give vague updates. Things like "She's stable" or "The doctor's moving to the next phase." Those words brought little comfort, and I predicted nothing would until the nurse said, "We're done and she's alive." But we were only four hours in, which felt like four days.

I tried to talk to my mom, but I couldn't. Every time I'd open my mouth, I either choked down vomit or saw the look in her eyes, which was probably the same as mine and meant *I don't want anyone talking to me.* So, I did the next best thing a son could do and went to the hospital café to buy stale pastries, which might've conveyed the same empathetic sentiment as talking or they could've simply just been stale pastries. Either way, eating them was at least something to do.

By hour eight, my head was permanently drooping into the palms of my hands, but I refused to sleep. Mom had been pacing the waiting room since the sixth update.

Finally, she stopped. I'd gotten so used to the squeak of her shoes on the linoleum that the sudden silence rang in my ears. I looked up at her.

"I can't stay here. I mean, I'm not running way—not really. I'll come back; I promise. I just—" She looked tormented, tortured. She looked how I felt. "I just can't stay here, Reed. I'm sorry. Can you—can you call me when there's news?"

I stared at her, my mouth slightly open. I couldn't believe she was taking off again—even if it wasn't far, even if it wasn't for long. Beatrice might not notice if she was here or not, but I would. As horrible as it was to wait for the news about the surgery together, it would be infinitely worse to wait by myself.

But it was pointless to say any of that. Mom looked like she'd tear out of here the moment we broke eye contact. She couldn't help but put herself first, just like always.

"Sure, whatever. Just go."

She clutched her purse so tightly, her knuckles turned white. "And you'll call me when there's news? Either way—you'll call me?"

I nodded and stared at the floor. I wished I had it in me *not* to call her, to leave her twisting and wondering if Beatrice was okay.

But I could never do that. I wouldn't wish that agonizing uncertainty on anyone.

Not even on our mom.

She squeaked her way down the hallway and to the elevators. When I heard the *ding* of the doors closing behind her, I finally let the tears fall.

FIFTY-THREE

SITTING BY MYSELF in that waiting room was just as bad as I knew it would be, maybe worse. I had too much time to think about Mom, about how I kept letting her break my heart over and over again. About Beatrice and the surgery. About Helena.

And then, as if my thoughts had somehow conjured her, I heard a familiar voice.

"How are you holding up?"

I stared at Helena, shocked to see her—but also so incredibly happy and relieved. "Fine" was all I could say.

"And how's Beatrice?" Helena asked, taking the seat next to me. The one my mom had been in—the one she should've still been in.

"She's good, I guess. The nurse gives us updates every hour or so." I looked over at her. "Helena, listen, I'm really sorr—"

"It's okay. You don't need to apologize."

"But I want to. I should've never treated you like that."

"Reed, my dad explained everything—about the deal he forced you into and all the rest. Anyway, I was already planning to forgive you when your mom called."

"My mom called you?"

Helena nodded. "Well, she called my mom, who then called me. She said she needed to get some air, but she hated leaving you alone to wait for news, so she asked if I might come sit with you after school let out. I was going to come anyway, though."

My mind reeled with the significance of what she was saying. My mom had taken off, true, but she hadn't actually abandoned me after all. She'd been looking after me the best way she knew how, by sending someone she knew would take good care of me. By sending Helena.

"Wait," I said, slowly processing the rest of what she'd said. "You were planning to come already? Why, for Beatrice?"

"For Beatrice, yeah. And for you."

I glanced at her, unsure.

"Mrs. Kapoor read your essay in class today," Helena said. "She said it was the best in the ten years she's been giving the assignment. I don't love that you got a better grade than me—*again*—but I think it's really cool you decided to write about the blanket fort."

"I wrote about you and me, Diet Soda Club. I wrote about the room I love the most."

"Since when did you become so sentimental?"

"Someone once told me that if you don't care, then nobody else will."

"Who told you that?"

"Jared Poolio."

"The guy who works at the Cheap Check?"

"Yup. He's actually pretty wise."

We both laughed but softly, so we didn't disturb the other people who were waiting. Helena laughed like she used to when we were hiding under her blankets.

"I want you back in Diet Soda Club," I said. "Not the one that makes fake IDs or sells test answers, but the club that just drinks diet soda."

"Hmm." Helena tapped her finger on her chin. "Okay, but only if I can call you Yo-Yo."

"Deal."

The remaining hours went fast. Helena went out and bought us dinner from a burger place down the block, and we passed the time chatting about summer plans. Mr. and Mrs. Shaw were going on a monthlong vacation to Tahiti. But Helena, it turned out, would be going to a photography camp.

"Photography?" I asked, glancing up from my burger. "How'd you manage that?"

Helena grinned. "It turns out that you can be quite persuasive when you want to be. Apparently, you said something to my dad that made him—and I quote—'reconsider the role that photography plays' in my life." She laughed. "You know, Reed, you'd make a good lawyer if you put your mind to it."

"Yikes, no thanks," I said before I could stop myself. "I mean, no offense if that's something you still want to do someday," I added quickly.

Helena laughed. "None taken. Trust me, I totally get that it's not the right path for everyone. And I think my dad is starting to accept that now, too."

I'm not saying that everything between Helena and her parents was perfect. Probably her mom was drinking a martini at that very moment, and her dad was definitely still a jerk in a lot of ways. But this one small thing—which was also kind of a huge thing—had clearly improved, and I was really happy about that. It reminded me of the ways in which Mom had been better since she'd been back.

She obviously still had a long way to go, but things *were* getting better, and that gave me hope.

Eventually, Dr. David and Dr. Jenson made the long walk toward us, their expressions stone-cold. As they got closer, though, they smiled. Not a smile of pity or sympathy but a smile that said everything was going to be okay—a smile that had me reaching for my phone to tell my mom the good news.

They smiled like Beatrice could eventually go to school, make friends, and fall in love. They smiled like maybe one day she'd become the next great white hat or choose to do something else—something even more amazing or something totally, wonderfully mundane. Either way, now she had the chance, all because of diet soda.

ACKNOWLEDGMENTS

This book has pivoted more times than I can remember from a story about vigilante teenagers doing parkour to a murder mystery. But at the heart of all of those quick-lived iterations was always Reed and Beatrice. It just took some polishing to make sure they and their love for each other shined the most.

That being said, I want to give my first round of thanks to my rock-star editor, Kaylan Adair. Thank you for giving me the space and time to figure out what I wanted to say to the world next. Most importantly, thank you for giving me the freedom to write the stories I want to write and develop the characters that I know we both feel deserve their spotlight. It was a bit of a risk to write an entire manuscript before you even read a word of it, but I truly appreciate your trust and how quickly you were on board to become a member of Diet Soda Club. Each Zoomie Zoom session and email we exchange truly makes my day when they happen because I know we're building something special together. Above all of that, thank you for being so damn good at your job!

Big shout-out to my agent, Stephen Barr, for being a true friend through the process of writing this book. Thank you for always just being awesomely there whenever I need some encouragement.

Trust me when I say that not a day goes by where I don't think about how I wouldn't be able to do any of this if you hadn't initially believed in me. You helped my dreams come true and continue to do so. Forever and always, here's to you, good sir.

If you know me, then you know my life would not be possible without either of my parents, Sheri and Alan. Their selfless care and love are the reason I'm even able to pursue my dreams in the first place. You both are definitions of what it is to be a caregiver, and I want to thank you for being the complete opposite of Reed and Beatrice's mom. And thank you for putting up with my crap on a daily basis. It does not go unnoticed.

As always, my mom deserves her very own paragraph not only because of how much she sacrifices for me, but because she played a pivotal role in helping create this book. We spent many hours sitting in the living room, scheming ways to make fake IDs and how someone might efficiently sell test answers. This is a scary thought, but we'd make a very good crime duo.

Thank you to my brother, Jacob, and my sister-in-law, Kailey, for your love and support. And thank you to my nephew and niece, Asher and Iris, for making me smile on the days when I just need a good smile.

Hugs and high fives to everyone at Candlewick who worked on this book. Thank you for letting me be a part of your amazing roster of authors, and thank you for believing that authentic stories about disability deserve to be published.

Thank you to my dearest friend, Michele. I truly would be alone in the world without you. Knowing that you exist brings me a lot of comfort.

And the biggest thanks goes to everyone who reads this book and lets Reed, Beatrice, and Helena into their lives. From the genuine depths of my heart, thank you for allowing me to share another piece of my soul and for being curious enough to read this far past the ending. You are now all honorary members of Diet Soda Club.

Last and certainly least again (inside joke but becoming less inside), thank you to Steve Stoma for giving me the power and energy to write every day.

With that, I will not say goodbye but instead part with a humble see you later.

Much love.